I0628953

DEATH
AND A FEW
DAYS OFF

Copyright 2016 Kevin Lamport. All rights reserved.

This is a work of fiction. Names, characters, businesses, places, events, and incidents are either the products of the author's imagination or used in a fictitious manner. Any resemblance to actual persons, living or dead, or actual events is purely coincidental. The author acknowledges the trademarked status and trademark owners of various products referenced in this work of fiction, which have been used without permission. The publication / use of these trademarks is not authorized, associated with, or sponsored by the trademark owners.

I'd like to thank Sherry for introducing me to Kathy, a critique partner who became a friend.
Check out Kathy's website at www.kathysteffan.com

Special thanks to:
Chad
Colin
Elyza
Jason
I'm lucky to have friends such yourselves.

Thanks to Shona, who believed and supported me in this writing endeavour, both vocally and silently but always unwaveringly, even when I didn't believe myself.

Thank you to the good people at Scribendi https://www.scribendi.com/ for their editing and Damonza https://damonza.com/ for their formatting and cover art.

This is for Jack Lamport

DEATH
AND A FEW
DAYS OFF

KEVIN LAMPORT

PART 1
EARLY SPRING THROUGH LATE SUMMER
2005

CHAPTER 1

JAKE HARRIS LOOKED from the map covering the steering wheel to the puffy cumulous clouds tumbling across Lake Michigan and asked himself, *Is an evening with Sofia Gianolo worth interrupting my trip?*

The unconsidered answer was, yes. Only a crazy man would give up a night with an insatiable, hot-blooded Italian girl. She knew the restaurants and clubs and liked to hang on his arm and tell all her friends, "This is the airline pilot I told you about."

On the "con" side of the equation, Sofia wanted him to pick her up at work—an auto-wrecking business her family owned—so she could introduce him to her older brother. The idea interested Jake like a dose of the clap. A couple of months back, he'd met her two younger brothers, twins but most definitely not identical. They probably weren't mobsters...

Gino had stared at him out of hard eyes and a stony face. He adjusted his tie. Brushed his palm over a haircut that was as slick as the suit he wore and the shoes on his feet. He told Jake how everyone in Chicago knew who the Gianolo family was, how he'd best proceed with caution. "You don't treat Sofia right, you might find yourself floating in Lake Michigan with cement shoes." He snapped his fingers. "One phone call. That's all it will take."

While Gino rambled on, Paolo glared at him out of a face crisscrossed with impossible-to-ignore slashes of puckered flesh. The scars glowed bright white and shiny pink. Paolo habitually stroked the vertical marks, drawing attention to his face rather than hiding it.

Sofia ordered them both to behave. Later, from behind her hand, she told Jake that Paolo had fallen on a barbeque doing a B&E when he was a teen.

Jake shook his head at the memory. He refolded the map and tossed it on the passenger seat, where it joined his cell phone, a selection of CDs and half a bag of pizza-flavored Doritos. He uncapped the bottle of water between his knees and took a deep slug. Gino and Paolo were more than enough Gianolo men for him. He really didn't want to meet a third. On the other hand, it had taken some backtracking to find A1 Auto Wreckers. The place wasn't a common Chicago tourist stop. After all that effort, it seemed a shame to drive on by.

He dragged his fingers through dark, wavy hair and absently scratched the back of his neck. All this weighing of pros and cons was nonsense. It was time to act like the decisive airline pilot he was, or at least used to be, thanks to the questionable skills of the executives managing World Ways. The choice was simple. Did he want to get lucky?

Yes.

Did he think the Gianolo twins were dangerous, connected mobsters?

No, of course not. The idea was too ludicrously Hollywood to believe.

He swallowed another mouthful of water and re-capped the bottle. He started the Mustang, turned the air conditioning up to max and headed for A1 Auto Wreckers, driving with a wry thought in his head: *What's the worst that could happen?*

CHAPTER 2

A S500 MERCEDES, SHINING as bright as Lake Michigan under an early May sun, idled into A1 Auto Wrecker's enormous parking lot. It rode close to the ground on lowered suspension and trailed dust clouds like tumbleweeds in its wake. The vehicle came to a halt near one end of a mobile home. A peeling, hand-painted sign that once read "Office" was screwed to the side of the trailer. Time, weather, and vandals with neon green spray paint had altered the sign. It now read, "Orifice." When all traces of dust in the air had settled, the driver opened the car door and stepped out.

Eric Dalrymple placed his fists in the small of his back and stretched all the driving kinks away. He brushed his hands down his chest, smoothing wrinkles out of a jacket that hung perfectly on his large frame. Tugging back a lapel, he lowered his head and sniffed his armpit. The sweet and sour stench of sweat was barely noticeable but he jerked his head back and cut a glare through his Ray-Bans at the blistering blue sky. He loved the winter, the snow so crisp and clean, like bed sheets fresh from the laundry. He especially loved winter's sub-zero temperatures. Chicago's summer heat was unbearable. He had gone Muhammad Ali on the last smart ass who said, "Yeah, well, it's a dry heat."

He briefly considered changing into his second T-shirt of the day. After a moment's hesitation, he reluctantly decided to wait until he finished his business at A1. Violence tended to raise a sweat.

An older model Intrepid pulled into the parking lot. It came to a halt behind the S500. Without even a crumpled quarter panel to distinguish it from hundreds of other Intrepids on the road, the faded green Chrysler was as unremarkable as the Mercedes was noticeable.

The driver climbed out of the Intrepid, complaining. "Air conditioning don't work in this piece of crap. Why don't I ever get to drive the Mercedes?"

"Seniority," Dalrymple said. "Get her shit."

Under Dalrymple's watchful gaze the second man opened the Intrepid's back door. He pulled a backpack off the seat, as well as a baby blue hoody. A cellular phone fell out of the sweatshirt pocket and landed in the gravel at his feet. He picked the phone up and stuffed both it and the hoody into the pack. Using the button on the lower dashboard, he opened the Intrepid's trunk lid, tossed the pack in, then hurriedly backed away from the car.

Dalrymple said, "You get everything from her apartment?"

"Like you asked. Anything with her name on it is in the backpack. Anything I could find," the second man qualified. "Clothes, jewelry, what-not, I left all that stuff."

Dalrymple nodded his approval. He removed his sunglasses and slipped them into his breast pocket. Staring into the sedan's trunk the entire time, he swiped his wrist across the bridge of his nose, grimaced at the dirty smear of sweat and then wiped his hand dry on his T-shirt. He unwrapped a travel-sized Wet Ones, dropped the foil package on the ground, and disinfected his hands with elaborate care, one finger at a time.

The woman in the trunk lay on her side. Her wrists were bound behind her back with duct tape. She kicked when they tossed her in, so Dalrymple had used some more of the tape and bound her feet together too. She peered up at him out of panicked eyes as huge as cymbals in her ashen face. Her eyes were pretty, and it wasn't just the terror that made them look that way. It was the color. Cinnamon. When the light hit them just right they glittered like rusty autumn leaves.

"You scared, Chloe?"

She shook her head slightly.

Dalrymple allowed himself a tight, brief grin. "You should be."

He dropped the Wet Ones. The towelette floated away in a hot gust of wind. He slipped a latex glove onto his freshly sanitized hand. "You know, I never liked you," he said and in one smooth motion that bespoke practice and skill, he bent over and slugged her in the face. He hit her hard enough she'd know about it, but he didn't give it his all. He wanted her conscious and aware, ready for what came next.

Chloe's head snapped back and smashed into the floor of the trunk with a metallic thud. She let out a muffled shriek. Her eyes filled with tears and overflowed. Blood poured from her nose, coating the duct tape gag and soaking the neckline of her shirt. The muscles in her throat worked spasmodically.

Dalrymple giggled, knowing she was swallowing a mouthful of blood.

The second man said, "Damn! What you hit her with?"

Dalrymple held up a roll of coins. The back of his gloved hand glistened with wet blood. "You smack someone in the mouth with these, they're spitting Chiclets. Better than knuckle dusters, too." He sounded proud. "Cops don't look sideways at a roll of nickels."

"Why don't you use quarters? Be heavier. More bang for your buck."

Dalrymple nodded, thinking about the question, giving it serious consideration. "That's a valid point. But, if a roll of quarters breaks open, you're out ten bucks. You only lose two if a roll of nickels comes apart."

"Fiscal prudence. Can't argue with that," the second man said. After several seconds, he said in a deferential tone, "Eric, this ain't the best idea. Should we be wasting time like this? Let's make tracks."

Dalrymple rolled his head in a tight quarter turn, listening for the snapping click of neck bones. He peeled off the bloody glove. Without looking at his partner, he dropped it into the trunk. "The name is, Mr. Blonde, okay? Nobody calls me Eric." His voice was low and dangerous. "And, I don't recall asking your opinion. Go wait in the Mercedes, you don't like seeing pretty little Chloe get what's coming to her."

The second man stiffened. Glanced quickly at Chloe and pointed with his chin. "You don't want her to drown before you kill her, you better pull the tape off her mouth." He strode away without looking back.

Mr. Blonde called after him, "Pussy." He laughed, a short nasty sound devoid of mirth. Leaning into the trunk, he grabbed a corner of the duct tape gag and ripped it away from her mouth. Blood and drool spilled onto the carpet in the trunk. She gulped in deep, raspy breaths.

While he waited for her to recover, Mr. Blonde probed his scalp with the tips of his fingers. Clipped close to his skull like it was, his head stayed cooler on days when the sun beat down with such relentless insistence. He felt a layer of sweat building but when he inspected his fingertips they came away clean. No black residue. Drug store dye kits were okay except they took a couple of hours to work and son-of-a-bitch did they stink. Instead, he used shoe polish to instantly touch up the roots, keep his naturally red hair from showing. Not a perfect solution. Shoe polish wasn't permanent and in hot weather it ran, but at least it worked fast and didn't smell like ass.

Chloe finally stopped gasping and choking.

Mr. Blonde said, "Couldn't keep your mouth shut when it counted, could you? All you had to do was spend the Boss's money. Look pretty. But you're too smart for your own good, aren't you? I was gonna just shoot you." He made a popping sound with his lips and stabbed her on the bridge of the nose with his index finger. "Right between the eyes—"

Chloe interrupted him with a howl of pain.

"—but that's entirely too easy." He paused. The next part was fun. He liked to draw it out, enjoy it. And, he liked to think there was value in giving the victim something to think about while they waited to die. After all, actions had consequences. "You want to know where we are?"

She shook her head apathetically. Hopeless tears cut lines through the dirt and blood on her face.

"We're at A1 Auto Wreckers. A minute from now I'm gonna head into the office." He hooked a thumb over his shoulder, showing her where it was. "Mario Gianolo owns the place. He's a fuckwit but he's gonna crush this car. Then chip it. I'm telling you so you know what to expect."

He paused, gave her time to think about what was coming, and was pleased to see her eyes widen in panic as the idea took hold.

"The first thing you'll hear is the rumble of heavy machinery. Lying in the trunk, you'll probably feel the ground shake as it gets close. There'll be a big clang. That'll be a huge magnet latching onto the roof. The car will swing around some until it lands on the conveyer belt."

She squirmed and twisted in the trunk.

Mr. Blonde smiled. No way she'd loosen the duct tape binding. But it was entertaining watching her try. "You'll ride the conveyer for maybe ten seconds. I suggest you use the time to think about how you should have fucked the Boss, instead of fucking him over. If you're lucky enough to survive getting flattened into a twelve-inch layer of aluminum, you go through the chipper." He sighed deeply, theatrically. He shook his head. "It's a shame really. I would have enjoyed some private time with you. Would have liked to tango." He shriveled inside as he spoke. Sex was noisy, sweaty, and, for it to be really pleasurable, out of control—things Mr. Blonde couldn't tolerate. Sex was the last thing he wanted from Chloe.

A flicker of optimism appeared on her face. She snuffled. With the tip of her tongue she wiped a film of pink blood off her teeth. "You want to tango?" she asked in a timid voice. "Let's tango."

Mr. Blonde laughed, this time with genuine mirth. She'd given him the reaction he wanted. "You kidding me? You're a mess." He ripped a six-inch strip of duct tape off the roll. "You're so ugly right now I couldn't get it up." He made a face and shuddered. "And, you stink. Now shut up and hold still." He reached into the trunk with the tape taunt between his fingers.

Chloe thrashed her head from side to side.

"Keep that up and I'll give you another smack."

The tears and thrashing stopped, as if she knew there was no point to either. She took a deep breath, sniffling bubbles of snot and droplets of blood up her nose.

Mr. Blonde's stomach wobbled. He quickly taped her mouth then slammed the lid of the trunk shut. An uneasy chuckle burst free. How was it he could knee cap somebody with a DeWalt hand drill and a quarter-inch bit, but he didn't have the stomach for natural bodily functions? Bacteria was the answer. It was everywhere. Millions of miniature bugs with hundreds of legs and hundreds of eyes, all of them carrying suitcases full of diseases.

He rapped his knuckles on the lid of the trunk, and started toward the Orifice.

After a couple of steps, he paused. He planted his fists on his hips and stared thoughtfully at the Orifice door. Maybe he should just pop Chloe. Get it done fast and easy. He reached beneath his coat and found the grip of the revolver in the holster under his arm.

The Boss never specified how he wanted a job done. The onus was always on Mr. Blonde and he took the responsibility seriously. He thought each killing out carefully. When he needed to deal with a piece of garbage, some lowlife street loser, popping the guy and tossing him in a dumpster was appropriate. When he needed someone to vanish or a problem to go away, (or several problems for that matter), Lake Michigan was a very big, very deep, body of water.

But occasionally a killing was less about the victim and more about sending a message. That's when he liked to get creative.

He'd never fed anyone to a crusher. In Chloe's case, it felt right. Imaginative. Full of finesse. Killing her fast and easy didn't sit well. After she went through the chipper, the man waiting for him in the shiny black Mercedes would spread the story. Mr. Blonde's reputation as a cold-stone killer would grow and a message would be sent: *Don't poke your nose where it doesn't belong. You listen in on private conversations, voice opinions, you're going to get dead. Not even the Boss's girlfriend is exempt.*

Mr. Blonde pushed away his reservations. What could go wrong? Mario Gianolo was a lapdog desperate to impress the Boss. His business was crushing and chipping cars. Put those two facts together and this was an almost impossible job to botch.

Almost.

Mr. Blonde tapped his index finger against his lips a couple of times. If Mario's younger brothers got involved all bets were off. The twins were fuck-wits of galactic proportions. It was worth encouraging Mario to take a personal interest in destroying the Intrepid. Impress upon the fat fuck that destroying the vehicle was his job. Nobody else's. The Boss was counting on him.

Mr. Blonde dropped his revolver back into its holster. He resumed his walk toward the mobile home.

Two by eight planks across cinder blocks served as the first step into the A1 Auto Wreckers office. They creaked and bowed in the middle when he stepped on them. With his hand on the doorknob, he hesitated, steeling himself to the filth he knew he'd find on the other side of the door. After a deep breath, he tugged it open.

A cloud of blue smoke and stale sweat billowed out. Mr. Blonde immediately started coughing. Through watery eyes, he spotted Mario, the man sitting behind an industrial-type steel desk, basting in his own lard like a Thanksgiving turkey. The sparse hair on his head glistened with oily sweat. He glowed a celestial shade of crimson, more scarlet than Mr. Blonde ever remembered seeing him. A pair of red, white, and blue suspenders, still attached to his pants, drooped over each arm of his chair. He stared at Mr. Blonde with an indecipherable look on his face.

Contempt? Dislike? Mr. Blonde narrowed his eyes. He knew Gianolo felt both for him. He didn't care. Today something else about Mario's demeanor put him on alert, like maybe the dislike and contempt had swollen and the jellyfish had suddenly grown a spine. Tension radiated off the man in waves.

The fuck was going on?

"Have a seat," Gianolo mumbled, motioning with his left hand to an empty vinyl armchair opposite his desk. White stuffing, edges dirty gray, exploded out of a slash running the depth of the olive-green cushion.

Unwilling to take his eyes off Gianolo for long, Mr. Blonde barely glanced at the armchair. "I don't think so."

Gianolo shrugged. He dropped his left hand onto his soccer ball belly. His right hand still dangled by his side, hidden below the top of his desk.

Suddenly Mr. Blonde knew why Gianolo was ignoring the cigar smoldering in an upside-down piston that served as an ashtray. There'd be a weapon in his right hand. Probably a nine-millimeter, something compact with lots of ammunition in the magazine. Judging by Mario's attitude, it wouldn't take much for him to use it... The wrong tone. The wrong move. Mr. Blonde trusted his sixth sense when it came to stuff like this. It had kept him alive and out of serious trouble in the past. He'd seen the inside of a jail cell, obviously—that was a rite of passage—but he'd never done hard time, not even after his gang initiation, when he killed the cop. What a debacle that night turned out to be. Still, he skated because of his sixth sense.

Neither man spoke. A fly buzzed and bumped into the single, grimy window. It wouldn't be long before it joined a host of other fly corpses on the windowsill. Seconds slowly ticked away. A shaft of dirty sunlight sliced into the office. Mr. Blonde squinted at it, silently chastising himself. Mario Gianolo was almost as big a fuck-wit as his brothers but eventually even a whipped dog bites back.

Desperate for his revolver, Mr. Blonde's fingers twitched. Could he get it out in time if Gianolo decided to make a play? Probably not. Gianolo could shoot him right through the desk. What about the roll of nickels? Maybe leap across the desk and...? He dismissed the idea. Not practical. The computer monitor was in the way, paperwork, the telephone. Plus, he'd get filthy.

He had nothing. No options.

Gritting his teeth, Mr. Blonde forced down his growing rage. It was time to be the timorous guy. He could do that. Usually it happened when he was looking for information, just before he went super-nova and beat a guy into a coma or bounced someone's skull off a scrap of railway tie. Staying in control and letting the situation play out didn't sit well. For the moment though, it was his only move. He rolled his head in a half circle.

"It's just me, Mario," Mr. Blonde said blandly. "How long you plan on sitting there with the piece in your hand?"

Gianolo slumped forward with a noisy sigh. He coughed, the sound gurgling deep in his chest. His hand came up from beneath the desk slowly and without intent, his index finger on the frame of the pistol rather than inside the trigger guard. Mr. Blonde saw he'd guessed correctly. It was a nine Gianolo held between his fat, sausage-like fingers, a Smith and Wesson SW99.

Gianolo rested both hands on the swell of his belly, the barrel of the SW99 pointing harmlessly toward the wall. He said weakly, "I wasn't sure if…" He stared off to the side, refusing to meet Mr. Blonde's eyes. "Never mind."

"Look at me, Mario." Mr. Blonde kept his tone light and easy. He glanced without interest at the two-year-out-of-date wall calendar Gianolo was studying. "Miss March, she's fine, but I'm over here. Who'd you expect I'd be with, you'd need a gun?"

While he waited for an answer, he unwrapped a Wet Ones. The undefined citrus aroma mixed with the sweaty, smoky stench of the Orifice, creating an interesting olfactory cocktail. He couldn't decide which was worse—the smell or the way polluted air caught in the back of his throat and made his mouth taste like the bottom of a birdcage. Scanning the room, he didn't see a place to discard the wrapper. A sudden panicked thought hit him: *I might have to put garbage in my pocket.*

Gianolo kicked a trashcan out from below his desk. "I'm never sure who's gonna come through my front door. It's good to be prepared."

Mr. Blonde nodded. He cleaned his hands, concentrating on the hollows between his fingers. Without looking up he said, "Where's Gino and Paolo today?"

"When you said you'd be dropping by, I gave them the morning off."

"Sofia?"

Gianolo's voice changed to one of affection. "I told Sofia to grab a coffee. She'll be gone a while." He tapped the ashes into the piston top, and stuffed the soggy end of the cigar into his mouth like a cork.

The urge to leap over the desk and plunge the burning cigar into the fat fuck's eye was almost overwhelming. Mr. Blonde pushed it aside. "The Intrepid we spoke about earlier?" He rocked his head back, over his shoulder. "It's parked out front. The Boss doesn't ever want to see it again. He's counting on you. It's your responsibility. Nobody else's. Chip it before sunset."

Gianolo waved a dismissive hand. "It's as good as done."

Mr. Blonde dropped the soiled Wet Ones. It fluttered to the floor, missing the garbage can entirely. He nodded. As angry as he was, he had to grant Gianolo a grudging grain of respect. The man hadn't shown any interest in why the Intrepid needed to be destroyed. He hadn't asked any questions. "Chipped before sunset, Mario. Make sure."

"I get that," Gianolo snapped, his voice rising sharply at the end of the sentence.

Mr. Blonde's patience vaporized. Nobody, fucking nobody, spoke to him using that tone of voice. Hardly realizing what he was doing, he grabbed his lapel, tugged his coat open, and reached for the .357 under his arm.

Before his hand found the butt of the revolver, Gianolo raised the SW99. The barrel wavered, etching small circles in the air, but it was pointing at him nevertheless and Gianolo was only six feet away. If he started yanking the trigger he wasn't going to miss. Mr. Blonde let his coat fall shut. He slowly raised both arms, palms open. "Let's both take a second here, okay Mario?"

Gianolo's breath came in rapid, wheezy puffs. Sweat stains the size of a three-person Jacuzzi had formed under each arm. The cigar in his porky face looked like a valve used to blow up bath toys.

"It's the heat," Mr. Blonde said. "It makes us guys crazy, this kind of weather." He waited a moment. "I'm gonna get going. Tell the Boss you did what he asked." He backed to the door.

"The Wet Ones you threw on my floor," Gianolo said. "You

want to put it in the trashcan. Please?" His voice was as weak as green tea but the SW99 was still pointed in Mr. Blonde's direction.

Mr. Blonde nodded. Once. Rage bubbled like magma pushing on the earth's crust, tinting everything red. Blood thundered in his ears. He bent at the waist, retrieved the towelette, and dropped it into the can. He reached behind him searching for the doorknob, eyes locked on Gianolo's unpredictable face the entire time. When he found the knob he twisted it and backed out of the office.

His fury was a barely controlled fire. He wanted to slam the door, smash the windows, punch the wall until his knuckles were bloody and the siding splintered. Most of all he wanted to whip the .357 out and unload six rounds into Gianolo's face.

But it wasn't the time.

The Orifice door closed behind him with a click.

He stamped down the two by eight steps, clenching his fists until his knuckles turned white. At the bottom, he stopped and sucked an enormous calming breath through his teeth.

It wasn't the time. Once Chloe was disappeared, after a week or a month went by, he'd pay Gianolo a visit and the greasy wop would pay big.

CHAPTER 3

JAKE HARRIS WAS thinking about the Gianolo twins rather than concentrating on the road in front of him. When the turn into A1 Auto Wreckers came up, it came up way faster than he expected. Surprised, he reacted quickly, spiking the brakes and sawing the steering wheel hand over hand. The Mustang responded, carrying him precisely, although too rapidly, into the auto wrecker's driveway...

... directly into the path of a black S500 Mercedes fishtailing out of the parking lot.

"Holy shit," Jake shouted. He frantically cranked the steering wheel and immediately realized turning wouldn't do it—the angles were wrong. They were going to collide. The S500 rocketed toward him like a ground-to-ground missile. Gravel spewed from the rear tires in twin rooster tails. Jake needed more space. He slammed his foot on the gas pedal. With a deep growl the Mustang accelerated, throwing him back in his seat with neck-snapping force. The car bounced across lunar-sized potholes.

The Mercedes was inches away.

For a nanosecond Jake was sure they'd trade paint, maybe scrape off each other's side mirror but somehow they passed without touching, then the parking lot in front of him disappeared in the cloud of dust the Mercedes left behind in its wake. Above the rumbling engine Jake heard stones pelting his car with metallic tings. He jumped on the brake and came to a skidding, teeth-rattling stop. He lowered his window, rammed his arm out and raised his middle finger. "Asshole," he hollered.

He took a deep breath, trying to slow his pulse. He forced himself to loosen his grip on the steering wheel. Sure, he hadn't been paying real close attention but then again, who expected someone to be driving ninety miles an hour out of a parking lot? He'd have to find a car wash. Hopefully, when he cleaned the Mustang, he wouldn't discover fresh rock chips. Shaking his head, he looked into the rear view mirror.

A feeling of amazement washed through him.

The Mercedes hadn't driven away. It sat idling where the parking lot and the road met, red brake lights glowing brightly in the shiny black paint. Without warning, the brake lights went out and the reverse lights lit up. The Mercedes accelerated backward in Jake's direction.

Anger sent Jake's heart rate north a second time. Whoever was driving the Mercedes had stones the size of Patagonia, because one thing Jake knew from his brother—Mark was a driving instructor in Tampa and saw every variety of driver—the guy who causes the accident never thinks he's to blame. Mr. Mercedes wasn't coming back to apologize.

Jake turned off the Mustang, unbuckled, and climbed out. Fists on his hips, he stood beside his car and waited.

The Mercedes came to a stop. With a quiet hum the window slid into the door. Jake looked at the driver and the man stared back at him out of hooded eyes, his white face made paler by his short, unnaturally ebony hair. A nerve twitched in his tightly clenched jaw.

The man said, "You got a Florida plate on your car, friend.

And, I got one question. Does the heat in Florida make everyone as big a fuck-wit as you?"

Jake started at the man's high-pitched, almost teenaged voice. It didn't harmonize with his bulk or obvious rage. *He almost wrecks me, and it's my fault?* "Are you on crack? You nearly killed us both," Jake said, in a voice filled with tightly controlled anger. "I don't see any reason to be going that fast in a parking lot."

The driver's pale face flamed scarlet. He rolled his head in a swift quarter turn. There was a series of audible snaps. A second later the Mercedes door flew open and the driver exploded out of his seat. He took two fast steps, swinging a vicious right cross.

Somehow through his surprise Jake saw the fist coming. He pulled back to avoid the worst of the punch. For the briefest slice of time he smelled artificial citrus. The punch landed, pulverizing his upper and lower lips. His head snapped back like it was on a rubber band. His teeth carved up the inside of his mouth. An intense pain blasted through his head. For a moment, everything went black. He staggered, but didn't fall.

Step back. Keep moving. Another blow is coming.

Scrambling, feet dancing for balance, Jake flung a steadying arm out, and raised his other hand to his mouth. His fingers came away sticky with blood. He shook his head briefly, trying to clear his vision. If he could see this nut, this freak attacking him over a simple road rage incident, maybe he could hit back. Defend himself. But something was wrong with his eyesight because now there were three people swaying back and forth in front of him, and each apparition had black paint, some shit like that dripping from his hairline down his cheek.

"You don't flip me the bird," the Freak said. "Ever. Especially not today."

Once again Jake was surprised at the timbre of the man's voice. He didn't have long to consider it. The Freak swung a second time.

Still overwhelmed at the speed of the attack, Jake curled his own hands into hard fists. All he had to do was get inside the next punch and he'd be able to throw a jab of his own, maybe slow the Freak down. Concentrating on the middle apparition in front of him, he timed it the best he could and ducked.

About a day too late.

The pain from the first blow was nothing compared to the nuclear explosion inside his head. He heard the crunch. Felt his nose flatten on his face. The bright Midwest sunshine went black as space. For a terrifying moment, he knew he'd gone blind. Standing was impossible. His feet went out from under him. He landed on his back. The air rushed out of his lungs in a noisy whoosh. He rolled onto his side and drew his knees into his stomach, chest heaving instinctively, every inhalation a breath of fire. One thought filled his head.

I can't see.

I can't see!

Slowly the darkness brightened. In a relieved rush he realized his vision was returning. He saw a silhouette standing in front of him. Over the roar of blood pounding in his ears like ocean surf, he heard a car door open and a moment later slam shut. Footsteps crunched in gravel, growing louder as they approached. From what seemed like a great distance away Jake listened to a nonsensical conversation.

A voice, respectful and firm at the same time, said, "Eric. Uh, I mean, Mr. Blonde. Popping this guy ain't the best idea. Out here in the open, like we are."

"First I get to fuck up Chloe Sheridan. Now this guy. I'm having a banner day. Don't ruin it for me."

"Put the gun away and let's get out of here. You don't know who he is."

"I don't care."

Hazy with pain and shock, Jake raised his hand and wiped

his eyes clear. Put the gun away? Mr. Blonde? What the hell was going on?

The Freak stood in front of him, a body's length away. He held an enormous chrome revolver down along his thigh, his thumb tense on the hammer. A second man stood to his left. His hand was wrapped around the Freak's bicep. He appeared to be pulling him toward the Mercedes.

Gravel gouged into Jake's flesh. His right cheek was on the ground, wet like he was lying in a puddle, only there was no water in the A1 Auto Wreckers parking lot. Without thinking about it, he knew the puddle was a gelatinous mixture of his own saliva and blood. Never before had he experienced violence of this magnitude. It happened to other people, but somehow he was the one lying in the dirt with his mouth wide open, trying to suck air through his pulped nose, while two complete strangers discussed "popping" him.

"Shoot him and then what?" the second man said. "Drive away? Leave him where he is? Throw him in the Intrepid? What? It's not clean enough."

The Freak—the one the second man referred to as Mr. Blonde—blew air through his lips in a noisy, exasperated sigh. "You might be right. Just doesn't sit well."

The second man nodded, a sympathetic look on his face.

Mr. Blonde seemed to consider his partner's advice and after a quick nod, he dropped his revolver into the holster under his arm. He fished a Wet Ones out of his pocket. He tore the packet open with his teeth, removed the wipe then rolled the foil wrapper into a tiny silver marble and flicked it at Jake.

Jake jerked back reflexively when the garbage bounced off his forehead.

Mr. Blonde's girlish giggle filled the air. A trail of black dye dribbled down his cheek. He swiped it away impatiently, and cleaned his fingers with the antiseptic towelette. "You're one lucky tourist," he said, still sounding pissed off. "I suggest you go back to Florida. Don't ever let me see you again."

He snorted hard through his nose, hawked and spit a gooey mouthful of saliva and snot at Jake. It splattered on Jake's chest. Then he rotated on his heel and followed the second man back to the Mercedes.

The phlegm burned like acid. Jake didn't move. Not to wipe the goo away. Not to swallow. He didn't do anything to draw attention to himself. Instead he waited motionless, hardly daring to believe that Mr. Blonde would just drive away, leave him sitting in the parking lot without so much as a backward glance. He watched the man tug the car door open then hesitate. Instead of climbing into the Mercedes he shot Jake an evil glare.

Jake's breathing shallowed. The Freak wasn't leaving after all.

CHAPTER 4

ROUND ONE HADN'T gone well and if Mr. Blonde wasn't going to simply drive away, Jake didn't expect to fare much better in the second round. But, he had to try. He met the Freak's stare from across the parking lot without blinking, waiting apprehensively, thinking if the Freak decided to come back, this time he'd make sure he landed a punch of his own. Assuming the man kept his chrome revolver stowed in his holster. He licked his lips, tasted parking lot dust, then dug his heels into the ground, and pushed himself to his feet. Getting ready. Fighting dizziness.

An inaudible voice drifted out of the Mercedes.

Mr. Blonde glanced into the car. He said, "Yeah, yeah. I'm coming." Then he turned his laser glare back to Jake. "I guarantee if we cross paths again, you won't be so fortunate." He slid into the S500. Slammed the door. With a throaty rumble from the twin exhaust pipes, the car came to life. A second later gravel squirted out from beneath the rear tires. The car paused, turn signal blinking, before pulling onto the road and disappearing into the shimmering waves of heat radiating off the asphalt.

All very sedate and polite. Not at all like four minutes before when Mr. Blonde and Jake nearly collided.

When the Mercedes was nothing but a black dot in the distance, Jake closed his eyes, dropped his chin to his chest, and silently thanked the second man's calming influence. The shock of the attack was waning, giving him time to think. He was only alive out of convenience. If the second man hadn't climbed out of the Mercedes and pointed out how difficult a corpse would be to deal with, Jake knew he'd be dead. A shudder of fear rippled up his spine. That's all he was to Mr. Blonde. An insignificant problem.

It was a terrifying thought.

The single shudder became trembles that shook Jake's entire body. His pulse was suddenly stratospheric, his breath coming so rapidly he felt like he was suffocating. He tightened his hands into fists. Clamped his teeth together. Told himself, *He's not coming back. It's over.* He concentrated on inhaling through his nose and exhaling out his mouth until his heart rate dropped and the feeling of panic faded.

He looked at the glob of phlegm on his shirt and flushed with humiliation. He wanted to dive under his car and hide from the world. What a month. It just kept getting worse. Four weeks ago he was flying a Boeing in and out of the world's biggest cities. Now he was deeply thankful for the floatplane job a friend arranged for him in northern Canada.

And, he'd come within inches of losing it all.

A foot closer to the Mercedes and he was on his way to the hospital without medical insurance, instead of Sioux River and his new position with Tundra Air. That close. Twelve inches. No way of supporting himself. No way of helping his brother.

The sun pressed down. Blood dripped intermittently from each nostril, turning into a burgundy crust beside the snot stain on his chest. Jake tugged his shirt over his head and threw it into a pothole. With probing fingers, he examined his face. His first tentative touch made him flinch. He scowled. Took a deep, steadying breath, gritted his teeth and continued his inspection. His nose was split horizontally, displaced to the left side of his face. His lips felt huge but when he touched them he found them less puffy than he first thought. His mouth was sticky, as if he'd gargled interior enamel. He was desperate for a drink of cold water.

Without warning he heard his brother's voice in the back of his mind, Mark saying, "Get to it. You can't just hang around all day."

Jake sighed. Listening to Mark was a hard habit to break.

He looked up and studied A1 Auto Wrecker's operation for the first time. The parking lot was expansive, large enough to accommodate several semi-truck and trailers loaded with vehicles for disposal, but other than a tired green Dodge Intrepid and his own Mustang, the parking lot was empty. A mobile home trailer sat on the opposite side of the parking lot. Stretching away from both ends of the mobile was a wooden fence separating the scrap yard from the parking lot. Behind the fence, a steel boom stretched skyward. Likely a crane or magnet. A cable as thick as his arm hung motionless, straight down from the tip of the boom.

He turned his attention back to the mobile. A sun-bleached sign with indistinct lettering was attached to the side of the building near the door. It seemed obvious the mobile was A1's office.

He'd find water in there.

And, a phone to call the police.

With luck he'd find Sofia too. He wouldn't be kissing any of her tender spots tonight. Not with his swollen lips but it would be fun seeing her anyway. With luck, the rest of this crappy day was salvageable.

"Time to make something happen," Mark the pragmatist urged from the back of his mind. Jake huffed out a second noisy sigh. Constant motion described his brother best. He was happiest when he was making something happen. Or reacting to it. For years, Jake was only a step behind him. It was comfortable leaning motionless against the front fender of his car, letting the sun slowly toast his neck and shoulders, but it wasn't what he did.

He pushed himself away from the car and took a couple of slow steps toward the rear of the Mustang. Pain pulsed through his head, radiating out in concentric circles like the lines from the epicenter of an earthquake. He fought back a surge of nausea and blinked away the sudden shower of stars in his eyes. Once he regained his equilibrium, he opened the Mustang's trunk and found a fresh golf shirt in his roller bag. He pulled it over his head, tucked it into his Levis, and gave the mobile home another skeptical look.

Why was the wrecking yard so quiet? There wasn't a sound behind the high wooden fence. No wailing circular saw. No rattling pneumatic gun. Other than the green Intrepid, A1 looked deserted. It was like the business had been closed for the day. He shook off an inexplicable feeling of foreboding.

He shuffled toward the office, fastening the buttons of his jeans while he walked. He passed the Intrepid. Up close to the mobile the lettering on the sign was clearer. It read Orifice. Despite the way Jake felt, a slight grin tugged on the corners of his mouth. The throbbing in his face instantly deepened. The grin became a wince.

Behind him a phone rang, one of those annoying musical numbers instead of a real ring.

He skidded to a halt. Nervous despite himself, he whirled in place, his dusty, worn-out sneakers scuffing the gravel.

Other than the faded Dodge and his own car, the parking lot remained empty. Was someone in the car, maybe sleeping in the back seat? A witness?

Despite hoping at a very base level that nobody had seen the assault, he knew a witness would be a good thing. He had no excuses. There'd be no escape. He'd have to stand there and fight back the mortification and admit he hadn't landed a single blow in defense of himself. But a witness would lend credibility to his story when he spoke to the police.

He took a couple of uncertain steps toward the Intrepid. Peered into the back seat. Then the front. The vehicle was empty.

A second muted verse started. Closer now Jake could tell the sound came from the vehicle's trunk. "What the hell?" he muttered. He frequently left his cellular on the console of his car. It was there right now. Some people left their phone in a purse or a backpack. Mark lost his several times a day, although as far as Jake knew his brother had never once locked it in the trunk and walked away.

The phone played a third verse.

Jake scratched the back of his neck. Frowned. After several more seconds of uncertainty, he hiked his shoulders. Storing your phone in the trunk of a vehicle was unusual, but if that's what someone chose to do, it was up to him or her.

He clomped up the wooden steps leading into the Orifice, hoping Sofia was in there, and hoping the older brother she insisted he meet had at least a fraction more personality than his two younger siblings.

CHAPTER 5

JAKE TUGGED THE Orifice door open. He paused. One look and he decided he didn't want to step into the haze of blue cigar smoke that clung to the ceiling of the mobile. He was weirdly happy about his flattened nose. It kept him from smelling the stink that caught in the back of his throat.

The proprietor, an overly generous description of the Cabbage Patch adult behind the desk, glanced up fast, a surprised expression on his face. He inhaled sharply, and coughed. The wet, gurgling sound made his eyes water and bulge like major league hardballs. He slammed the desk drawer closed with a ringing metallic clang. In the same motion, his right hand dropped below the level of the desk.

Jake ignored the man's obvious shock. He scanned the room, searching for Sofia. The office was devoid of the female touch. No ferns in the corner. No colorful baubles on the desk. With his damaged nose he couldn't even smell a hint of her perfume. Disappointed, he walked all the way into the room. With a forced smile he said, "Hi. I'm here to see Sofia." He paused. His face ached. Pain thrummed behind his temples and at the base of his skull. "You must be Mario Gianolo?"

The man nodded once.

Jake leaned forward across the top of the desk with his weight on his front foot. He thrust his right hand out. "I'm Jake Harris."

Mario didn't move.

Jake swayed. It was an awkward position to hold. Just about the time he decided Gianolo wasn't going to shake, the man slowly raised his right arm from beneath the desk. He grabbed Jake's hand limply in his own, pumped once and dropped it. He stuffed his cigar into the corner of his mouth and immediately leaned back in his chair.

The rest of the man was as slimy as his hand. Trying to be polite, Jake resisted the urge to wipe his palm dry on his thigh. Already he disliked Sofia's picture-of-health older brother. Perhaps it had something to do with pre-disposition, but Jake guessed it was more about first impressions. One look at Mario and he knew the guy was letting life pass him by. Everything about him said, "I don't care."

Mario stared at him out of slit eyes. "The fuck happened to you?"

"Some guy just assaulted me. Right out front." Jake tossed a thumb over his shoulder in the direction of the parking lot. "Listen, is Sofia around?"

Mario shook his head imperceptibly. All of his chins wobbled. Speaking fondly, he said, "I had a meeting this morning. Sent her out for coffee. Means she'll be having lunch with her friends for the next three hours." His thin eyes narrowed and his tone became defensive. "I'm not liable for what some private citizen does in my parking lot."

Jake manufactured a laugh. The office was ten degrees hotter than the air outside. The heat and the smoke brought the dizzy, light-headed feeling rushing back. Black dots swam in his eyes and sweat beaded on his back, scalp, and face. All he wanted was a sweating mug of water. If Sofia were standing behind him, resting her consoling hands on his shoulder while a doctor re-centered his nose, that would be nice too. Thirty seconds and already he was tired of pretending to be in a good mood. Especially if Sofia had stood him up.

"I'm not going to sue you," he said. He pointed to the phone on Mario's desk. "But if you don't mind? I really should call the cops."

The cigar was clamped between Mario's index and middle fingers. He waited a few long seconds before gesturing at the phone. A cloud of ashes dusted his desk. "Be my guest," he said grudgingly. "Don't tie it up. It's a business line." He brushed away the ashes with the edge of his hand and left a long gray skid mark across the blotter.

Jake perched on the edge of the desk. He reached for the phone. "Have you got any water?"

Mario exhaled heavily. "Yeah." He put both hands on the arms of his chair and pushed himself up with a grunt. The effort deepened the red in his face. "Let me get you a bottle," saying it like the enormous favor he was being asked was taking him away from something important. He hiked his pants up past his narrow hips as far as his bulbous belly would allow. One by one he slung the patriotic suspenders over each shoulder. Finally, he started a slow shuffle deeper into the mobile home. After a few steps, he came to an abrupt halt. "The guy that did this to you. What he look like?"

Jake shrugged. "Big guy. Had a girly voice. Black hair, except I think it was dyed. The color was running down his face. Driving a nice car. An S500. He called himself Mr. Blonde."

Mario's entire demeanor changed while Jake spoke. Before Jake finished, the fat man swiveled and marched back into the office. He straightened as he walked, squaring his shoulders. At the desk, he snatched the phone out of Jake's hand and replaced it in the cradle.

"You don't want to call the cops on that guy." Now it was Mario dishing out labored smiles that didn't reach his eyes, seemingly friendly all of a sudden, except his voice was edged with tension.

Jake compressed his lips into a thin line and tried to control his patience. "Yeah. I do. The guy came this close," he held his thumb and index finger an inch apart, "from wrecking my car. He assaulted me. He was going to shoot me." He still couldn't believe that part.

"I get that." Mario's voice was forceful. He shook his head. All the fatty parts jiggled in time. "But really, you don't want to involve the cops." After a big, exasperated, I-can't-believe-it-either sigh, he said, "Here's how it'll go. They'll take your statement. Soon as you describe him, they'll know you're talking about Eric Dalrymple. They'll ask about witnesses—"

"None." Jake raised a questioning eyebrow. "Unless you saw something?"

"I didn't see fuck all." Mario spoke so fast the words tripped on each other. He paused. Seemed to think about what he'd say next. "The cops will pick him up. They've wanted him behind bars for some time. They'll question him. A lawyer and ten friends will come in and say how they were fishing with Dalrymple all day. Then the cops will let him go."

He stuck the cigar into his mouth and puffed mightily. When he'd finished exhausting all the smoke out his nose and mouth, he coughed, that deep wet cough. Jake had a vision of boiling lava. Only instead of burbling and churning crimson, the lava was green and yellow mucus. He clenched his teeth together holding the nausea at bay.

"You know what happens then?"

Jake crossed his arms and waited impassively without answering.

"The crazy-man will come looking for you. When he finds you it will be more than your pretty mug he busts up." His tone changed. Suddenly it dripped sincerity. "Trust me. I know him.

I'm doing you a favor." Mario's lips pulled back from his yellow, smoke-stained teeth in what could hardly be described as a smile. He gave Jake a friendly slap on the shoulder. He slid his thumbs from shoulder to waist, up and down behind each suspender. "Okay?" He stared at Jake, waiting for an answer, obviously seeking acquiescence but trying to be casual about it.

Jake closed his eyes and exhaled heavily. He scratched the back of his head with annoyed impatience. "All right. I won't call." *Until I get back to my car and my cell phone.* "I'd appreciate that water."

Mario stared at Jake with a doubtful look. "I'll get it." The reluctant, you're-making-me-work, tone was back. He snapped the suspenders on his chest and disappeared into the other room.

While he waited for the water Jake flipped through an out of date girls-in-a-garage calendar, trying to decide if he preferred exotic May with her pneumatic drill or trashy September with her pneumatic wrench. Nothing about the calendar made sense and he was too busy mulling over Mario's mirror image attitude changes to dwell on it.

Something was happening. He couldn't figure out what. How successful was the Gianolo operation? A dented four-drawer filing cabinet. A plywood floor in need of paint. A big, old-fashioned monitor on the desk. An olive green armchair covered in cigarette burns and Pennzoil 10W30. Not only did the place look shabby, it wasn't exactly overrun with customers. Stranger still was how quickly Mario Gianolo's personality flip-flopped from lazy and abrasive when Jake walked in, to helpful and friendly when the police and Mr. Blonde were mentioned in the same sentence. Mario clearly didn't want either within a fifteen-mile radius of his place.

"Your water."

Jake let the calendar pages fall back to Miss March. He took the bottle, unscrewed the cap and took a deep swallow. It was about the best thing he'd ever tasted. He felt it flow all the way to his stomach. Almost immediately, the pounding in the back of his head lessened. He knew the feeling was temporary. He swished a second swallow around, cleaning his mouth.

"Makes sense, right? What I said about calling the cops?" Mario said.

Jake nodded noncommittally. "Sure." Every time Mario spoke, dialing 911 became a better idea.

Mario blew the air out of his mouth in a great noisy breath and collapsed in the chair behind his desk. He interlaced his fingers across his balloon of a belly. "So, I guess if that's all… I'll tell Sofia you dropped by."

Jake knew he was being chased out of the office. He didn't mind a bit. "Yeah. Let her know."

He opened the door, took half a step out and saw the Intrepid. He paused. Since he was the only person in sight, Jake assumed the Intrepid belonged to Mario. Maybe the man forgot his phone in the trunk when he waddled into the Orifice at the beginning of the day. He said, "One more thing. When I came in I heard a phone ring in the trunk of your car." He shrugged. "You might want to get that. Maybe some more business."

Mario's lazy man bearing disappeared as rapidly as it had earlier. He sat up straight, eyes riveted on Jake. A fresh film of sweat instantly appeared on his face. The stains beneath each arm darkened. "Uh, Good. Yeah. I'll take care of it," he stammered.

Jake shook his head. The Orifice door slammed behind him. Strange, but it wasn't any of his business. It was time to get on the gas, leave the entire Gianolo family behind. If he never saw any of them again, Sofia included, it would be too soon. First though, he needed to talk to the police. After he told them about the assault, perhaps he'd mention the Intrepid, although he was unsure what he'd say about it.

CHAPTER 6

MARIO GIANOLO ROCKED back on the rear two legs of his chair. He twined plump fingers together behind his head and mentally patted himself on the back. He smiled smugly. The morning was shaping up. Eric Dalrymple had made a mistake. Mario let the smile widen. Next time he spoke with the crazy-man, he planned on working the blunder into conversation. After all, you want to crush and chip a car with a body in the trunk, you don't fly a big, colorful banner that says, "look inside," and a ringing phone was pretty much a big, colorful banner. Most people get curious when they hear that sort of thing. Just like Jake Harris did.

Until that moment Mario, hadn't been one hundred percent sure there was a body in the Intrepid. But, just in case there was, he'd made a concerted effort to ignore the vehicle. Assuming someone was locked in the trunk was far different than knowing for sure, and if the Boss wanted the vehicle chipped before sunset, who was Mario to ask, "Why the rush?" Now, after Harris mentioned the ringing phone, and after years of dealing with Dalrymple, little doubt remained. The only question left was…

Who?

He had to admit, he was curious. Not curious enough to

remove his ass from his perfectly molded office chair and look, but curious just the same. He suspected Chloe Sheridan. Word around the water cooler was, the Boss had grown tired of her. Too bad. Turning a fine piece of real estate like Chloe into mincemeat seemed a terrible shame.

Mario whistled softly.

He opened the top drawer of his desk and slid out the *Penthouse* he'd hastily stuffed in there when Harris walked into his office. He flipped to the photo layout and picked up where he'd left off. His hand fell to his crotch. He slowly started rubbing.

Did Chloe have belly button jewelry? He couldn't remember. He imagined she did. She dressed younger than she was, in torn-at-the-knee jeans and tops that showed off her nice flat stomach. Like an adolescent, which was backward, really. Chloe just shy of thirty and trying to look younger, while teenage girls everywhere dressed to look older.

Drinking in the photos, thinking about young girls with their pants hung low on their hips so everyone saw their thongs, Mario's breath shortened. His hand moved with more urgency. Mr. Blonde would have delaminated if he'd seen him, no doubt about it.

Tough shit.

Mario figured if he wanted to spank the monkey instead of getting busy with the Intrepid, it was his privilege. He had until sunset. Plenty of time to phone Paolo and Gino. He liked to delegate the sensitive tasks to the twins, rather than the other yard-apes who scrapped and parted out the wrecks. He trusted them. It wouldn't take long to drain the fluids and strip the Intrepid of the shit the magnets and sifters couldn't handle when the vehicle was chipped. Certainly not past sunset, so, Dalrymple could get stuffed.

Mario had stroked himself a fair-sized tent in his trousers by the time he moved from the photos to the letters all the authors swore were God's honest truth. He undid the top button of his pants and unzipped. He inhaled mightily. With his gut sucked in as far as it would go, he slid his hand down the curve of his belly, under the waistband of his shorts. He managed to wiggle his fingers in as deep as the second row of knuckles before his breath rushed out like a warm Chinook.

Damn.

It wasn't going to happen. Sitting at his desk, there was no way to get his hand on his unit without pushing his pants and shorts out of the way. Why was everything so hard? He sighed, then chuckled. Wrong choice of words. Why was life so difficult? Nothing came easy... which, on further thought, was also the wrong choice of words, Mario supposed.

He planted both hands on the arms of his chair and pushed himself up with a grunt. He scooped up the *Penthouse* and hustled down the hall, the swell of his belly leading the way, his erection following closely behind. The red, white, and blue suspenders dangled down by his knees.

He smiled. After he enjoyed five or six solitary minutes in the bathroom, screwing Dalrymple over in an almost literal fashion, he'd call Gino and Paolo. A short time later, the Intrepid and Chloe, or whoever it was in the trunk, would get crushed and chipped and it would no longer be his problem.

CHAPTER 7

WHEN HE WALKED out of the mobile home, the heat of the midday sun hit Jake like a physical blow. A wave of dizziness made him stagger. He sat down on the lowest plank, waiting motionless for the feeling to pass, listening to hot air and distant traffic and to Mario shuffling around the trailer. He hoped the dizziness wasn't a symptom of a concussion. He didn't think so. It was more likely a combination of bad air in the Orifice and the heat of the day rather than something as serious as a concussion. He swallowed dryly. His face throbbed. When he touched his cheeks, angry flares of pain radiated away from with the tips of his fingers.

Don't call the cops? Like hell.

After several minutes, he straightened. Stood. So far so good.

He cautiously started toward the Mustang, planning his next course of action. Driving to the hospital in his condition, in a strange city, wasn't the best idea but the alternatives weren't much better—he could call an ambulance and have it meet him at A1 or he could do nothing at all. Calling an ambulance seemed a touch melodramatic and doing nothing wasn't an option. Which left him back at choice one... drive himself and hope a big, recognizable H sign would show up before assault-induced double vision.

A hollow, metallic thump rang through the silent afternoon. Deep in thought, Jake kept walking, only dimly aware he heard the unusual noise. A second and a third thump quickly followed and these were loud enough to break into his thoughts. He stopped, planted his fists on his hips and glanced around out of questioning eyes. Aside from the Mustang and the Intrepid, the parking lot was still empty. There was nobody else in sight. He cocked his head, listening. A warm gust of wind ruffled his hair. Where did those sounds come from?

Thump.

Suddenly he knew. The Intrepid! First, a ringing phone. Next, metallic thumps. The phone was one thing. Easy to ignore. He did it all the time when he was trying to avoid telemarketers or the World Ways crew-scheduling department. Metallic thumps weren't as easy to disregard. Jake hurried back toward the Dodge. A nervous tingle shimmied up and down his spine. Standing with his knees against the rear bumper he hesitated a moment then rapped his knuckles on the trunk lid twice.

Twin thumps answered him.

He rapped again. Three times this time.

Thump.

Thump.

Thump.

After the third thump, Jake heard stifled squealing. He couldn't identify the sound. It didn't matter. The noises emanating from the trunk were clearly not mechanical. Since an animal couldn't make that kind of measured response, whatever was in the trunk had to be human.

The nervous tingle bloomed. Why was someone locked in the trunk of a car in a wrecking yard parking lot? He rushed around to the driver's side of the Intrepid. Pulled the door open. Crouching, he searched for a trunk release. Some cars had buttons on the dashboard or in the glove box. Others had levers along the doorsill. He didn't know where Chrysler hid theirs, but it was there somewhere. After a short search, he found it. He pushed the button, glancing over his shoulder as he did, in time to see the trunk lid bob up.

The squealing sounds instantly increased in volume. Their distraught quality raised the tiny hairs on his arms and on the back of his neck. Suddenly he wasn't so sure he wanted to see who was in the trunk, or see the person's condition.

It was too late to stop.

He had to know.

Curiosity made him forget about his pulped face. He stood up fast and stars filled his vision and the pain rushed back, making him gasp. He slammed his eyes shut and sucked a huge breath in through his teeth. Willing himself not to keel over, he braced himself with both palms flat on the roof of the car.

After several seconds, he cautiously opened his eyes. When it was clear he'd regained his equilibrium he crept toward the rear of the Intrepid, dragging the fingertips of one hand along the side of the car as though worried his balance would desert him a second time. His footsteps crunched in the gravel.

The frantic squealing intensified.

He risked a fast glance at the Orifice, hoping the sluggish Mario Gianolo hadn't strayed too far from his chair. Then, licking dry lips, Jake peered around the side of the car into the open trunk.

Two panicked eyes stared up at him, sparking copper in the afternoon sunshine. A strip of silver duct tape was smeared tight across a woman's mouth.

Jake felt his jaw draw drop. Without thinking he reached into the trunk, going for the duct tape gag, thinking, *As bad as I feel, she's got to feel worse.* Her face and shirt were caked in blood. Black eye makeup streaked down her face like bony, graveyard fingers. Tears cut lines through the dirt on her cheeks. The Intrepid had seen gravel roads and the trunk was thick with dust and grime. Her jeans were a grungy no-color. Her top, once yellow, Jake guessed, was muddy ochre.

"Shit," he muttered. "What's going on?" He pulled the duct tape away, moving slowly, knowing it would take skin with it.

The girl in the trunk wasn't so patient.

She twisted her head sideways, ripping the tape off in a single fast movement, taking strands of loose, red curls with it. Her eyes brimmed with tears. She rolled onto her side and raised her arms as much as possible in Jake's direction, sucking in great gasps of air. "Hands," she said between gulps.

Her terror was palpable and contagious. "I don't have a knife," he said, his voice strained. "We'll have to do it the hard way." He found the end of the tape wrapped around her wrists and scraped at it with his fingernail, loosening a corner. He swallowed dryly. Mr. Blonde had beaten him without effort or thought but it looked like he got away lucky, compared to what the Freak had planned for… "Who are you? What the fuck is going on?"

"Chloe Sheridan," she snapped. "Is that relevant right now?"

He started unravelling what seemed like an entire roll of tape from her wrists. The Orifice was a magnet to his eyes. He saw Mario Gianolo's huge silhouette cross in front of the window. His breath hitched. His trembling hands fumbled. The tiny corner of tape slipped away. He swore, searched with fingers the size of fence posts and found the loose end.

The distant murmur of an approaching vehicle slowly changed into a rumble. He cut a hasty glance at the road, sure he'd see the black Mercedes pulling into A1's parking lot, the chrome revolver coming up in the Freak's hand.

The driveway was clear.

"Hurry up." Chloe's voice squeaked with terror. She twisted when she spoke, yanking the tape away from him once more.

The approaching vehicle drew closer, the engine note low and throaty. Just like the Mercedes. Already shaky from the earlier beating, Jake's legs suddenly felt watery and unsubstantial. He shook off the feeling. Mr. Blonde *wasn't* coming back with his chrome hand-cannon and his high-pitched, maniacal laugh.

Or, maybe Mr. Blonde is coming back, a little voice in the back of his mind said. *Maybe he's storing Chloe in the trunk, while he grabs a coffee and a bagel, some shit like that.*

"Hold still," Jake said.

She stopped squirming long enough he somehow managed to get all the tape off her wrists.

The car drove past A1 without stopping.

Chloe swung her arms in front of her, shaking the feeling back into them. She slid to the left side of the trunk and extended her legs, moaning with relief as she straightened them. "My feet. They're taped too."

Jake found the end of the tape around her ankles and started unwrapping it. He flicked a glance at the Orifice. The window was empty. He turned his attention back to the tape around Chloe's ankles. As he did he caught a flicker of movement out the corner of his eye. His gaze snapped back in time to see Mario's profile cross the Orifice window, moving in the opposite direction it had only minutes before.

Only this time the silhouette paused.

Jake groaned. They'd run out of time.

CHAPTER 8

MARIO GIANOLO TOSSED the *Penthouse* at the plastic milk crate that served as the bathroom's magazine rack. It hit the side of the crate and fell to the floor. With the now pointless magazine lying forgotten at his feet, Mario stood with a grunt and hauled his pants up from his ankles. Foregoing the sink and in lieu of an anti-bacterial towelette similar to those Dalrymple favored, he simply swiped each palm down his thighs a couple of times. He wished the man were in his office right now. He would offer his hand as a friendly, conciliatory gesture to make up for the unpleasantness of their meeting. The idea of shaking the crazy-man's hand immediately after spanking the monkey made Mario laugh out loud.

Puffing slightly with fading exertion, moving in an awkward bowlegged shuffle, he walked out of the bathroom with less urgency than he'd entered four minutes earlier. He tugged down the fabric at the crotch of his pants with one hand. With the other hand he pulled up on his zipper. Part way up the zipper jammed. He tugged several more times but now it wouldn't move up or down. He guessed it had snagged on a piece of fabric but he couldn't see around the globe of his belly to be sure. After a couple of attempts, he let it go. He'd worry about it later. The time had come to call Paolo and Gino, get them busy with the Intrepid.

He dropped one shoulder and pulled a suspender over the top, wondering why he always got the crap jobs. Hold this briefcase, Mario. Scrap this car, Mario. Meanwhile Mr. fucking Blonde was dropping the Boss's name every day. The Boss this. The Boss that. And, in his spare time he's watching *Reservoir Dogs*. Mario owned *Goodfellas*, all three *Godfathers*, and seasons one through five of the *Sopranos* on DVD. He figured it begged the question—who was more qualified to work for the Outfit?

As Mario reached for the second suspender, he happened to glance out the office window and holy shit he couldn't believe what he saw and, if he thought his heart was going clippity-clop in the bathroom a minute ago, it was racing like Secretariat now.

Jake Harris stood at the bumper of the Intrepid, reaching in, helping Chloe Sheridan climb out of the car.

Shock sent Mario's blood pressure soaring like a homerun ball in Wrigley Field. Panicked sweat beaded on his back and under his arms. For an eternal five seconds he stood frozen, unable to absorb what he was seeing, but understanding it at the same time—how any chance of working full time for the Outfit was escaping out the back of a Dodge Intrepid.

How Dalrymple would go nuts.

How next time it could easily be him in the trunk of the car.

How he needed to stop Harris and Sheridan at this exact moment because it was the only way this situation would turn out favorably.

Mario forgot about his fly stuck halfway between here and there. He forgot about the dangling suspender. Cursing Dalrymple for getting cute rather than simply shooting Chloe Sheridan, he leaned over the top of his desk and grabbed the Smith and Wesson. He spun around and after several shuffling steps, flung his office door open.

CHAPTER 9

"THIS WON'T BE good," Jake mumbled under his breath.

"What did you say?" Chloe asked breathlessly.

Trying not to scare her worse than she already was, Jake made an effort to control the tension in his voice. "Mario. He's seen us."

Her eyes widened. "Oh shit, oh shit, oh shit, oh shit." She shoved Jake's hands away, yanking at the tape around her feet in terror, instead of unwinding it.

"Don't pull it," Jake said. "It won't break. You've got to unwrap it."

The Orifice door flew open, slammed on the side of the mobile with a ringing metallic crash. Mario Gianolo's round bulk filled the frame. His eyes bulged. His sparse hair had come unglued and stuck out in unlikely directions. A flap of shirt poked from his open fly like a White Sox pennant. One suspender was over his shoulder, the other still dangled by his knee. Jake noticed it all like it was the background of a painting. It was there, but it wasn't what he focused on. It was the pistol in Mario's hand that grabbed his attention. He couldn't take his eyes off it.

"You two. Stop right there," Mario yelled, and maybe he thought the order and the pistol was enough. Maybe he thought

Jake and Chloe would stand there and wait for him to lumber down the steps and bundle them back into the Intrepid's trunk.

"Help me out," Chloe said. Her voice, bordering hysterical, sounded like glass scraping on metal.

Jake's head flashed around. The tape around her legs was gone. She held her pack in one hand and reached for him with the other. He linked his hand in hers, held on firmly and towed her out of the trunk.

"My car," he said, "let's go." He pivoted and rapidly stretched his legs into a sprint, more than ready to leave the Windy City behind. That fast he lost sight of Chloe. Couldn't even sense her near him. He cut a quick glance over his shoulder. Saw her down on one knee, only a step or two away from the Intrepid.

Jake immediately realized her legs hadn't recovered. Shit! He just wanted to run, get away before bullets started flying, before the Mercedes reappeared. What was he thinking, coming here after Paolo and Gino's threatening, man-to-man talk? He should have known nothing good could happen. The twins were nuts. Why did he expect the older brother to be any different?

But he couldn't just leave Chloe to fend for herself. She was struggling and if he left her, she'd be back in the trunk before he disappeared over the horizon. Skidding to a halt, he spun. In three long steps he stood beside her. He put a hand under each of her arms and hoisted her to her feet. She staggered once, nodded her thanks and was off like a thoroughbred.

"I said stop," Mario hollered with what sounded like pure desperation. He wobbled down the cinderblock steps. "You can't do this to me." His face glowed brilliant red, his blood pressure climbing like the space shuttle Endeavour.

Jake looked back in time to see him raise the pistol. A sharp pop rang out. Mario's arm jerked skyward. Chloe screamed. Had he hit her with his first bullet? Jake slowed momentarily, expecting to see her stumble, to see a crimson carnation of blood bloom on her back. He'd have to stop, pick her up and carry her to the Mustang. Dead or alive, there was no way he was leaving her behind to the cast of the Wrecking-Yard-of-Horrors.

Chloe just kept running, the backpack slamming her in the side with every step. Two more shots cracked in the afternoon air. Jake ran too, as bullets split the air around him. Chloe made it to the Mustang and he was only a single step behind her. She yanked frantically on the passenger door handle like maybe she'd over-power the lock and he thought, *why did I lock my car in an empty parking lot?*

He stuffed his hand into his Levis searching for keys. They weren't in his right pocket. Or his left. When did he use them last? He couldn't remember. His mind was frighteningly empty.

Think!

After the confrontation with Mr. Blonde, he'd opened the trunk to get a clean shirt. That was the last time he used them. He circled to the rear of the car. Saw the keys sticking out of the trunk lock. He snatched at them.

"Hurry," Chloe screamed. Her eyes, wide with dread, stared over his shoulder.

Jake didn't want to look. He couldn't help himself. He saw Mario break into an ungainly trot, his right arm stretched out in front of him, the pistol leading the way. It twitched twice as he squeezed off two more rounds. Both shots kicked up dirt near the Mustang, Mario's accuracy improving as he drew closer.

Jake fumbled for the key fob. The key chain slipped out of his fingers. He dropped to one knee. Scooped it up. Stabbed the unlock button on the fob. The electric locks released both doors. He jumped into the driver's seat, expecting Chloe to dive in beside him but her gaze was pinned on Mario.

"Chloe," Jake yelled. "Let's go already."

She tugged on the door handle and maybe she still didn't expect it to open because when it did she stumbled backward a couple of steps and fell to the ground on her rear. Flailing at the door handle like it was a lifeline, she hauled herself back to her feet. She lobbed her pack into the car. A split second later she dove into the passenger seat after it. Before she had a chance to close the door, Jake dropped the gearshift into first. The Mustang shot forward, pounding through potholes with teeth-jarring force for the second time that day, leaving Mario behind in a cloud of dust and gravel.

At the edge of the road, Jake looked both ways and, wouldn't you know it, almost no cars all morning, and now there were vehicles coming from both directions. He slowed, hoping the timing would work, hoping he wouldn't have to come to a complete stop before easing into traffic.

Mario's enormous profile rapidly filled the rear-view mirror. His arm snapped skyward several more times. Jake couldn't hear the shots over the Mustang's engine. How many damn bullets were in the pistol? The man was relentless. And, there it went again…

A metallic thud rang through the Mustang. A slice of a second later a neat round hole appeared in the rear passenger window. The glass spider webbed around it. Chloe howled. She pushed herself back, shrinking into her seat. Jake hammered the brakes, sending her flying into the dashboard.

"My car, you son-of-a-bitch," he shouted. He slammed the car into Park, and went for the door handle. He couldn't explain why but he was ready to climb out of the car and take on Mario and his pistol barehanded.

Until Chloe snapped him back to reality.

"What are you doing?" she shrieked. "Go. Go. Go. Or we're both dead."

Mario squeezed the trigger.

A second clang. A third. The back end of the Mustang seemed to twitch. Was he aiming for the tires? They wouldn't get far if Mario shot a hole through a tire. Jake looked at Chloe, then glanced over his shoulder in time to see Mario's arm jerk skyward one more time. Then he jumped on the gas and threaded the needle between two cars crisscrossing in front of A1 Auto Wreckers. One vehicle swerved out of his way. The driver barely slowed before speeding away. The second vehicle veered into Jake's path, then abruptly slued off in the opposite direction leaving empty asphalt in front of the Mustang.

The rear tires squawked and three hundred and ninety horses slammed Jake and Chloe back in their leather seats, torpedoing them away from the wrecking yard.

CHAPTER 10

FOR MARIO IT all happened like a slide show, someone's impatient finger on the button. Click. Harris and
Sheridan sprinting for the car.

Click. Yelling at them.

Click. Chasing them.

Click. Heedlessly popping off shots as he ran.

Mario thought he got lucky, maybe hit Harris when he put a
bullet through the wide side post behind the driver's seat, because
the Mustang came to a stop. For a brief moment, grim elation
spurred him. His lungs burned. His chest heaved. He wasn't a
sprinter and every step sent knives of pain slicing from his feet to
the base of his spine. He closed the distance between himself and
the Mustang in one last concentrated effort knowing if he didn't
capture Harris and Sheridan before they hit the open road, he'd be
lucky to ever see them again.

The slide show ended. Time sped up.

With an angry snarl, the Mustang leapt to life and launched
itself out of the parking lot. It slowed briefly, long enough to avoid
a Mazda 626 coming from the other direction, then with two
loud squeals the rear tires grabbed traction on the broiling asphalt.

Wisps of blue smoke curled away from the wheels and the car rapidly shrank into the distance.

Mario screamed, "No," and fruitlessly pulled the trigger again and again and again. The pistol only barked once before the slide slammed back, ejecting the last empty casing. The brass twinkled in the afternoon sunlight at the height of its parabola before landing on the ground near his feet. He dropped his arm to his side, the SW99 still loose in his fingers. He stood there for several seconds, panting. As his breath stabilized, the realization of what had just happened crystallized in his mind. An icy fear, like winter's first breath washed over him.

Chloe Sheridan had escaped.

Dalrymple had given him specific instructions and Mario had failed to follow through. The crazy-man would take it poorly, like it was a personal insult, like Mario deliberately screwed him over. He briefly considered ignoring the problem, pretending like he'd done exactly what Dalrymple wanted. As quickly as the idea appeared, he dismissed it. If he lied and Chloe re-surfaced, like he knew she eventually would, Dalrymple would lose what little was left of his mind. So would the Boss. Mario wouldn't be the only one who'd end up dead. The Outfit would go after Paolo, Gino, and Sofia too. Dalrymple would need to send a message.

Alternatively, he could call Dalrymple and get in front of the problem—immediately tell the crazy-man Sheridan escaped. With a shudder, Mario dismissed this idea as well. He wasn't working retail, where admitting your mistake meant everybody walked away happy. Dalrymple's wrath would be just as fierce today as it would be in a week or month, whenever she showed up again.

There was one other choice and Mario thought it was his best and only chance. Since he couldn't ignore the problem, he would handle it himself. He'd let Dalrymple believe the job was done and find Jake Harris and Chloe Sheridan on his own. When he found them, he'd have Paolo and Gino take care of them.

In the silent heat of the day, Mario suddenly became aware of a baby's desperate cries. His head swung around. He stared down the road and his mouth fell open. One hundred yards away, a white jet of steam hissed and sizzled out of the Mazda 626. The front of the car was caved in, bent around a telephone pole.

Mario haltingly staggered toward the Mazda, wondering what happened, thinking when the driver swerved to avoid the Mustang, maybe he lost control and hit the pole. The baby's shrill howls poured from the broken rear passenger window, growing louder as he approached. There was no reason for a rear window to be smashed, he thought. The driver hit the pole head on.

Slowly, with sickening comprehension, it dawned on him. His final shot hit the 626, not the Mustang.

The baby's cries reached out and ripped at his heart. He sucked in his stomach, stuffed the slim-framed SW99 into his waistband and broke into an awkward trot. *Oh mother of God, please, please let the baby's parent be alive.* Some faceless schmo driving by in a pickup and he wouldn't have given the wrecked vehicle a second thought. But he had siblings. He knew how important a baby was to a family. The phrase, "innocent bystander" seemed very applicable to an infant. The schmo who drives through the middle of a firefight and hits a telephone pole, he's paying for something. Karma. Or bad luck. Whatever. A baby doesn't owe a nickel or a favor to anyone.

He saw movement in the driver's seat and the wave of relief was overwhelming.

The driver's door swung open. A woman stepped out. She held a cell phone to her ear with her right hand. The other arm crossed her chest, clutching her right shoulder. Blood seeped from a cut on her forehead, contrasting harshly with white powder that coated the upper half of her body—talc from the exploded airbag. She wobbled into the side of the Mazda but her motherly instinct was strong. A firm look of determination crossed her face. She stumbled around the car to the passenger side where her infant cried in the car seat.

In the distance sirens wailed.

Mario knew immediately to whom the young mother was speaking. He wasted a few precious seconds looking up and down the road searching for the cops before he turned and lumbered toward the Orifice. The pistol in his waistband stabbed him in the belly with each step. He slowed his gait long enough to tug it out of his pants. Where could he lose it?

With only seconds to decide his first thought was the Intrepid, maybe under the seat. He dismissed the idea immediately. The Dodge would be searched. No other place popped to mind, except maybe tossing it under the steps on his way into the Orifice.

He was nowhere near fast enough. He stood in the parking lot wracked with indecision still clutching the empty handgun when two cop cars came to a screeching stop. Officers boiled out of their cruisers clutching their own weapons. Mario raised his arms high above his head. The Smith and Wesson fell from his slack fingers and clattered in the gravel near his feet.

He wasn't as upset as he might have been. The afternoon's fiasco would have serious ramifications but he couldn't help thinking he was better off in jail where Dalrymple couldn't touch him.

CHAPTER 11

FIVE MILES AND three stoplights later Jake unclenched the steering wheel. The adrenaline was wearing off, leaving him bone weary and aching all over. He suppressed a yawn and glanced sideways at Chloe fidgeting in the passenger seat. Curiosity burned. Who was she? Why was she locked in the trunk of a car?

She saw his look and said sourly, "Why do guys do that? Use the passenger seat like a suitcase?"

Jake raised his eyebrows. It wasn't exactly the "thanks" he was expecting. He forced himself to ignore a quick flash of irritation, knowing fatigue made him impatient. She'd been through a lot. Certainly more than him. She had every right to be touchy, even if it was his car and using his passenger seat for whatever he pleased was entirely up to him.

Chloe pushed her backpack between the seats, dropping it on the floor in the back. The partially folded Chicago map followed. Jake's cell phone found a comfortable place between her thighs. The box that held the books on CD landed in her lap. Finally, she flipped the bag of pizza-flavored Doritos over her shoulder. Chips spilled out of the airborne bag littering Jake's spotless Mustang.

"Hey, hey, hey," he snapped. "Cut it out. My car is clean. I want to keep it that way." He softened his tone. "Pick them up, please."

Chloe squinted at him. "Who am I? Your maid?"

Jake took a deep breath. Managed to contain his irritation with the thinnest binding of thread. "I don't know who you are. But you're in my car. I drove twelve hundred miles without dropping chips on the floor. I don't care if your vehicle is a garbage truck. Mine isn't. So, pick them up."

She crossed her arms over her chest. "I'm not a waitress." Clear. Succinct. Non-negotiable. A fiery red glow heated her high, prominent cheekbones.

Jake saw granite stubbornness and knew as surely as night followed day that a debate with Chloe was something he'd never win. He wiped an annoyed hand down his face. "Shit," he muttered. At that instant there was nothing he wanted more than to go home. Just kick Chloe out of the car, leave her on the side of the road and drive home to Tampa. He wouldn't stop for anything but gasoline. When he got home, he'd kiss his landlady's feathery, powdered cheek and he'd mow her lawn or water her flowers or wash her New Yorker, whatever she wanted, and after Mark finished his shift, they'd play nine holes. Some shit like that.

Unfortunately, none of that was possible.

Unless... There was still an employment opportunity with Executive Flight Charters. The company hadn't come through with a flying position before he left Tampa, but the chief pilot had suggested he stay in touch. A tenuous flicker of hope flared to life. Was it worth calling Executive again? Why not? He was due for some good luck. Perhaps he could turn around and go home, and put an end to any more homicidal Mercedes owners, self-involved hitchhikers, and mosquitoes the size of crows he was certain to find in Ontario, Canada. Perhaps he could end this nonsensical road trip right now.

Jake shoulder checked. Slowed.

Chloe's gaze swung from his face to the road behind them, and back. "What are you doing?"

With the car in Park, idling on the side of the road, Jake unsnapped his seat belt. Staring straight ahead he thrust out his arm, palm flat. "My phone. Please."

She slapped the cell into his hand. He climbed out of the car, flipping the door shut behind him with more force than he intended. It crashed shut and he winced. He pushed speed dial nine, Executive's number memorized in his phone. While he waited for someone to answer, he drummed nervous fingers on the roof of the car. After several rings, a voice he recognized answered.

"Good afternoon. Executive Flight Charters. This is Becky. Can I help you?"

"Hi Becky. Jake Harris calling. Is Gary in?"

"Hi Jake. Please hold."

Jake waited with his heart banging like an artillery barrage in his chest, his hand clammy on the phone. He didn't know why asking for a job affected him this way. Maybe it was the fear of rejection. Job-hunting was demeaning. It smacked of groveling. Especially when he wanted it so badly. Mark laughed at that, told Jake to get over himself. The world revolved around people working a job and spending what they made. Didn't matter if you were a teenager flipping hamburgers or a CEO managing a Fortune 500 company. At some point, everyone asked someone else for a job.

"Gary Lewis."

"Gary, it's Jake Harris calling."

"Hi Jake."

"Hi. I'm in Chicago. On my way to northern Canada. A place called Sioux River to fly a Navajo and a Beaver. I was wondering..." Jake's voice trailed away. This was where it got difficult. "Well, I was wondering if there were any—"

"Keep driving, Jake. There's no positions available. Not yet."

Jake closed his eyes and dropped his chin to his chest. He

paced beside the Mustang trying to walk off his disappointment. Little clouds of dust puffed up with each step. A sticky film of sweat moistened his forehead and the small of his back. He wasn't sure if heat or nerves were responsible.

"Jake," Gary said, his voice patient but firm, "I get two, three resumes a day. Most of them from guys right out of flight school. The rest are from people with experience. Guys like you. You have an advantage over them because you took the time to come in and meet me. To see our operation. That's the only reason I took this call. This is the last time. I've got your resume. I like it. I'll call if a position opens up. Okay?"

Completely defeated, Jake nodded, although there was nobody to see the gesture. "Sorry to bother you."

"It's no bother. You get a new number, give Becky a call and leave it with her. She knows who you are."

"Sure thing."

"Good luck up north. I've got to run." He disconnected.

Jake closed the cell, ending the call. He grit his teeth against a hopeless surging anger. "Shit," he yelled at the top of his lungs. He kicked the Mustang's rear tire.

Pain lanced through his ankle.

He swore again, hopping beside the road on one foot, breathing rapidly while waves of pain radiated up and down his leg. After a couple of minutes and several deep, calming breaths he climbed back into the Mustang. Without really thinking about it, he handed Chloe his cell phone like it was Mark sitting in the passenger seat and not a complete stranger.

She took the phone without comment.

He dangled his wrist over the steering wheel. Lost in thought, he blew out a heavy sigh. The airline industry was flat. At best, the majors were maintaining the status quo. Many of his colleagues took nonflying positions after World Ways went bankrupt—Home Depot, landscaping, contracting. That sort of thing.

Against those odds, Jake managed to find a flying job. Tundra Air was small. It was miles away from World Ways, both literally and figuratively. The owner didn't think air regulations mattered in the bush. On the other hand, the cash was good, the living expenses next to nothing. Above all, it was a flying position.

"Those guys, they'll be coming." Chloe's voice climbed an octave as she spoke. She glanced out the rear window, a hopeless expression on her face. "We've really gotta get out of here."

Jake said, "Where can I drop you? The police station?"

"What am I gonna tell them?"

He cut her a confused look. Wasn't the answer obvious? "Tell them why you were locked in the trunk. Tell them who put you in there."

Chloe snorted. "Yeah, right."

"Okay. No cops then," Jake mumbled. Louder he said, "Hospital then? That suit you?"

"Whatever. Let's just go."

"You didn't pick up the chips."

She gave her eyes a little roll and her head a little shake and she turned away, stared out the window, and muttered, "Obviously."

Jake pressed his lips into a thin hard line. After everything else, it was the impatient little mutter that used up all his remaining patience and sympathy. Despite how far out of his way it would have taken him, he could have traveled north via Montreal and visited Marie-Claude. She helped him get the job—it was her uncle who owned Tundra Air. Or, he could have chosen St Louis. Last time he was in town he traded numbers with a lady named Sandra. Neither of them had a pen so she gave him her lipstick and he wrote his number on the inside of her leg. The last three digits ended up high on the creamy white flesh above her thigh high stocking. But, no. Instead of Marie-Claude or Sandra, he ended up with Chloe Sheridan throwing Doritos around his car like confetti.

Well, if she wanted to get stitched up, he'd drive her to the hospital because that's what a decent person did. If she didn't want the ride, that was her choice too. Either way, orange Doritos crumbs speckling black leather was the final straw, the culmination of the entire crappy month.

He said, "You don't get into a stranger's car, trash it, then order him around like a taxi driver. Clean up the mess you made. Do it now or we'll wait right here. All night if we have to." He shut the Mustang's engine off, emphasizing his point.

The haughty attitude from moments before vanished. "What are you doing?" she asked incredulously.

"You heard me." He watched her squirm in the seat, probably remembering what she'd lived through, thinking about what she might have to face again. A duct tape gag. Feet and hands taped together. Imprisoned in the trunk of a car. It must have been suffocating in the trunk. With her mouth taped and her nose bloody she would have labored for every breath. He felt his resolve slip. In a softer tone he said, "Just pick up the chips."

Tears filled her eyes.

Her fear was infectious. Nerve spiders scurried all over Jake's back. His stomach felt unpleasantly hollow. Mr. Blonde was out there. Jake wanted to look behind them, needed to look just to be sure the Mercedes wasn't eating up the pavement, Mr. Blonde coming fast with his polished revolver and uncontained rage. He resisted, knowing if he looked Chloe would see he was as scared as she was.

Suddenly he felt like a total heel. "Listen, Chloe. I'm on a timeline here. I was supposed to meet someone tonight. Looks like I'll be in emergency instead. Either way, I don't have time to waste. I've got to keep moving. Could you just clean up the mess you made? Please? Then we're on our way."

"You're an asshole," Chloe said. She started picking up the pizza Doritos.

He helped.

When all the chips were back in the bag where they belonged, Jake started the Mustang and pulled back onto the road. Chloe stuck her hands out the window and rubbed orange Doritos crumbs into the wind. Finished, she crossed her arms over her chest and stayed twisted sideways in the seat with her back to him. Eventually, without looking at him, she said, "What did you think you were doing back there?"

Jake didn't like her tone one bit, sort of calling him a dumb-ass without saying the words. "You mean when I rescued you from the trunk of a car?" He didn't expect an answer. Chloe didn't surprise him. She slipped back into her childish sulk.

Likely she was wondering about why he stopped when Mario shot the car. Narrowing his eyes, he thought about the question. He quickly gave up. He couldn't explain it to himself. There was no way he'd even try with Chloe.

After another long stretch of silence, she shifted. The leather squeaked as she settled into a more comfortable position, her back no longer facing Jake. "I wasn't kidding, you know."

Jake shot her a questioning look. "Pardon me?"

"Dalrymple. Mr. Blonde," she explained. "When he finds out I didn't go through the crusher, he'll go wild. The Boss wants me dead. Dalrymple was supposed to kill me. The sick bastard finds out I'm alive, he'll go wild."

A killer who works for the Boss? "I don't know what you're talking about," Jake said, fidgeting in his normally enveloping leather seat. He had an idea he knew exactly what she was saying.

Chloe made a vague, dismissive gesture. "Maybe you can understand this. Stay of execution? You know what that means?"

Jake thinned his lips. Throw condescending into the friendly mix of personality traits she'd shown him. He didn't bother responding.

"I appreciate you pulling me out of that car. I do. But you just killed yourself." She raised a finger and said, "One, Dalrymple will come after us because he screwed up a job for the Outfit and the Boss won't accept that. He'll come after us because, two," she held up a second finger, "I might have told you something. And finally, three," she looked at his battered face, "he'll come after us because you rescued me and he'll consider that a personal insult." Three fingers stood straight up, wriggling in Jake's direction.

"I can tell you're grateful." His voice dripped sarcasm. "I really can. But Mr. Blonde is never going to see me again. If he looks, he won't find me. You know why?" Jake didn't wait for an answer. "Because after I drop you at the hospital I'm leaving Chicago. I'm not coming back. I'm going so far from here he won't know where to start looking. So, I'm not too worried about Mr. Blonde."

For a while she didn't say anything. Jake drove, savoring the silence and hoped a sign for a hospital would show up before he had to ask Chloe for directions.

"Who were you meeting?"

"What?" Jake asked, confused.

"Tonight. Who were you meeting at A1? It's not the kind of place people stop on their way through town."

"Believe it or not," he said, "Mario Gianolo's got a sister." He added unnecessarily, "Our date's off."

Chloe nodded. "Sofia. I've never met her. I bet she's a nice girl, judging from her brothers."

"If she was a nice girl I wouldn't have been going out with her."

Chloe smiled slightly and rolled her eyes. There was no malice in her expression. "You were just hoping to get your oil changed. Is that it?" She played with her hair, tugging down a long strand of unruly red curls, letting it boing back up. "Where do you know her from?"

Jake shook his head, uncomfortable discussing his personal life with a complete stranger. "Doesn't matter."

"Who'd you call back there?"

"None of your business."

"What happened to your face?"

Shit, he was starting to wish she'd get angry once more. Once she started talking she never shut up. Jake let go of the gearshift long enough to point to his face. "Your buddy, Mr. Blonde—"

"He's not my buddy."

"—did this. He said he busted up someone named Chloe Sheridan. Then he went to work on me. He said he was having a good day. Freak."

"Why's he mad at you?"

"He almost drove into me with his car so I fingered him." Jake shrugged. He managed a short chuckle. "He didn't like that much." Chloe cracked a second grin, wider this time and despite the blood and bruises, Jake saw a pretty face.

"Not too many people get away with flipping Dalrymple the bird."

"How do we get to a hospital?"

"Where are you going?

"A hospital."

"You're a tourist, right? What I mean, if you were traveling north, it'd be better to find a hospital in that direction. No point going south and having to backtrack."

Jake nodded. "Okay, I am traveling north, as it turns out. North until the road ends."

Chloe gave him directions. When she finished, she said, "I don't know your name."

He lifted his hand off the gearshift and stuck it out for her to shake. "Jake Harris."

She grabbed it and shook briefly, getting the formalities out of the way. "Where is it you're going Dalrymple will never find you?" Skepticism in her tone and etched all over her face.

"Doesn't matter. We'll get checked out at the hospital." He peered at himself in the rear view mirror. "Hopefully they can center my nose. After that you and I are never going to see each other again."

"But you're positive, one hundred percent, he won't find you there?"

Jake shoulder checked, flipped his signal on and slid into the right hand lane. Traffic was thick. Moving fast. He shook his head and blinked, trying to concentrate on the road despite the occasional wave of dizziness and Chloe jabbering in his ear, asking questions he'd already answered.

"There is absolutely no chance in hell he'll find me," he said with complete conviction. There was no way the Freak would find him in northern Canada because he wouldn't have the first clue where to look, if he even bothered looking, which seemed unlikely to Jake.

After about three seconds of silence Chloe said, in the same non-negotiable tone he heard earlier, "In that case, I'm coming with you." Without missing a beat, she gave him the same wide smile he'd seen earlier. "Come on. Tell me who you called."

CHAPTER 12

JAKE JERKED IN surprise. He flashed an astonished glance at Chloe, sitting so contentedly in his passenger seat.

She gazed out the windshield with a small, faraway smile on her face. "Eyes on the road, Jake. It's the next exit you want."

Jake dragged his eyes back to the freeway unfolding in front of them. There was no way in hell he was driving to Ontario with her tagging along. The Outfit, what Jake was beginning to understand meant the Mob, was chasing her. The Boss, whoever he was, wanted her dead. And, there was Mr. Blonde. Jake didn't know what to think about him. After taking a deep breath, he opened his mouth to object. Words failed him. He shook his head.

"Yes, Jake. I am."

He risked a second glance at his passenger. Her jaw was set, her face unyielding, the same non-negotiable expression as earlier. His knuckles turned white on the steering wheel. His fist clenched, released and re-clenched the gearshift.

Chloe picked up the pendant on her necklace, some sort of abstract fish shape, and began sliding it back and forth on the chain. "You said you were going someplace Dalrymple will never find you. That's what you said." She finally looked at him and shrugged. "I don't want him to find me either. I'm coming with you."

"Chloe—"

"Next left."

Jake signaled then jerked the steering wheel left.

Chloe's expression remained impassive. She raised her arm and braced herself against the dashboard. "Right at the lights."

Hand over hand Jake cranked the steering wheel. He mashed the gas pedal. The rear tires squawked and the Mustang leapt through the corner.

"See the big H hospital sign? We're almost there!" Her voice was chirpy. She looked at him with a smile that shone through the dirt, blood and swollen nose. "Let's go in, get fixed up. Then we can hit the road."

He pulled into a vacant spot in front of the hospital meant for dropping off and picking up. He kept both hands on the wheel and stared straight ahead. "You get out. I'll find a parking spot."

There was a long silence. Jake felt the heat of her gaze boring into the side of his head.

Finally, Chloe said, "Okay, Jake. But you're not thinking about dumping me then leaving, are you?" She watched him closely while she spoke.

Jake pressed his lips into a hard thin line. He wouldn't meet her eyes.

"I thought so," Chloe said, nodding. "You could do that. But if I don't see you in about ten minutes I'm telling the cops, the nurses, the doctors, everybody in the waiting room, even Jerry Springer if I can get him on the phone, that you did this to me." She pointed at her face while she spoke.

Jake wiped his wrist across his forehead. He just wanted to put the miserable, pain-in the-ass, Windy City behind him.

"Or," Chloe continued, "we can go in together, tell them I walked into a door. Or, missed a catch playing softball." There was a moment of silence. She reached out, touched his arm and said excitedly, "How 'bout this. We tell them we were in a car accident?"

"Shit," Jake muttered, feeling completely defeated. She held all the cards, at least until they were checked out and it was on record he hadn't laid a hand on her. Or, maybe he wouldn't make up stories when he walked into the Emergency Room. Maybe, when the nurse handed him the clipboard with the androgynous human outline attached, he would draw arrows pointing to all the places that hurt. And, while he waited for a doctor to re-center his nose and examine all those aching body parts, he would phone the cops. Tell them exactly what happened, providing detailed descriptions of both Mario Gianolo and Mr. Blonde.

Jake explained all this to Chloe, adding he might describe the Mercedes while he was at it.

Chloe said simply, "You're not going to do that, Jake."

Jake orbited the parking lot in increasingly larger circles, thinking a guy would be in real trouble if he was bleeding out the ears, some shit like that, because there wasn't a parking spot in sight. "Why not?"

"Because police reports slow things down. Here's how it will go. The cops will—"

"Let me guess. The cops will arrest him. His friends will alibi him. The cops will kick him loose," Jake said, paraphrasing Mario Gianolo's earlier explanation. "Is that about right?"

"That's exactly right, Jake."

"And, what?" He was tense with annoyance. Through clenched teeth he said, "We look like we do, and Mr. Blonde never pays for it?"

Chloe nodded with a sympathetic look. "Sorry. The cops won't have any reason to hold him. But it won't end here. You know that, right?"

She spoke gently and he knew she was trying to ease him into the bad news. An almost indiscernible tingle of fear gnawed at his belly. "What do you mean?"

"If it were just a matter of pissing Dalrymple off, you'd never see him again. He knows you'll call the cops. He knows the cops will kick him loose. He'll lose an afternoon. That's as much an irritant as you are to him. The only way he wastes another minute on you is if he sees you on the street." Chloe cracked a crooked grin. "If that happens he'd probably give you another thumping. Just to make up for the time he lost."

The fish pendant between her fingers made a soft buzzing sound as she slid it back and forth on the chain. She dropped it long enough to shake an index finger in the air between them. "But, when you helped me out of the trunk it stopped being about you. Now it's about us. Whether you like it or not, we're on borrowed time. You for being in the wrong place at the wrong time. Me for…" She looked away, avoiding his sudden interested glance. "Sometimes pretty artwork hanging on a wall disapears if it's been there for too long. I was like that. Let's just say, I heard things."

When she looked back her copper eyes flashed with intensity. "It will start with Mario Gianolo. He'll want to find us fast. Before Dalrymple hears we're gone. To minimize the size of his screw-up, you understand? 'Yeah, they got away but I got them right back.'"

Jake nodded. He slid into a parking spot and let the Mustang idle while he scanned the lot, searching for a pay machine. "How do you pay for parking here? You think they validate?"

Chloe ignored his question. "Right now Gianolo is on the phone calling everyone he's ever met. Telling them to watch the hospitals and police stations, keep an eye open for a nice Mustang with a couple of fresh bullet holes. While you're busy wasting time with the cops, those guys will be looking for us. They'll find us. It's just a matter of when."

"So, to sum it all up," Jake pointed back and forth between his and Chloe's battered faces, "the cops won't do anything about this. And, us hanging around gives the Outfit plenty of time to prepare a decent burial for us in a Chicago repository?"

Chloe nodded. "Yeah."

"Not me. Not if I took off on my own."

She looked serious while she considered the question. "I'm not sure. The Outfit might go looking for you whether I was with you or not. Although, I doubt it." She puffed out her cheeks and let the air out in a noisy whoosh. "I just don't know about the Outfit." Her voice firmed. "Dalrymple though, he finds out I escaped and you helped, he'll be coming. He takes embarrassment poorly. Gianolo. You. Me. We all made him look bad." She nodded a second time and there wasn't a shred of doubt in her voice. "He'll find some time and look for us."

Jake cut a look at Chloe sitting beside him, arms crossed over her chest hugging herself, goose bumps pebbling her arms. She was silent for once, giving him time to work it all out. He turned the AC off and then absently scratched the back of his head. He needed his nose re-set. If it didn't take too long, and he forgot about talking to the authorities, he could be on the road in a hurry.

The way Chloe told it, Mario would find them in Chicago. Jake was still convinced nobody would look for him in Sioux River. "Let me drop you off at the police station," he said, trying one more time to get rid of her and salvage his trip. "You tell them he tossed you in the trunk. Tell them why—"

"No, Jake." She shook her head. "I know some things but I don't have proof. The cops won't arrest him on my word alone. Who am I? And, they won't arrest him for putting me in the trunk for the same reason they won't arrest him for beating you up."

Jake sighed. "Because his friends will say it wasn't him and alibi him."

"Exactly. They'd thank me for the info, say goodbye and I'd be back in the trunk by nightfall."

Jake blew out a second noisy sigh of exasperation and resignation. "All right," He shut the car off. "Let's get checked out and then get out of here." He climbed out of the Mustang and closed his door with a firm click. Chloe followed, giving hers a hard hip check while she settled her pack over one shoulder.

He shot her an irritated glare. "Take it easy. You don't have to slam it."

She stuck her tongue out at him and made a face.

"Real mature." After a rueful glance at the bullet-pocked rear quarter panel, he aimed his key chain at the car. The doors locked with two quick chirps. "Listen, Chloe—"

"You're not going to start with me again, are you? How you're not gonna let me go with you?" Angry color bloomed in her cheeks like mini carnations.

"No. Actually, I was going to say, you can't go in there wearing that shirt. It's bloody. Covered in dirt. One look and the nurses will run screaming the other way. But if you're good with it, fine by me."

"Oh. Sorry."

"You want," he said, "I'll get you one of my shirts to wear over top of your own. You can change inside." He popped the trunk. He opened his roller bag, placed some neatly folded chinos off to one side and put the two ball caps Mark bought him at Sports Authority on top of the pants. Then, like he was rifling through a Rolodex, he thumbed through layers of shirts, finally selecting a white polo with World Ways embroidered in blue on the breast. "How about this one? You'd look good in that."

"You mind if I borrow a hat too?"

Jake faltered, not because he minded her borrowing anything, more because the hats were gifts from his brother and he hadn't planned on wearing them right away.

"It's okay," Chloe said, with a confused sort of lilt in her voice. "I don't need one, I guess."

"No, Chloe, take a hat. My brother bought them for me the day before I left Tampa. I was…" He was going to say he missed Mark, he wanted to savor the caps, put them on a shelf, some shit like that. He didn't really know what, just that he hadn't planned on wearing them yet. But he couldn't bring himself to tell her that. It sounded weak. He settled for, "Who do you like? Yankees or Boston?"

She stood there, hip shot, sucking noisily on her lower lip while she thought about it.

"He bought me two caps because no matter where you go, most people either like the Sox and hate the Yankees, or the other way around. Either way, you'll always be able to make conversation. He loves sports, my brother."

Chloe took the Yankees cap.

"Yankees fan, huh?"

She tugged an unruly tangle of red curls through the opening at the back. While she was arranging it she said, "I don't care. It's blue and white. It sort of matches your shirt. What's his name?"

Jake shook his head. It was a hell of a way to choose your team. "Mark."

"What's he do?"

"He teaches people how to drive."

They walked toward the hospital entrance and Jake thought the hat looked better on her than it ever would on him.

"Chloe, I've got to ask. What are you going to do when we get there? What about your friends? Family? Clothes? You haven't packed." The more he thought about it the more the complications piled up, leading to the one big question on his mind. "You want to leave town, some place the Outfit," he felt strange saying that, "won't find you, why not use your own car? Or buy a bus ticket, or a plane ticket."

"Those are obvious choices. Places Dalrymple will watch. Not only that, if I get on a train or a plane, it's easy to have people meet me when I get off. Who's going to look for me traveling north in a black Mustang with Florida tags?" She answered her own question. "Nobody. Not right away. Anyway, what's the big deal? Just drop me off when you get to Fargo. I'll figure it out from there."

He looked at her confused. "Fargo?"

Chloe shrugged impatiently, letting him know he wasn't keeping up with the conversation. "You said you were driving north until the road ended."

"The road goes a little further than Fargo."

Her eyes widened and her mouth formed a perfect circle. "Oh!" She rapidly clapped her hands a few times. "You're right. They won't look for me in Brainerd. Not right away. This will be so much fun. I've never been there. Why are you going to Brainerd anyway?" Her voice dropped, took on a vacant quality similar to Mark's, when he was listening but thinking about something else entirely. "Even still, I'll only have a couple of days head start…" Her voice faded. "Jake. You live in Florida, so I guess you don't know. Dalrymple will find you in Brainerd. It's not that remote."

"Uhm, Chloe? You ever hear of a little place called Canada? About a million square miles bigger than the U.S.? Located just north of Brainerd? I might stop in Brainerd for gas. That's it."

For the first time Chloe looked doubtful. Jake felt a warm thrum of elation. Had he talked her out of it? Could he leave her behind and continue enjoying the drive? Soaking up scenery he'd only seen from thirty-three thousand feet. Listening to the radio or the books on CD, phoning Mark with progress reports and describing the crappy hotel in which he was staying?

Jake studied her face as her internal struggle raged. He almost saw the course of her thoughts. If it took the Outfit two, three days to find her in Brainerd, it would probably take them even longer to find her in Canada. They might not even look for her there. On the other hand, Canada was the great, snowy unknown. A mystery to most Americans.

He knew the moment she made her decision. Her face hardened with resolve. Jake's spirits dropped like a manhole cover.

"I'm coming with you." Her voice was tight and unsure. But, determined too.

Jake said, "What about your job? Your apartment?" *Or cave, you crazy woman?* "Money? Identification? Valuables?" Then it came to him. A technicality. He could end this nonsense on a technicality she wouldn't know about. "You'll need a passport to cross the border," he said, grinning while he waited for her step to falter.

Chloe yanked on the door handle. The door swung open. She strode for the hospital admittance counter. "Only by air. If you drive between the U.S. and Canada all you need is a birth certificate." She smiled over her shoulder at him and patted a pocket on her backpack. "When Dalrymple's buddy 'packed' for me, he put everything with my name on it in my backpack. When you're planning on killing someone, it doesn't make much sense to leave all kinds of identification lying around, does it?"

Jake wasn't certain he knew the answer to that question, but he had to agree. What she said made sense. He sighed heavily.

Chloe said, "Nice try though."

CHAPTER 13

A FTER AN HOUR or more in the hospital, Jake found himself back in his car, Chloe sitting comfortably beside him in the Mustang's shotgun seat. "I don't have the first clue what you should bring," he said, peering at his reflection in the rear-view mirror. The white strip of bandage holding his nose in place contrasted crazily with his two black eyes. How long did the nurse say it needed to stay there? Seven to ten days? It would be an uncomfortable week and a half. Turned out breathing with a broken nose wasn't the easiest thing in the world.

"Why are you being so difficult? Just tell me what you packed."

He looked at her. Chloe held a compact mirror inches from her nose and patted on makeup, effectively concealing the purple bruise on her face. She said her lips felt like Oscar Mayer Wieners pasted to her face. The damage must have been on the inside, because Jake couldn't see any swelling. With the bruise hidden and only three visible cuts marring her mouth, she didn't look too much the worse for wear.

He gave the back of his head an irritated scratch. "I packed bug spray. And, my brother bought me some fishing gear. I brought that."

She made a face. "You know, Dalrymple is coming. The sooner we get out of town the better."

"Why are we at a mall, then?" He swung his gaze away from her face and looked at rows of parked cars stretched out in front of him, all the way to the shopping center entrance. He shook his head with distaste. Took a deep breath. Released it. "We got out of the hospital in record time. Let's not waste it." He hoped it didn't sound like he was pleading. He suspected he sounded exactly that way. "You said Mario would have people looking all over for us. Going shopping won't speed things up."

"No. I said his people would watch the hospitals and cop shops. They won't look for us in a mall." Chloe closed her compact with a click. She dropped it into her backpack on the floor. She rotated her bare feet north, and wriggled her toes in the flip-flops. "I'll need shoes, of course."

Shoes?

A nervous shudder rippled Jake's body. For some reason he thought of an old oak standing tall in the face of an approaching storm, digging in as the gusts came harder, hoping it would be strong enough to survive. That was mall shopping as far as he was concerned—digging in, trying to survive. He had a friend in San Diego who liked to drag him to the Horton Plaza. Two hundred plus stores, open to the elements. Architecturally the mall was interesting. But it didn't have a single shop that was different from what you'd find in any other mall. No DeWalt tools. Not a Cabela's in sight. There were no exotic European sports cars with scantily clad car babes draped over them like expensive accessories. Just the standard boring clothes and shoes.

"What else do I need in the northern parts of Canada? Besides bug spray and a fishing rod?"

"Blue jeans," he said.

Chloe nodded. Glowed. "Now we're getting somewhere. Jeans. Shoes. What else? I haven't shopped for myself in a while."

Jake didn't know what that meant and for the moment he didn't care. He threw his hands in the air. "A jacket, I guess. A fleece. There are stores up there, Chloe."

"Do they have a Gap?" She removed the Yankees cap, flipped the sun visor down and checked her hair in the mirror. Her expression clearly indicated she wasn't happy with what she saw. She raked her fingers through a tangle of red curls. With a practiced twist, she bundled it all into a ball and pinned it in place on the back of her head with a comb. "I don't wear fleeces," she said. "I'll get some sweaters instead."

"I don't know if there's a dry cleaner up there. You're better off with a fleece. You can throw a fleece in the washing machine." He paused. "What do you plan on doing when we get to the end of the road?"

"Where is the end of the road?"

"Sioux River. A small handful of white folk live there, along with several hundred Native Indians and most of the black-flies in the world."

"Why are you going there?"

He wasn't sure how the conversation worked its way back to him. "Work."

"Maybe I'll work too," she said, sounding skeptical. She planted her pack on her lap as she spoke. After some rooting around, she found her wallet and smiled triumphantly. "Never leave home without it." She opened it, licked her fingers and started counting under her breath.

When she hit fifteen hundred dollars, Jake couldn't take it anymore. "You carry that much around at one time?"

"Thanks." Chloe glared at him. "Now I have to start again." She moistened her fingers a second time and started recounting, finally stopping at twenty-two hundred dollars. She looked at Jake with a worried expression. "Only twenty-two. I don't think using my credit card is a good idea. They're always able to track people in the movies when they use their credit cards. Maybe I should take some more cash out. As much as the card can handle."

Jake stared at her, his mouth hanging open a little. "Why do you need that much cash?"

Chloe looked at him like he had two heads. "Shopping. And, we're going to have to eat. And sleep."

"You plan on staying in a Wyndham every night?"

"Jake, I plan on staying in the same hotel as you."

She wouldn't like his choice of hotels. When you pack around twenty-two-hundred in cash, just in case Neiman Marcus has a surprise shoe sale, it means you've never heard of the Empress Motel, out by the airport. Burnt-out neon and rooms starting at twenty-nine bucks. There was no point broaching the subject. He'd set the ground rules. Cheap hotels. Subway. If she was still determined to come with him she'd have to suck it up. Room service was down the street at 7-Eleven.

"Unless you find someone willing to pay you in cash, you can't work. You're an American. There won't be any jobs—"

"What are you talking about? You're from Florida."

Jake waved a dismissive hand in her direction. "I have dual citizenship. My mom was from Detroit. My dad from Windsor. I can work in either place. You can't. Not unless it's under the table. Anyway, I doubt you'll find a job that pays the kind of cake you're used to."

"What do you mean?"

"Most people don't pack twenty-two hundred dollars around, just in case. There'll likely be two convenience stores. The Northern and something else, locally run. There'll be some bars. A hotel or two. There will be an assortment of people who live there because it's a job. Cops and nurses. Teachers. Some government workers and some airline employees. That sort of thing. There is absolutely nothing for you to do up there."

Chloe had one hand on the door handle, making Jake think of

a kid standing outside the gates to the Magic Kingdom at eight-fifty-nine A.M. "I'll work something out. Let's go." The door opened and she hooked one leg over the doorsill onto the parking lot pavement.

"I'll wait in the car."

Chloe's face fell. "Don't you want to come in with me? Tell me what looks nice?"

"You'd make a potato sack look good, Chloe. Listen, I really hate—"

"Thanks, Jake. You're sweet."

He squinted at her, confused. Then he realized what he said and felt the heat of embarrassment warm his neck. He coughed slightly, looked away.

"You don't want to come in, just give me the keys."

"No way," Jake said flatly. "I'm not giving you the keys to my car."

"If I go shopping, leave you waiting in the car, you'll be looking at the mall in your rear-view mirror before I reach the front door. Right?"

Jake didn't answer.

Chloe leaned over and twisted the ignition key to the off position. Pulled it out of the column, all in one nice smooth motion.

Jake didn't see it coming. He dropped his hand fast, trying to grab the keys from her.

Too late.

She skipped out of the Mustang, slamming the door behind her.

He sprang from the car. "Don't slam the door! Fuck's sake, Chloe, how many times do I have to say it?" He reached over the top of the Mustang, palm open. More calmly he said, "Give me the keys, please."

"No."

"Give me the keys," his voice louder this time.

"No. I'm coming with you, Jake. You'll leave without me if I give you the keys. So, the way I see it, you have two choices. You can wait in the car without the keys. Or you can come inside with me. If you want, wait for me at Starbucks while I'm shopping."

"So you can take off in my car? I don't think so."

A thoughtful look crossed Chloe's face. "I hadn't thought of that. I guess you're coming with me." She sauntered away.

With no other choice, Jake followed. He swore, broke into a jog until he caught up with her and walked beside her without saying a word.

Chloe grabbed his arm with both hands, half dragging and half steering him toward the main entrance. She outlined her battle plan as they walked. "Shoes are the hardest, so we'll start there. After I get shoes I'll look for jeans. While I'm looking for jeans I'll keep my eyes open for anything else I might need. Socks. Tops." She wrinkled her nose. "A fleece, I guess."

"A new car to carry it all," Jake mumbled under his breath. As they got closer to the entrance his slouch deepened and his feet dragged like a death row inmate taking his last long walk.

Chloe ignored him. "This will be so much fun! I'll keep my eyes open for accessories, too…"

A second, larger shudder shook Jake's slumped-over frame. *Accessories?* What did that mean?

"…belts and scarves. Things to bring it all together." The mall door swooshed shut behind them. Chloe paused and scanned the area. "There," she pointed, "A map."

"All this stuff, Chloe. Can't we just go to your place, pick it up there?"

"I lived in an apartment the Boss paid for. That gave him the right to come and go as he pleased. Since he's the one who put me in the trunk, I can't really go there, can I?"

"Mr. Blonde, you mean?"

Chloe shook her head. "No. Dalrymple works for the Boss.

He's a leg breaker. He does the Boss's dirty work. Other than that, I don't know much about him." She tapped her finger on the map. "Nine West. Perfect. I love their shoes."

"Who's the Boss?"

"I don't really want to get into this, Jake," she said as they walked into the Nine West store.

"Yeah, well, I don't want to waste an afternoon in a suburban shopping center with someone I've never met."

"It's my business, Jake. I'm not going to get into it," she repeated. The firm set was back on her face. She handed her back-pack to Jake. "Hold this. I want to try these on."

He slung Chloe's pack over his shoulder with a sigh. Seemed her relationship with the Boss, whatever it entailed, was too personal for her to discuss. Jake didn't really care about how the two of them were connected. However, the Boss's identity did concern him. "When you say the Outfit, you mean the Mafia, right? The Mob?" The words sounded ridiculous coming out of his mouth, when they weren't associated with a movie or a novel.

Chloe bobbed her head, a combination shake and nod. "Kinda. The Outfit is a slang term for a family in the Mafia." She twisted and pivoted in front of the mirror, looking at the boots on her feet from every possible angle. With one leg stretched out, hands on her hips, she said, "How do these look?"

Exactly like the last four pairs of black boots you put on, Jake thought. He mumbled, "Good. Real good," but he was too distracted to pay much attention. Obviously the Mob existed, but it had always been a great distance away, far enough to be theoretical or fantastical. How was it, that in a matter of hours, it had moved from an almost fictional entity to a first-hand conversation?

Eventually Chloe finished trying on Nine West footwear but she hadn't found everything she wanted so she dragged him into another shoe store and bought hiking boots with thick heavy soles. Contrasting nicely with boots that made sense in Sioux River was everything else she purchased… There was a pair of sandals, a pair of tall leather boots that looked real sexy and were good for absolutely nothing, and a pair of what Chloe called "everyday shoes." Finally, she picked up a pair of patent leather pumps with the three-inch heels, told Jake they were, "cute and I can't resist them." When Jake muttered something about high heels being real practical in the bush, she ignored him.

The ass kicker was, after all the shoe stores they drifted in and out of, she still wore her flip-flops. "I like to savor new shoes," Chloe explained. "Sometimes I'll put a new pair in the closet and every now and then, I'll just go in and look at them. You know?"

Unfortunately, they weren't done yet. Jake trailed behind her like a whipped dog. The storefronts blended into a kaleidoscope of colors. Chloe finally picked up the thread of her Mafia explanation. "You've heard about organized crime, right? Asian gangs. Bikers. That sort of thing?"

"Of course."

"Okay. Take the bikers, for instance. Cities all over the world have groups of guys who get together and ride bikes." She smiled when she said this, and rolled her eyes. "Most people call them a gang. They call themselves a club. Whatever. Technically they're known as a 'chapter.' Collectively all these chapters form a worldwide group called the Hell's Angels.

"Similarly, there are groups of Sicilian criminals scattered in cities across the U.S. Instead of chapters, these groups are called 'families.' Put all those little family units together and the whole big group is called the Mafia. Or Mob, if you like. Somewhere along the line, one of the families was referred to as 'The Outfit.' The name stuck. The head of a family is the Boss. Make sense?"

Jake said, "I guess." He paused. "You were his wife?"

Chloe burst out laughing. "No. The guy is like fifty. So is his wife. I was his girlfriend."

There wasn't much to say to that. Jake kept quiet. They paraded from store to endless store. He listened to her happily chatter on about mundane shit, like how she always found something to wear in Anne Taylor Loft but never found anything in Anne Taylor. Eventually he zoned out to the same place he went on the long flights when the autopilot was doing its job, the place where he had to be conscious and aware but not concentrating heavily. Occasionally he nodded and made the right mouth sounds, a skill he was quickly refining in the hours since he met her.

Eventually Chloe lost steam and decided it was his turn to talk. "This job you're going to, what is it?"

"I'm a pilot. I'm going north to fly for a company called Tundra Air."

"Cool," she said, sounding impressed.

Jake was used to this reaction. Everyone seemed to think he had a glamorous profession. It certainly wasn't tedious, like sitting in front of a monitor in a sterile cubicle from nine to five every day. Like any job though, once you've done it for a while, the shine wears off. He found that particularly true now that he was moving backwards in the industry into a smaller company, getting away from the majors.

"Hey! There's the Starbucks. Let's get a coffee." She grabbed his arm and towed him into the line-up.

"Oh, for…" Jake's voice faded into a quiet groan.

"What kind of plane do you fly?"

"I'll be flying a Cessna, a Beaver, and a Navajo."

She looked at him with a blank face.

"Small bush planes," Jake explained. He watched some of the confusion disappear.

"With pontoons?"

"Floats," he corrected her. "On the Cessna and Beaver. They're small. Only enough room for four or five passengers. The Navajo is referred to as a Light Twin, because it's really small and has two engines. It carries seven passengers. It's good for medical evacuations."

Side by side they shuffled forward in the Starbucks line-up.

"Would you like to be a real pilot one day? Fly for a real airline?"

Jake sighed inwardly. He explained this to people everywhere he went. "I am a real pilot, Chloe. Tundra Air is a real airline. A real small airline. If you mean, would I like to fly a big airplane for a major airline like," he hiked his shoulders, "United, for instance, I've done that. I flew a Boeing 767 for World Ways."

"Do you know what you want? I'm going to have a grande, non-fat, extra—"

Jake interrupted her with a second, much louder groan.

"What?"

"Didn't you say we had to hurry? That we needed get out of town? Remember? Dalrymple?"

"Two minutes to get a coffee won't make any difference."

"Two minutes, huh? I'll wait over there." He pointed to the small seating area and walked away, muttering under his breath, "A two-minute Starbucks? Not in this life time."

He sat at a table with his chin cupped in his palm, waiting much longer than the promised two minutes. He tried to be annoyed with her. After dragging him into a mall it should have been easy, but somehow the feeling wouldn't stick. She was interesting and when she wasn't being rock-head-stubborn, she was friendly. She was so enthusiastic about everything—the road trip, shopping, even his job. Her coffee must have tasted great too, because the smile she shot at him after her first sip made the bruises and cuts vanish. It was difficult to stay annoyed with someone whose cup is always half full.

He stood. "You ready? Can we go now?"

"This is yummy," she said, waving the cup under his nose. "You want a taste?"

He shook his head.

"Didn't you like flying a big airplane?"

Jake sighed. "I loved it." The longing in his voice surprised him. "World Ways went bankrupt. I was furloughed. There are a lot of furloughed airline pilots out there. None of the majors are hiring. Which means none of the smaller airlines are hiring either. While I wait for them to start again, I took this job."

"Who's flying around way up there?"

"Tourists."

Chloe laughed, until she realized he was serious. She scrunched up her nose in an unconscious expression that said, "Really? I sort of believe you. Who goes there for a holiday?"

"Fisherman and hunters. The guy I'll be working for has a lodge with guest cabins on a lake. It's called Deep Cove."

"Like a resort?"

"Sort of. It's not a five-star Club Med in Puerto Plata, like what you're thinking. This is more rustic. Animal heads and stuffed fish hanging on the walls. Shit like that. Tourists drive up to Sioux River and stay in the guest cabins. They take out little boats, go fishing or hunting. Some guys want to rough it. I'll fly them even farther north, into remote places without road access."

Chloe still looked skeptical, like the idea that people paid good money to go camping in the northern Canadian wilderness didn't make sense. She sipped from her Starbucks cup. "That's it?"

"No. That's not it. The road ends in Sioux River. Literally. But there are all kinds of tiny villages north of that. They're called hamlets. Tundra Air flies people in and out of them."

"How many people live in a hamlet?"

Jake shrugged. "Five hundred. Maybe. They're so small they don't have a hospital. If someone gets hurt, I'll fly up there, pick 'em up, and bring them south to a hospital." He paused. "Can we please get out of here, Chloe?"

She thought about it, head tilted, hand on her hip. She studied the bags in Jake's arms like she was running a mental checklist—socks, shoes, pants, underwear, belt… She nodded. "Let's go."

Jake thought he heard reluctance in her voice, like maybe she hadn't finished having her way with the mall. He bee-lined for the entrance doors before she decided to try on another pair of jeans. When he needed jeans, he went to Sears or Target, grabbed two identical pairs of Levis and bought them without trying them on. Not Chloe. She tried on eleven different pairs in six different stores. The first pair was too loose. The next too tight.

Too high.

Too low.

Too faded.

Too blue.

Mind-boggling.

"Tell me, Jake. How does a guy who lives in Tampa get a job flying in Sioux…" She hesitated.

"Sioux River," Jake answered, then said, "Nepotism."

CHAPTER 14

MARIO GIANOLO WALKED down the hall toward the visitor area, a cop one step behind, escorting him with a hand clamped on his tricep. The orange jump suit pinched him under the arms and squeezed him around the gut. He yawned expansively without bothering to cover his mouth. The day had stretched out, and it wasn't going to get any easier or any shorter. The stained and dirty mattress in his cell was a mere three-quarters of an inch thick. The guys in the cells surrounding him snored and farted and laughed and cried. Sleeping tonight was doubtful.

The cop held the door into the visitor's area open. Mario walked through, then paused and scanned the mostly empty room from one end to the other. He spotted Gino sitting at one of the tables and Mario thought it may have been the single best thing that happened this entire shitty day.

Initially he wanted to call every contact he had, from one corner of Chicago to the other, perhaps find Chloe Sheridan and her hapless getaway driver within hours of their Daytona-esque escape from A1. Unfortunately, the cops wouldn't let him near a phone until they completed the mug shots, fingerprints, questions, and reports. He also suspected they were dragging their heels. It took until early evening for them to finish. By then Mario's panic had decreased. Common sense took over. Rather than calling those who might not be loyal, not being family and all, he called the only two people he trusted. Gino and Paolo had a vested interest in not allowing news of Chloe's escape to get back to Eric Dalrymple.

"Talking only," the cop said. "No physical contact."

Mario ignored him, tried pulling away and heading in Gino's direction. The cop tightened his grip, stopping him in his tracks. "Hey shit-heel, you hear me, or you wanna turn around, go back to your cell right now?"

"No physical contact," Mario said. "Got it."

"You get ten minutes."

Gino looked as uncomfortable as Mario felt—Saturday evening in jail did that to a man—and his brother's nervous ticks were on full display. He kept smoothing his hair and fussing with his tie, as usual way overdressed for his surroundings. He was freshly shaved and as Mario got closer to their table, he smelled the cologne his brother preferred, incongruous given the surroundings but for once, not overpowering or unpleasant.

Mario dragged a plastic chair the same color as his jumpsuit away from the table and flopped down with a grunt. It was a flimsy thing, unstable and non-threatening—it would never be considered a weapon—and it wobbled side to side under his weight. "Thanks for coming," he said.

Gino ran his hands across his wavy hair. "No problem," he said, sounding strained.

Mario ignored a stab of annoyance. It better be, "no problem." Gino wasn't the one in jail. He tried nodding away his irritation but wasn't entirely successful, despite how grateful he was that Gino actually showed. "Where's Paolo? I expected you both."

"Parking. This fucking town, you know how much it costs to park here?"

Mario waved his hand back and forth, cutting him off. "You

got a cell phone, right?" Mario asked the obvious—it might as well have been attached to Gino's ear with an umbilical cord.

Gino cocked his head and furrowed his brow. "You know I do."

"Why wasn't it turned on this afternoon?"

Gino's look of confusion deepened. "You called me earlier?"

Mario shot him a glare, then let his gaze roam around the room. "What do you think?"

"Sorry, bro. I didn't recognize the number."

"Next time it rings, answer it." Mario forced a softer tone into his voice. There was more to gain with sugar than salt. "They don't allow me unlimited calls in here."

"What's going on? Why are you here?"

"Nothing important. A misdemeanor." Unloading eleven rounds into mid-morning traffic and being directly responsible for putting a young mother in the hospital would hardly be considered a misdemeanor in a judge's eyes. But his lawyer could sort that out when the time came. First, and far more important, was Chloe Sheridan. Mario took a deep breath. It was hard admitting such a monumental screw-up to the twins, boys he'd looked after for years, but there was really no choice. The entire family was in a world of hurt if Dalrymple found out Chloe had escaped.

"We can't wait for Paolo. They don't give me much time. You'll have to fill him in." He stared at Gino, pinning him in place with his eyes, making sure he was paying attention, making sure he'd understand the seriousness of the situation. "I need you guys to do something for me. Something for us. The family."

Gino straightened his tie. He leaned forward with his forehead creased in concentration. "No problem," he repeated.

Mario's level of irritation ratcheted up another notch. "You two have to find Jake Harris."

Gino looked blank. "Who?"

"Jake Harris," Mario snapped. "Sofia's latest sport fuck."

"Why?"

"Gino, you know how Eric Dalrymple ended up working for the Boss?"

Gino hiked his shoulders. "I've heard stories."

"Word around the water cooler is, he killed a cop. When he was eighteen. A gang initiation."

"Yeah?"

Mario was pleased to see Gino's perplexed expression. It meant he was paying attention and would therefore understand the seriousness of the situation. "Well, that cop killer, crazy-man came by A1 this morning. He left something in the trunk of his car. Something we were supposed to take care of." He needed to be subtle in case the guards were listening to the conversation. None of them were standing too close and as far as Mario knew his conversations were supposed to be private, but that rule may have only included his lawyer and not a family member. "Subtle" was the smart play.

Mario pushed on. "Harris also stopped by. He took what Dalrymple left in the trunk. He probably doesn't have it anymore but we find him, we find what he took. This has to happen as soon as possible. Definitely before Dalrymple finds out we didn't do as he asked. That would be bad for all of us." For emphasis he added, "Sofia included."

He waited several long seconds until a look of realization crossed Gino's rapidly paling face. He could see the light bulbs coming on in succession. *A known killer left something in the trunk... the Gianolo family was supposed to take care of it... they did not do so... whatever was in the trunk disappeared...* Mario knew it was a ton to digest at eight-thirty on a Saturday evening when you're inside a cop-shop instead of the Reggae Lounge.

On the other side of the room, a door opened. Scraps of conversation drifted in a couple of steps ahead of Paolo Gianolo.

"…no physical contact. You get ten minutes, less the time your shit-heel brother has already been here."

Paolo's barbeque-burned visage was stretched tighter than normal. He pulled out a chair and flopped down beside Gino. Said, "Parking. This fucking town, you know how much it costs to park here?"

Gino raised his hand. "Not important, bro," saying it like he hadn't said the exact same thing five minutes earlier.

The scars pulled the flesh on Paolo's face taut until his skull became visible beneath his skin. Color rose in his cheeks. "Show me the back of your hand one more time, Gino, you and I are gonna have a problem." He looked at Mario. "What's going on?"

Jesus, these two. They hadn't gotten along since Paolo's barbecue accident. Like a thin layer of frost, the control the two of them exercised was never far from melting. At first, when the burns were healing, Paolo had rubbed his face for relief from the constant itchiness. Later, when his face healed and he realized he'd always have a visible crosshatch, he developed a habit of bringing his hands up to hide the scars. Particularly when Gino was around; Gino always so concerned with his appearance. The contrast was extreme, and Gino played it up with his not-so-innocent comments: "He might not look it, but he's my twin brother."

Gino scrubbed his hand over his chin several times, the frown of concentration firmly in place. "How are we supposed to find him, Mario?"

"Didn't you just tell me, 'No problem?' Twice? Use your head. Sofia's rattled on about him. Talk to her. She'll tell you everything she knows. Then get your asses, both of you," Mario pointed at Paolo, "on a flight to Tampa."

"Tampa?" Paolo asked uneasily.

"The guy flew for World Ways. That's a Tampa-based airline."

"They're bankrupt."

"Only a few weeks, now. The guy hadda live somewhere, right?

The only idea I have is using Tampa as a starting point. Someone, maybe a relative, maybe his landlord, knows where he's going. Find out."

Paolo asked, "What was he doing in Chicago, anyway?"

Mario shrugged. "Don't know. Don't care."

After a little more conversation, the cop strode over. He towered over the table, arms crossed high on his chest. "Time. Let's go." He jerked a thumb at the door.

The twins said their goodbyes. Mario watched them leave, Paolo with his head thrust forward, stabbing his index finger at Gino, and Gino with both hands near his shoulders, palms open like he was surrendering.

Mario slapped his breast pocket, searching for a cigar or cigarette. He shouldn't have bothered. They wouldn't let him smoke in the visitor's room, but he still scowled when his hand came away empty. He shoved away from the table. The legs of the chair scraping across the floor sounded like a rusty chainsaw on a metal flagpole. He rose to his feet with a groan. He hoped, prayed, Gino would check his arrogance and Paolo would control his temper long enough for them to find Chloe. It was an iffy hope. A weed of fear sprouted in his belly and stretched its roots.

CHAPTER 15

THE BACK SEAT of the Mustang was littered with bags, all of them decorated with expensive brand names and braided rope handles. Jake could barely see out the rear window. He backed out of his parking space at the mall and headed for an exit that would take them to 163 North, white knuckling the steering wheel and vowing, "Never again." Next time a woman insisted he go shopping, he was going to shake his head and say, "Nope, I got something fun to do." After that he planned on strolling into a Miami crack house waving hundred dollar bills in the air, some shit like that.

Chloe on the other hand, couldn't have been more relaxed. Her eyes were closed, her seat reclined. She twisted curls of red hair around her finger like she was tugging on a spring. With the other hand she absently plucked at the pendant on her necklace. There was a satiated little smile on her face.

"What?" she asked, without opening her eyes.

"Nothing," Jake answered, keeping his thoughts to himself. As much as he disliked spending time at a mall, Chloe enjoyed it and he didn't want to ruin her mood.

She'd given him back his World Ways shirt and traded her own stained and bloody top for one of about ninety she bought. The ripped jeans were gone. Now she wore a pair of blue cotton shorts with B.U.M. written across the back in white letters, like there was any doubt. Typically, when there was enough space back there for a billboard, the look wasn't one Jake appreciated, but Chloe pulled it off easily.

"Why are you looking at me? You should be watching the road."

"I was wondering if your face was as sore as mine."

"It hurts, all right. From the inside out, you know?"

"I know. Mine hurts on the surface too. The air on my skin makes it sting."

Chloe opened her eyes. She twisted around in her seat until she was kneeling on the soft leather cushion. The B.U.M. shorts stretched tight and didn't quite hide the abrupt curve where her legs ended and her rear began. Soft afternoon sunlight filled the car, coloring her legs with an even caramel hue, backlighting almost indiscernible gossamer filaments of hair.

A vision like that... Jake forced himself to concentrate on the road.

After several seconds pushing shopping bags from side to side across the back seat, she rescued a Walgreen's bag and settled into her seat facing forward. She rattled a container of aspirin at him. "Drugs?"

"I'll power through, thanks." He shot her a quick glance in time to see her flick her right foot. The flip-flop dropped to the floor. She planted one heel on the edge of the seat. "Chloe, please don't—"

The chemical smell of nail polish remover filled the car's interior, wrinkling Jake's nose. He snapped his head around and gaped at her out of wide eyes. "What do you think you're doing?"

"What does it look like? I'm taking the polish off my nails. Then I'm going to repaint them copper." She waggled another small bottle with a copper-colored top in his direction. "Pretty, right?"

His gaze flicked back and forth between Chloe and the road

like a metronome. He chopped his right hand down. "No way. No way. You don't know what that stuff will do to the upholstery."

"Don't hit a bump."

"Chloe—"

"Watch the road."

"Shit, you're a pain in the butt."

Chloe smiled brightly at him. "Speed up a little bit. We spent longer in the mall than I expected."

"You want to drive? Is that it?"

"I'm busy." She paused, waved a cotton ball stained red at him to prove her point. "So, what's the plan?"

"Be careful with that," he cautioned unhappily.

"Yeah, yeah. The plan, Jake."

He scratched the back of his head. "We'll drive until about nine, long enough to get out of the city. Then we'll start looking for a cheap hotel—"

"Why so early?"

"Because I was up at five-thirty—"

"Five-thirty? Are you insane?"

"—and by nine I'm tired. It's a hazard an airline pilot has to deal with. Early check-ins. Pretty soon getting up early is a habit. We'll hit the road by six. Find some—"

"What?" Chloe wailed.

"—thing to eat for breakfast," he continued, like he hadn't heard her protests. Suddenly he felt a little better. Not as much as he expected he would when he finally gained the upper hand, but better all the same. "We should see the border late tomorrow—"

"Whoa," she shouted. She made a T with her hands, the cotton ball still pinched between her thumb and index finger. "Whoa. I don't get up before nine. Ever."

"Wow, that stuff stinks."

"I'm not getting up at five-thirty," she continued. Her tone made it clear she was digging in her heels.

"You are if you want to travel with me," he said simply. "I'm not changing my whole schedule because you don't feel like dragging your ass out of bed."

"Jake—"

This time Jake interrupted her. "No, Chloe. Listen. My car. My schedule. Period. I have a job to get to. This is important. At six I'm pulling out of whatever cheap-ass dive we find tonight. I don't care if you're in bed or in the shower. I'm leaving."

Angry buttons of crimson lit her cheeks. Her face hardened. She bent over and silently continued scrubbing the cherry-colored polish off her toenails. He stole the occasional glance and saw her open her mouth a couple of times and abruptly slam it shut. Likely she was running through the same list he was and just like him, she couldn't find any fresh ways of manipulating him—no keys to steal, no threats of abuse. Nothing. He didn't even need directions out of town anymore.

"I guess we're not talking now, huh?" he said.

Chloe shot him a withering glare and turned her attention back to her toenails.

Jake shrugged. If they weren't talking he was listening to the book on CD. Maybe he could get back to enjoying his road trip. He pushed the "play" button.

She didn't stay quiet for long. "What's this?"

"*The Stand.*"

"I thought books on tape were for blind people."

"CD. Maybe when they first came out. Not anymore." He reached over and tweaked up the volume.

She raised her voice. "Who wrote it?"

"Stephen King. A lot of people figure it's his best book. I disagree. I prefer *The Dark Tower* series. I waited a long time for him to finish writing the last book."

"Uh-huh." Chloe nodded without interest. "I don't read much. It takes too long. Well, except for magazines. I like reality

TV. I got right into *Survivor*. Never missed an episode until *The Bachelor* and *The Bachelorette* came out. Now that was good—"

"Chloe, if we're not talking, I'd really like to listen to this CD."

She went rigid, crossed her arms and looked out the passenger window. "Asshole," she muttered, just loud enough for him to hear.

In profile Jake saw her jaw, angry and hard. He sighed inwardly and turned off the CD, wondering why her anger mattered to him. "*Survivor*, huh?"

She shifted in her seat. The leather squeaked. One hand rose to her neck and she fingered the fish pendant. She didn't answer.

"I've never watched a single episode," he said. "I did watch *Temptation Island*. Once." He found it so unbearably bad that he hadn't made it through the entire episode.

Her shoulders dropped almost indiscernibly. She scrunched her nose. "Probably for the T and A, right?"

He shrugged a second time. "The TV commercials kind of play up that angle."

"It was okay, but I really like *The Bachelor*. When the runner-up became *The Bachelorette*, then I had to watch it too. They were so good."

"Really?"

She gave him the details and he managed to ease an occasional, "Is that right?" or, "Huh!" into her oration. When he couldn't think of anything else to say he resorted to mouth noises. By the time she finished she was twisted in her seat facing him, her left foot with the clean toenails tucked up comfortably on the seat beneath her.

Jake said, "You know they're not real, right? Even though they call them reality shows."

"I know they're produced. But there's plenty that's unscripted. It's entertainment, that's all. Better than family dramas." She hiked her shoulders. "They're way more real than the book you're listening to."

"One big difference. The book doesn't pretend to be anything but fiction."

"What's it about?"

Jake outlined the premise of *The Stand*. When he was finished Chloe surprised him.

"Turn it back on."

He did and the two of them fell into a comfortable silence, listening as the story unfolded.

For about three minutes.

"Why are they going to Colorado?"

"There's a lot going on in this book, Chloe. Too much to explain. The more you listen, the more you'll understand."

"Start it from the beginning."

"No."

"Ja–ke," she said, drawing his name out like a child losing a negotiation with a parent. "Please."

"There's like ninety CDs in this book. I want to listen to them all."

"Are they important?"

"Of course."

"Well then, I want to hear them too. If the book is that good, you shouldn't mind listening to them again," she said reasonably.

Jake shook his head and waved a vague hand over his shoulder. "Back there. Somewhere. Under all your bags."

She undid her seat belt, swung around, kneeled on the seat and started pushing packages and boxes aside. When she found the box of CDs, she ejected the one in the deck and dropped it onto the center console, then she slid in disk one of Stephen King's opus.

"Hey, hey, hey! Put the first one in the box where it belongs. My brother spent a lot of money on that book. I want to keep it in good shape."

Chloe did as he asked with a roll of her eyes. "Hats and fishing gear at Sports Authority. Books on CD. Where'd he get those? Borders?" She reclined her seat, rolled her new fleece into a tight cylindrical pillow and put it behind her neck. "He spoils you."

Jake considered explaining how the gifts were more than simple going away presents. They were close, he and Mark. But they never got gooey about it and Mark still needed a way to say, "Thanks for looking out for me." Jake acknowledged his brother's gratitude and encouragement by treating the gifts with special respect. He wasn't certain he could have verbalized all that with someone he barely knew and he wasn't about to try. Instead he said weakly, "He bought himself a baseball bat."

Chloe shifted in her seat again, planted her bare feet on the dashboard.

Jake's eyes bulged. "Are you comfortable?"

"Yep. Thanks for asking. You were right about the fleece. I'd never do this to a cashmere sweater."

"You mind not putting your feet on my dashboard?"

She blew out a loud, exasperated sigh. "You're so anal. Be quiet so I can listen."

That was rich, Chloe telling him to be quiet. He followed her orders, and listened to the story, happy for some reason that she was listening with him. It was a definite improvement over bullshit reality TV. Suddenly he felt bad about the hard line he'd taken. If they left whatever hotel they ended up in an hour later than he originally planned, would it make any difference? He'd still arrive in Sioux River on the day Lawrence Stevenson expected him. He gave the steering wheel a gentle frustrated thump with the heel of his hand.

"Okay, Chloe. How about this. I'll get up at five-thirty, six. I can't sleep much later than that. I'll go for my run. That's about forty-five—"

"You're going to run? With a broken nose? How you going to breathe?"

"I didn't think of that." After a second or two of thought, he shrugged. "I'll manage. Maybe I'll only go thirty minutes. Anyway, when I get back to the motel I'll jump in the shower. I'll wake you up when I'm done. You'll be up earlier than nine, I know, but..." He shrugged. "While you're getting dressed I'll go find us something to eat. We'll plan for an eight-thirty departure. Okay?"

She looked back at him and her face was a warm soft smile. "I like chocolate chip bagels," she said. "And, I absolutely need a grande, non-fat, extra hot, no foam, sugar-free, vanilla latte before I can get my day going."

A don't-push-it remark rose to his lips. When he looked at her, she wore a wide grin. He said, "You're messing with me, right?"

"Yep." She yawned into the back of her hand. "Uhm, Jake? What are the sleeping arrangements?"

"You. Me. Same bed," Jake answered, deadpan.

She looked at him with an eyebrow raised. "I don't think... You're messing with me, right?"

He laughed. "Two rooms. Or, if you're scared I'll take off on you, one room, two beds. You decide."

She seemed to think about it. "One room, two beds. That's fine with me."

"Your feet, Chloe. On the floor."

She sighed exaggeratedly, tucked one foot beneath her and stretched the other leg out. "Thanks, Jake," she said, and in a softer voice, mumbled, "Five o'clock to go running. Insane." She quickly fell asleep, snoring softly through her cut lips and inflamed nose.

The setting sun was still visible out the right side of the Mustang. With an hour or two to go and Chloe sleeping, Jake lowered the volume of the CD, quickly glanced at his passenger to be sure the noise wasn't disturbing her, and concentrated on the story.

CHAPTER 16

GINO GIANOLO PUSHED the button on his armrest. His seat reclined while, simultaneously, the footrest rose. He sighed with audible pleasure and settled into the warm leather. If the television screen were just a few inches larger, First Class would be better than his sitting room at home. The engines were so far behind him that their consistent, muted drone was relaxing.

He crooked a finger into the tie knotted at his throat, loosening it enough to undo the top button of his shirt. When he got off the plane he'd do both up, no point in looking sloppy. Until then he planned on enjoying the three-hour flight to Tampa. In fact, the pilot insisted on it. He told everyone on board to, "...sit back. Relax. Enjoy the flight." Gino planned on doing exactly that.

He picked up a glass, not a plastic cup, of Pinot Noir and sipped, letting the wine roll around on his tongue, savoring it pretentiously like he knew the difference between an expensive bottle and the kind that came out of a box.

He cut his eyes in Paolo's direction.

Even without a tie to loosen, his brother didn't look half as comfortable as Gino felt. Paolo clutched both armrests with white knuckles and barely contained anxiety. His biceps strained the sleeves of his Harley-Davidson shirt. He stared straight ahead while a nerve jumped rhythmically in his tightly clenched jaw. His face was the color of a wet napkin.

Gino reached over and patted Paolo's hand. "Take it easy, bro. We're in a Boeing." He glanced around the cabin, took another sip of wine and said, "not some Euro-trash Airbus. We got nothing to do for the next few hours. We'll get busy when we land. For now, we've got a waitress, entertainment, and comfortable seats. Enjoy First Class." He leaned into his brother. His voice dropped a level and he jerked a thumb over his shoulder. "Better than back there with the cattle, right? A waitress we don't even have to tip!" He patted Paolo's hand several more times, and pushed the flight attendant call button.

The Pinot Noir was excellent. It tasted like another glass.

"What," Paolo said through clamped teeth, "are we gonna do when we get there? To Tampa."

Gino nodded knowingly, like he had it all worked out, a simple matter of flying in, finding Jake Harris and flying out. The truth was he didn't have the first damn clue what they'd do in Tampa. Instead of answering he glanced out the window and watched the green patchwork quilt of some state he couldn't remember the name of, unfold below them. He brushed his hand across his hair. "Sofia didn't know too much about Harris, did she?"

Paolo shook his head once.

The flight attendant stopped at their row. She selected the call button off and said, "Can I help you?"

Gino beamed at her. He amended his earlier assessment. First Class was better than his sitting room at home. There were no attractive ladies in his condo, who came right to his arm chair and served him alcohol while he watched television. "This wine is excellent. I wonder if…"

Efficient and friendly, she smiled back. It didn't reach her eyes. "You'd like another glass?"

"Yes. Thank you."

She looked from Gino to Paolo. "Are you all right, sir?"

There may have been genuine concern in her voice. Gino was too busy struggling for a line to know for sure. It had to be original. Probably every businessman with time on his hands gave her a business card when he de-planed.

Paolo loosened his grip on the armrest. He wiped away the thin film of nervous sweat covering his forehead. He nodded once without looking at her. "Fine," he said faintly.

She raised her sculpted eyebrows. "Maybe a little fresh air would help?"

When Paolo nodded his thanks she twisted the overhead vent open. Air hissed out, ruffling his hair.

Gino let his smile widen. It was time to have some fun at his brother's expense. Smirking, he planted a hand on Paolo's shoulder and gave his brother a couple of gentle, sideway shakes. "My brother is a nervous flyer. Funny huh? We're twins. I love flying. He hates it."

A fleeting look of surprise cracked the flight attendant's heavy layer of make-up.

Paolo slowly turned his head.

Gino ignored the angry stare and asked her, "Have you tried the Pinot Noir?" It wasn't the strong line he needed. He knew it. Unfortunately, the right words weren't coming. A sixty-dollar haircut and a nine-hundred-dollar suit should have been enough, but he wasn't picking up any kind of vibe from her.

Still with the detached, clinical tone she said, "I'm told it's quite good."

Gino leaned into the aisle, watching her ass sway from side to side as she walked away. When she disappeared behind the curtain at the front of the cabin, he pretended to finally notice his brother's glare. "What?"

"Why you have to do that?"

"What?"

"You know what. Point out we're twins."

Gino suppressed a grin. He enjoyed watching Paolo squirm under a stranger's extra, unwelcome attention. He knew his brother believed people looked at him harder when they found out the two of them were twins. Instead of glancing at the scars and pretending they hadn't seen them, they looked twice searching for similarities. Always with questioning eyes: "What happened? How is it possible this good-looking fellow has such a hideous-looking brother?"

As he always did, Gino feigned innocence and hurt at Paolo's anger. He'd played the shtick for so long he had the act down pat. Innocence came first. He shrugged, palms upraised. "I was just talking. Making conversation. What's the big deal?"

"I've explained this before." Paolo's voice was low. Dangerous. His eyes blazed. He looked toward the front of the aircraft. "Pull that shit again, and I'm taking you to school."

Gino arranged his face into a suitable, hangdog expression. "I'm sorry. All I said was we're twins." He dry washed his face with both hands, wiping away the grin quirking the corners of his mouth. It was just so much fun getting under Paolo's skin. His tone changed from one of hurt indignation to brisk business. "You done feeling sorry for yourself? Maybe we could discuss what we'll do in Tampa. Would that be a suitable topic of conversation?"

"What do you have in mind?"

The question caught Gino by surprise; he had nothing in mind. Other than Mario's vague guidance, he didn't have the first clue what they'd do once they landed in Miami. "It's going to be too late to do much when we land," he said, speaking slowly, hoping Paolo would think it was for his benefit. After all, his brother wasn't the brightest bulb in the chandelier. He stroked his chin, sorting out a plan as he spoke. "I figure we'll check into an airport hotel. In the morning, we'll start working the phones. You can find out where Harris lives. Lived."

"How am I gonna do that?"

"Sofia said he lived with his brother. They rented from an old lady named Mrs. Edith Weatherly. Right?"

Paolo nodded.

"Get the phone book out. Call all the Weatherlys in the white pages until you find the right one. You do, get her address and drive on over. Wait for Harris to show up. Either one. Jake or the brother. I don't give a shit."

"That's gonna take all day."

"Why? You've seen the phone book? You know how many Weatherlys live in Tampa?"

"No."

"Then unless you got a better plan, shut up."

Paolo cut his eyes in Gino's direction. "Don't tell me to shut up, Gino." The dangerous tone was back.

Get to know Paolo and it was easy to tell when he'd become violent. It was never too far away at the best of times. Gino realized he hadn't given his brother enough time to calm down after embarrassing him in front of the waitress. Paolo was festering like an open sore. If he kept pressing, Paolo would go nuclear when they landed. Gino back-pedaled. "All I'm saying, if you don't have a better plan, don't be nitpicking mine."

"Say that. Don't tell me to shut up." Paolo paused. "And, just so you know, the brother's name is Mark."

"Mark. Right."

"We could call him directly," Paolo said, "but there's probably more Harrises in the phone book than Weatherlys. And, there's no point coming at him directly if we can find him without him knowing about it."

"It's what I thought," Gino said with a patient, condescending sigh, although he'd thought nothing of the kind.

"One other thing, Gino. They don't like to be called 'waitress.' They're flight attendants."

Gino shrugged. "Whatever."

"What are you gonna do while I'm hunting down the old woman?"

"I'll work the phones too," Gino continued. "Sofia said Mark was a driving instructor. I'll track him down. When I do, I'll follow him. Sooner or later he'll head home. Where you'll be waiting." Gino pointed at his brother when he said it. "If you see Jake before I get there, call me. I'll shoot on over. If Jake doesn't show up–"

"Don't expect he will."

"Me neither. But if he shows, you'll be there. I'll follow Mark home. Then you, me, and Mr. Glock will have a word with him. Find out where Jake is."

"Where we gonna get a Glock?"

"Mario gave me a name. I'll call the guy when we land. You want a piece too?"

Paolo nodded. "Be best if we each had one. What about cars? We're gonna need transportation."

"No problem. We'll rent."

"I don't want to be running around in some piece of shit compact."

He might look like he had no class, sitting there dressed like a mercenary in his black Harley t-shirt and camo cargo pants, but Gino had to admit, Paolo enjoyed some of the better things in life, just like he did. "Before we left," Gino said, "I called an agency. They only rent high-end vehicles. I got you a Corvette. Got myself a Beamer. The agency will meet us at the airport with the keys. Think that will suit you?"

The aircraft's engine note increased. Gino felt a pressure change in his ears. He watched Paolo blanch and stiffen in his chair. "Easy, bro. They're just changing altitude. It's smooth sailing from here."

Paolo's posture softened. He smiled. Slightly.

Gino smiled too. It was a good plan and as far as he could see, simple and foolproof.

CHAPTER 17

JAKE DROVE WITH his left hand draped over the top of the steering wheel, his right resting easy on the gearshift, enjoying the road, enjoying the low buzz of excited anticipation that always came with a new job. The sun warmed the interior of the car and the buttery leather wrapped him in comfort. The tires hummed on the road with reassuring constancy. After the previous day's insanity—from the wrecking yard to the shopping center—Chloe's quiet companionship was...

He straightened.

Quiet?

He glanced at his watch. Twelve minutes without a single word? He looked sideways. Chloe's soft round features were strained. She nibbled her lower lip and tugged on the curls hanging down past her ear. He took a breath, about to ask what was bothering her, then paused. Giving her an excuse to discuss the stick between her spokes seemed like lunacy because, if he asked, she'd tell him.

In excruciating, never-ending detail.

Still, he was curious. He shifted in his seat. A row of stitches knit a line of pain across the small of his back. It was time for a break. Time for a stretch. He kept his eyes open, searching for a rest stop and decided he'd ask what was on her mind when they got there, when he had a buffer zone larger than the interior of the car. It was cowardly, but the girl could ramble on and if they were to have a serious conversation, he wanted some external distractions.

Jake let the thought trail away.

He took a second look at his watch, added an hour for the time zone, and realized his brother would be on his lunch break. When he pulled into the rest stop, he'd call Mark. It was another stalling technique, no question, but what the hell. He hadn't spoken with his brother the previous day.

For a while he drove, watching the scenery pass, the power poles like pinpricks on the horizon, growing into towers before they flashed past. Eventually the unmistakable golden arches of a McDonald's rose above the horizon and he spotted a Mobil sign. When he slowed for the exit, Chloe asked, "What's up?"

"Nothing. I need a break, is all."

"You want me to drive? I can if you want."

"I just need a break." He parked the car. When he climbed out he put his fists in the small of his back and stretched with a groan.

Chloe stepped out and flipped her door closed with a crash. She headed for the store.

"Chloe…" It was on the tip of his tongue to tell her, for about the ninetieth time, to quit slamming the door. Instead he closed his eyes for half a second and took a breath and gave his head a little shake. He said, "You mind grabbing me a bottle of water, please? And, thanks."

She stuck her arm out and waggled an upraised thumb. Uncharacteristically, she didn't say a word as she resumed her walk toward the store.

He was going to have to ask. No two ways about it. Jake grimaced, opened his cell phone and hit speed dial one.

After two rings, Mark answered. "Speak."

"Hey man."

"Junior. How's things?"

Jake looked from the bullet hole in the side post to Chloe walking into the store. Her flip-flops slappity-slapped the pavement and the tangle of forest-fire red curls shone in the mid-morning sun. He smiled. "It's been an interesting couple of days."

"Tell me."

Jake leaned on the back edge of the trunk, crossed his legs at the ankle and quickly told his story. Mark didn't interrupt.

When he finished Mark said, "You sure you're done with this Mr. Blonde shit- head?"

Jake certainly hoped that was the case. The idea he'd run into the Freak a second time made a prickle of apprehension skitter up his spine. Thinking about the expensive sport coat and the luxury automobile, he said with as much conviction as he could muster, "Not an issue. Sioux River is a long way from Chicago. Be like I'm on another planet to a guy like him."

"Okay. What's the girl look like?"

Jake thought about the copper toenails, Chloe's nice round ass in her new Gap jeans, and the smile that lit up her face like the rising sun. "She's okay," he said.

As usual Mark interpreted. "Must be tough. A road trip with a hottie for company."

"Weren't you listening? She's a total pain in the butt."

"Here's what you do. Get up at midnight when she's down for the count and dump her. Just drive away." Jake didn't answer immediately and Mark laughed. "I think she's less of a pain than you're letting on."

It was time to change the subject. "What's up with you?"

There was a long silence. "It's been a rough day," Mark finally said with a sigh.

"Your turn. Tell me."

"I started my morning with a young lady named Ashley. She's got an aerobics instructor's body, makeup she applied with a drywall trowel and clothes so tight they'd make a street whore blush. One look and I thought, all right, she's twenty-five. Turned out she's seventeen. I don't know what her parents are thinking."

Jake smiled at his brother's old-fashioned attitude. "How'd you figure that out?"

"Her age? It's on the paperwork but she proved it when she opened her mouth. That's when the giggling started. The up-talking 'Likes.' 'Like, there was this time? Like, there was this guy?' You know what I'm talking about? Always ending her sentences with a question?"

"I know." Apprehension seeped into Jake's belly, making him shift on the trunk of his car. Days like these weren't good for Mark. The urge to punch out at five and hit the nearest Local Heroes, some sports bar with dozens of televisions hanging from the ceiling and neon beer signs in every window, was almost overwhelming. Jake pushed himself off the Mustang and paced nervous figure eights behind the car.

"She needed remedial English," Mark continued, "not a driving instructor. Ten minutes into her lesson I told her to shut up and concentrate on the road. I'd rather be lobotomized with a Sawzall than listen to any more adolescent babbling."

Nope. Not good at all. Jake massaged a knot in the back of his neck, ending the motion with an absent scratch.

"After Ashley I drew the short straw. Had to spend ninety terrifying minutes with Lin Ng. Let me tell you this, Junior. A fifty-two-year-old Asian woman shouldn't be driving an eighty-thousand dollar Lexus. Especially when they've never learned to read English road signs. Especially when they don't understand their driving instructor's commands."

"What happened?" Jake asked. Despite the apprehension, he sensed a funny story coming.

"She high centered the Lexus across a median. Front tires in the northbound lane. Rear tires in the southbound. I felt bad for her. She's a sweet lady. After that, I couldn't really understand a word she said."

"You gotta be kidding."

"Not at all. The cops came and re-directed traffic. People pointed and gawked. Poor Lin is crying her eyes out. The skid marks were fifty feet long. We hit the curb so hard… Parts everywhere." Mark paused. "Our session ended early."

Jake chuckled.

"I'm at Barney's trying to calm my nerves. I've gotta get right before this afternoon's session."

Jake imagined his brother at Barney's diner, the same place he went every day for lunch, the red vinyl squeaking as his brother shifted and twitched in the booth, right eyelid flickering rapidly with stress. He hesitated, hating to ask but knowing he had no choice. "You're not calming down with—"

"Coffee, Junior. Black and thick as roofing tar."

Relieved, Jake released a breath he didn't realize he was holding. Not too many people used caffeine to calm their nerves. Mark could settle down any way he liked, as long as it didn't involve a twenty-six-ounce bottle. "Sorry," Jake said. He returned to the comfortable spot on the edge of the Mustang's trunk.

"No sweat. What's the girl—"

"Chloe."

"What's Chloe plan on doing when she gets to Sioux River?"

Jake glanced at the store in time to see Chloe walk out carrying a bottle of water in one hand and a cardboard coffee cup in the other. Likely a grande, latté, mocha mixture, some shit like that. Something he'd be too embarrassed to order. Something of which he'd never remember the name.

She smiled when she saw his look and saluted with the coffee cup. Jake's insides gave a pleasurable little jump that caught him by surprise. He turned away from her and dropped his voice an octave. "She keeps saying she'll work it out. But she's a big city girl. I figure one look around Sioux River and she'll be on the next flight out of town."

"Good riddance, huh?" Mark said, still digging.

Jake thought about it briefly before answering. In a couple of days, they'd arrive in Sioux River. She'd look around the tiny town and realize she had nothing to do and no reason to stay. She'd leave, and that would be the last they ever saw of each other. That was fine. After their escape from A1 and their time on the road, Chloe was no longer a hitchhiker, but they couldn't be considered friends either. They didn't know each other. He'd be so busy learning a new job he wouldn't even notice she was gone, and like so many people with whom he'd crossed paths, all she'd leave behind was a memory.

"I won't miss her," Jake said with a shrug. "It won't be good riddance either. Listen, Mark, I gotta roll. I'll give you a shout in a day or two. Once I get settled in. When your shift ends go to the driving range and beat some golf balls to death."

"I might just do that. Drive safe, Junior."

"I will."

Chloe handed Jake the water and said, "You drink too much of that. Your insides are gonna rust." She hoisted herself up onto the trunk beside Jake, letting her heels bounce off the bumper. She wrapped one arm across herself like she was cold and held the coffee mixture with her other hand, propped on her forearm.

Jake said, "Come for a run with me. Water will be the best thing you ever tasted." Although he wasn't convinced. Her coffee cup steamed, making him wonder why he'd never acquired a taste for something that smelled so good.

"Why would I do that?"

Jake thought of telling her how running gave him more energy and kept him healthy and calmed his mind. Imagining her derisive snort, he hiked his shoulders. "Clothes."

Chloe sat up a little straighter. She looked at him with raised eyebrows.

"Shoes. Clothes. Gadgets. Sunglasses. All kinds of stuff. We hit one of those specialty running stores and you'll blow the rest of your twenty-two hundred."

She made a noncommittal noise but the interested look on her face didn't entirely disappear. "How's your brother?"

"He's good."

"You and him close?"

"I guess."

"You tell him you were traveling with me?" Her voice was filled with shy curiosity, a tone he hadn't heard from her before.

"I might have mentioned it."

"What he say?"

"He said it must be nice traveling with a hottie, so I told him, 'No, she's a complete pain in the butt.'"

Chloe stuck out her tongue at him. She was silent for a while. "I wish I had a big brother to look after me."

Jake didn't bother pointing out that for the time being, he was looking after Mark. "No sister either?"

"Nope. And, I'm not really in touch with my parents. They couldn't wrap their heads around my car and apartment and no visible means of income. It was easier to..." She shrugged and it was a sad little gesture. "I can't say I blame them. Let's face it. Being an old guy's girlfriend isn't..." She hiked her shoulders a second time. "Honorable?"

When it became obvious she wasn't going to say anything else, even though she clearly had more on her mind, Jake swallowed a sigh and opened the door. "Something else on your mind, Chloe?"

"I've never been to Canada."

"Is that right?"

"I've never been anywhere."

"The Boss set you up in Chicago, but he didn't take you anywhere? Didn't want to show you off?"

She shook her head. "Vacations are for families. He took his wife. Kids. He'd just buy me something. A Coach watch. Something like that. I've never left the States. Growing up, my family didn't have much money. We went camping. Road trips. That sort of thing."

Now she really did sound sad and Jake silently chastised himself for playing dodge ball for so long. Nerves and uncertainty were normal for someone who hadn't travelled before. It was the simplest problem he'd ever heard. Maybe he could alleviate all her fears and cheer her up with an equally simple answer. "If we were going to Toronto or Vancouver you'd be hard pressed to see any difference between them and any place in the States. The differences are there. But nothing significant. Sioux River on the other hand, I imagine the place will open your eyes."

Her head flashed around, cheeks flaming red. She glared at him. "I'm not some hick, Jake," she snapped. "You might be some big world traveler, but I've been to college. I've seen television and movies. I'm not stupid."

Taken aback, Jake didn't say anything. He squinted into the distance, lips pressed into a hard thin line. Clearly he hadn't figured out Chloe's problem and just as clearly, he'd forgotten how annoyed women get when you try and "fix" their problem. After several minutes he said, "You ready to go?" His voice sounded stiff even to him.

She sipped her coffee. She didn't move. "I've never been across the border."

Jake said nothing.

"I've never dealt with Customs."

He said nothing.

"I doubt they'll look at our bruises and the bullet holes in your car then just smile and wave us through."

It was a good point. She was right. They couldn't cross the border looking the way they did. The silence stretched while he thought about Canadians and their naive ideas about guns and bullet holes, and tried to come up with a plan on how to deal with the border crossing. He remembered reading a funny novel a couple of years back in which the main character hid real bullet holes with stickers that looked like bullet holes.

"Quit sulking," Chloe said.

Pot, kettle, Jake thought but wisely kept his mouth shut. He gave the back of his neck an irritated, frustrated scratch. "What did you study in college?"

"Interior design and decorating."

"You didn't like it?"

"I liked it. Turned out getting a job was almost impossible."

After another long pause, he nodded in the direction of the store. "Do they have merchandise in there? Stickers, that kind of shit?"

"Yep."

"We'll go in there, get some stickers. NASCAR would be good. Not number ninety-seven, though. I hate that whiner Kurt Busch. If they have stickers that look like bullet holes in glass, we'll get some to cover the hole in the window." He didn't like the idea of marring his beautiful black car with stickers, but a little elbow grease and a squirt of WD-40 and they'd come off.

Chloe brightened. "What about one of those yellow ribbons? The magnets?"

"Good idea." And, since they were on a roll, he said, "As for Customs, try not to worry about it. It's no big deal between Canada and the U.S. They'll look at our ID. Ask us where we're going and for how long." He shrugged. "Keep it simple and honest. We're going to a fishing lodge in Sioux River. They'll ask how long. We'll say a week. If they ask about the way we look, we were in a car accident. Sadly, your Cavalier was totaled. Okay?"

She nibbled her lip and nodded. "How long has Mark been a driving instructor?"

Jake thought the only reason she asked was to smooth his ruffled feathers. He appreciated her effort. "Eight months. He's had a couple of jobs since he got back from Afghanistan. He spent a few months as a security guard at JC Penny." Jake paused, then quietly made the understatement of the year. "It didn't work out."

He remembered standing there watching the cops drive away with Mark at his side and JC Penny management behind them, all frowns and crossed arms, telling them neither were welcome back. Not even as customers, and Mark saying, "Fine, I can't take the crowds anyway." Then they walked away, Jake silent, his stomach a burning knot of stress, and Mark railing on about shrieking two year olds, diaper bags as big as suitcases, and customers who didn't feel as though the sale price was low enough. The carnage he witnessed in the mall the day after Christmas made him snap.

"After JC Penny he worked for a contractor, putting roofs on condos. That went pretty well. Until our folks died. We found out later that is what is known as a trigger event."

Chloe reached out and gently touched his arm. "You don't have to tell me this, Jake."

"I know." Usually he avoided discussing his and Mark's relationship, but Chloe had the non-judgmental receptiveness of someone without any skin in the game. It made talking to her easy.

"Why didn't the roofing job work out?"

"He had a burger and a six pack of Coors for lunch." A smile tugged at the corner of Jake's mouth. "He stopped at a drive-thru ATM with a pretty good buzz on. With cash in his pocket he went to a drive-thru liquor store for a bottle of Polar Ice. Then he hit up a drive-thru pharmacy for some 7-Up and a bottle of Anacin."

"For the hangover."

"I guess. Back at the job site he stitched, 'This condo blows,' into the side of the boss's Ford Excursion with a pneumatic nail gun and some one-inch roofing nails."

Chloe scrunched up her nose in a clear expression of disbelief. "What?"

"My brother's bullshit tolerance is low," Jake said dryly. "Apparently the contractor was paying off the building inspectors. The thought of some poor couple spending five hundred K on a condo that wobbled in an onshore breeze and leaked water when it rained annoyed Mark."

"He didn't end up in jail?"

"The contractor couldn't afford the scrutiny. I paid to have the truck fixed. Everyone went their separate ways. Now Mark's at the driving school. He's doing fine. One on one he's good. It's the masses that grind him."

Chloe tilted her head back, draining the coffee cup.

"You want to go get those stickers?" he asked.

She jumped to the ground. Side by side they walked into the store. She grabbed his arm with both hands. "Jake, when we get to Customs, what about…"

He sighed softly.

CHAPTER 18

MARK HARRIS PUSHED the End button on his cell phone and plunked it on the table in front of him. How many guys met a cute traveling companion in a wrecking yard? Not many. A person couldn't help but smile at the improbability. A song he recognized from the local country station played quietly in the background. Mark swung his eyes up to one of the speakers hanging high in a corner. He let the smile grow. "New Country" was essentially "Old Country" with a modern, Rock and Roll vibe, which made *Back When* a little ironic he supposed, but Tim McGraw's lyrics were smart and the tune was catchy and in this case, "new" was definitely better than the twangy songs of "old." Maybe the day was on the upswing.

The kitchen door swung open and shut, wafting the stench of a hot deep fryer into the diner. Mark's stomach lurched. His smile faded. He hadn't told Jake everything. There was no point in worrying him. No point in telling him that by the end of Ashley's ninety minutes, his daily stomach ache had started. Not a stitch in his side like when you go for a swim after a meal but rather, a hollow, burning ache that left him squirming in the Neon's passenger seat. A double dose of Zantac between Ashley and Lin was barely keeping up.

He caught the waitress's eye, and held up his coffee cup.

She raised one finger and nodded.

Near misses. Pedestrians who didn't look both ways. Joggers who ran down the center line instead of on the shoulder... The stress level was indescribable. He wasn't sure how much longer he could put up with the pressure. Unfortunately, the other teachers at The Bay Driving Instruction refused to spend ninety minutes with Lin Ng so they drew straws. Mark knew the game was rigged. He always drew the short one when it came to elderly Asian women. The guys laughed and said, "You can handle them better than us. You were in Afghanistan."

"Let me tell you," Mark answered, "my life's in danger more often in Tampa than it ever was in Afghanistan." To be fair to elderly Asian women who couldn't drive for shit, their skills weren't any worse than the average adolescent—Ashley for instance, with her enormous Starbucks cup, or boys who all wanted to be Jeff Gordon.

Bloody hell he needed a holiday. Or a new job.

Or a real drink.

But, alcohol made him sprint through JC Penny singing *People Are Strange* at the top of his lungs, systematically decapitating mannequins with the billy club the department store gave him the day they hired him as a security guard. Melt downs such as those made for a compelling reason not to drink. How he avoided jail time after that deal was beyond him.

Back When.

A second, better reason to leave the bourbon alone, was the promise he made Jake. People got the wrong impression of Jake when they first met him. They thought the kid leaned toward shallow and self-centered. They weren't wrong. They weren't exactly right either. As long as there was a regular paycheck, a pretty girl, and recently, a clean Mustang in his life, Jake seemed happy just drifting. But the kid had a deeper layer. A determined, driven layer. He didn't end up becoming an airline pilot by drifting.

When he decided to put his mind to something, he was like an old dog with a fresh bone. The day World Ways filed Chapter 11, he flopped back in an armchair and rubbed his face with trembling hands. "Shit," he mumbled, then looked at Mark and said in a shaky voice, "What am I gonna do?"

As far as Mark was concerned, dealing with a furlough or a firing was nothing more than managing logistics. He planted both hands on his knees and pushed himself off the couch with a grunt. Pausing long enough to ruffle Jake's hair on his way out of the room, he said, "We're going golfing. Get dressed."

"I don't want to go golfing. Golf's nothing but a—"

"Frustrating walk. I know. But we need to figure out what you're going to do."

It took the better part of eighteen holes for them to agree that Jake's flying career could not go on hold. If he found another flying job, he had to take it. He could work his way back to Tampa whenever possible. He'd continue to help with Mark's psychiatrist bill. In return, Mark reinforced his promise to visit the shrink regularly and do whatever else it took to stay off the bottle and away from trouble. So, Jake left Tampa for Sioux River and a few more people saw the vein of iron running through the kid.

The waitress weaved through the diner carrying a steaming pot of coffee that made Mark's mouth water and a sandwich that dried it out again. She wore a dress the color of old mustard, her name embroidered in red cursive over her heart. The white apron tied at her waist held a writing pad and bristled with pens. "Here's your club, Hon," she said. She topped up his mug. "Were you talking to the kid?"

Mark nodded.

"How's he doing?"

"All right. Better 'n you and me, I guess. You look worn out."

A wisp of curly brown hair had escaped the bobby pins behind each ear. She exhaled a quick gust of air out the corner of her mouth, blowing it away from the tired shadows on her face. It immediately fell back and this time she absently pushed it behind her ear. "The baby kept me up late and this place opens early. You don't look so well rested yourself," she said.

He was getting four hours sleep a night, waking up regularly to stare at the ceiling then dropping off fifty minutes before the alarm shrilled. No. He wasn't well rested. "It was a hell of a morning."

"The second half has to be better than the first, right? Next time you talk to Jake, tell him I said, 'Hi.'"

"I'll tell him." He smiled. "He met a girl. In a wrecking yard."

"Jake met a girl? Really?" Her tone was mildly amused. She didn't look the least bit surprised.

Mark studied the club sandwich. It looked delicious. Thick slabs of multi-grain bread bulged with moist turkey, crisp bacon, and fresh vegetables. Two dill pickle spears and a generous pile of potato chips sat between the sandwich halves. His stomach did a long, slow barrel roll and a thin layer of oily sweat filmed his forehead. He said weakly, "Thanks for the sandwich, Linda."

"Yeah, well, I made it special." She walked away, sensible shoes designed for walking rather than style, silent on the tiled floor. The radio played, *She'll Leave You with a Smile.*

He nibbled the sandwich—it tasted like sawdust and stuck to the roof of his mouth like wallpaper paste—and he sipped his coffee and he wondered how he'd make it through to the end of the day. One more student to go. He pulled his schedule out of his breast pocket, closed his eyes, and took a deep breath before looking at it.

Phillip Mclean. A newbie. Sixteen years of inexperience.

Bloody hell. He tugged his right eyelid sideways with his index finger, slowing an uncontrollable flicker. Linda said the second half of the day had to be better than the first. Mark liked that kind of optimism. He didn't share it, but he liked it. He washed down a final mouthful of sandwich with a final gulp of coffee and headed for the door.

CHAPTER 19

GINO GIANOLO SHIELDED his eyes with the edge of his hand and stared across the street. How fucking long did Mark Harris get for lunch? The Dodge Neon with a "Student Driver" sign on the roof and "The Bay Driving Instruction" plastered across the side in block letters, still sat in Barney's parking lot, some retro-looking diner with weathered aluminum siding and neon Coca-Cola signs in the windows. Had to be twenty minutes Harris was in there now, probably sipping a sweating glass of iced tea while Gino invented ways to kill time, waiting in the suffocating Florida heat.

Seemed like all he'd done today was wait, starting with all the phone calls, pushing one for this and two for that, getting put on hold. It had taken the better part of two hours to find out where Mark Harris worked.

Gino did a one-eighty and pulled open the service station door, not much more than a walk-in closet propped up on three walls with cartons of cigarettes, snack food, and magazines. The temperature had to be twenty degrees cooler inside than out and he exhaled a heavy sigh of relief.

From behind the counter, a rail of a man wearing crossed flag tattoos (American and Confederate), and a white wife beater

stained with faded orange splotches, looked up from a *Guns &
Ammo* magazine. He eyeballed Gino quizzically.

"Your bathroom is disgusting. Needs to be cleaned." Gino
tossed him the restroom key. It was attached to a chunk of plywood. Someone with a black Magic Marker had written "sukc it"
and drawn an anatomically correct stick man with implausible
proportions on the plywood.

The rail easily caught the heavy key chain with one hand. He
glanced at Gino's BMW parked beside the pumps. He raised two
wispy eyebrows. His equally thin moustache twitched. "You buying anything? Smokes? Food?"

"No."

"How much gas you putting in the Beamer?"

"The tank is almost full."

"What the hell you doing using my shitter, then?" He pointed
at a hand-written sign on the wall, "Restrooms for Customer Use
Only." "I thought you were buying something. Get the hell out
of here."

Gino didn't move right away. He'd made a mistake and packed
for Chicago's cooler temperatures, not this eighty-six degrees and
climbing heat. Sloppy or not, he'd had no choice but to give up on
his tie. It hung loose at the neck now, his top button undone. He
hooked a finger into the collar of his shirt and tugged it away from
his neck. He softened his tone. "I'm waiting for a guy in the—"

"This look like a lounge to you?" The Rail nodded at the door.
Gino glared.

The Rail straightened on his chair and leaned forward, shooting Gino a glare of his own in return.

Gino clenched his jaw, wanting nothing more than to pull
the revolver out from beneath his coat and explain who he was
and why he wouldn't put up with the man's piss-poor attitude. His
only hesitation was the strong likelihood the Rail had a weapon
of his own under the counter, given his choice of literature. After

several long seconds locked in a staring contest, Gino spun on his heel and strode out of the air-conditioned service station, into a blast of heat that immediately raised fresh beads of sweat on his scalp and dampened the small of his back.

Behind him the Rail called, "You can't stay parked at the pumps, either."

Gino's step hitched and he almost turned around and walked right back into the store, revolver in hand, but after a second of hesitation, he continued to his car. Back in the BMW, he slammed the door and dropped into the seat. The leather upholstery scorched his butt. He arched up and away from the heat before settling down more cautiously, cursing in anger and frustration. Who did the service station putz think he was, talking to him in that manner? Kicking him out of the air-conditioned shop? Was that any way to treat a Gianolo?

No.

In Chicago, the family name carried some weight. That shouldn't have changed just because he was in Tampa. Granted, he wasn't a Dillinger or an Accardo, but in certain circles his name meant something. He had half a mind to… Well, he wasn't sure what to do.

His stomach gurgled loudly.

He swung his pissed-off stare away from the service station and aimed it at Barney's diner. He hadn't yet eaten a mid-day meal. And, he'd skipped the hotel's generously titled "Continental Breakfast." Instead, after his marathon on the phone, he'd driven directly to The Bay Driving Instruction and compared people walking in and out of the office to the photograph Sofia showed him. Around noon he finally saw a face that most closely matched the photograph. Turned out the man was on his way to lunch… which meant more waiting for Gino.

Barney's front door finally swung open.

Gino leaned into the windshield, squinting. Mark Harris—the

individual Gino assumed was Harris—walked out of the diner to his Neon. He was taller than Gino expected, but he had no frame of reference. Sofia's photograph only showed Jake from the waste up, with nothing to scale him against. Mark was slim bordering on skinny. He wore glasses. His haircut was cut short like a soldier's and was neither modern nor fashionable. His white button down was fastened all the way up to the collar. Not exactly the picture Gino had drawn in his mind, but he was confident he'd tracked down Sofia's latest boyfriend. When Harris drove away, Gino slid into the lane behind him.

Silently fuming at the disrespect, the heat, his rumbling belly, and what he considered the pointlessness of the mission in general, Gino decided he was done waiting. In the harsh light of day, Mario's problems and concerns didn't seem too critical. After all, how bad could Eric Dalrymple really be? Stories and reputations were embellished and exaggerated all the time. He was done chasing Mark Harris all over Tampa. He didn't need Paolo's help, not to force a geek driving instructor to answer one simple question. It was time to make something happen.

CHAPTER 20

"SO, PHILLIP," MARK asked, walking toward the Neon— probably one terrified little car if it were anthropomorphic. "You ever driven before?" His student had a zit the size of a raspberry on his forehead. Mark didn't want to make the kid nervous or self-conscious by staring at it, self-confidence was a fragile thing for a sixteen-year-old, but he couldn't un-see the pimple, it was a magnet for his eyes, so he gave his student only a fleeting glance and kept walking.

Philip shook his head.

Mark's spirits rose slightly. A clean slate. No bad habits to break before they started.

"My dad was teaching me in his Impala," Phillip said enthusiastically. His voice broke like an out of tune piano. Suddenly he sounded like an adolescent schoolgirl. "Plus, I've gone driving with our neighbor. He's got an Impala, too. My dad and him? They bought their cars on the same day. They're both white."

The kid's smile was huge.

Mark assumed Phillip meant the Impalas were white.

Out on the road he coached the kid through complete stops, shoulder checks, and lane changes. When it became clear Phillip had a better grasp of the fundamentals than either Ashley or Lin, he glanced at his watch. Lots of time left in the lesson. With a barely controlled tremor, he said, "Take a left here." He stretched the skin near the corner of his right eye with his finger until his eyelid stopped flickering. A nervous itch tickled the back of his throat. "I'm taking you to a nice quiet area where we can practice parallel parking. We have time before rush hour starts."

The nervous itch worsened, making him cough.

Philip cut him a fast glance. "You have a cold?"

Surprised, Mark looked at him. Teenagers were usually too self-involved to be aware of anything happening around them. Phillip noticing meant he had more going for him than most. It was a nice change.

"No. I don't have a cold. Thanks for asking. Now, keep your eyes on the road. Try and relax. Loosen your grip on the steering wheel. That will help. You're not trying to strangle the car."

Phillip nodded.

Mark said, "Good man." He swung his eyes back to the road…

… in time to see a glistening black BMW dive in front of them without signaling.

The Neon slammed into the BMW's right rear quarter panel. A screeching jangle of metal and squealing tires ripped through the air. The front corner crumpled like tinfoil. Mark rocked forward violently in his seatbelt then settled back a fraction of a second later.

There were several seconds of stunned silence.

Phillip stammered, "He… He cut me off. I couldn't do anything. There was no place for me to go." He looked at Mark with a stricken expression. The pimple on his forehead pulsed with an alien life of its own.

"I know. You did all you could. Put it in Park," Mark said, calmly. He reached over and turned off the ignition. "I'm going to take care of this. You got nothing to worry about. You understand? Nothing. Nobody will blame you. This accident is on him. Okay?"

He gestured to the BMW, and looked back at Phillip waiting until the kid nodded his understanding.

Mark knew exactly who'd take the heat, and it wouldn't be Phillip. It wouldn't be the guy driving the BMW either.

The Beamer's driver's door swung open. A tasseled, ebony shoe hit the pavement. The driver stood, a tall, slick-looking GQ type. He straightened. Centered his tie. With lips twisted into a scowl, he shot a glare at the Neon.

Mark unbuckled. "Stay put." Blinking, with his stomach tied in anxious knots, he climbed out of the car. He considered the Neon's front end while the slick, GQ type studied the backend of his BMW. Eventually Mark said, "Doesn't look too bad. I guess we should trade paperwork. My name's Mark Harris."

"I don't give a flying fuck what your name is." Slick's words were an angry snarl. "One thing's for sure. You're going to regret the day you hit me."

Mark cocked his head and narrowed his eyes, knowing the situation had just deteriorated from not-good to damn-bad.

Slick's voice rose. "Look what you did to my car. You're supposed to be teaching him to drive. How to stop when someone's in front of him."

Mark's blinking right eyelid was a blur of motion. He cleared his throat. "Sir, you—"

"Don't give me, 'sir.' What kind of instructor lets his student tailgate?"

Slick strode forward until he stood only a few inches away. The urge to back pedal was almost overwhelming. Mark held his ground and looked impassively into Slick's blazing face. He knew the nonsense the man was pulling. He'd seen it before in the military, one guy trying to intimidate another using his height, weight, and proximity as a weapon.

"You didn't signal." Mark's voice was as level and unemotional as a concrete sidewalk. "You cut us off."

Slick stabbed Mark in the chest with his index finger, his anger gaining steam. "You're blaming me?"

Mark looked at the finger probing his chest. A low thrum, like a busy wasp nest hanging on a branch, resonated through him.

"This car is worth more than you make in a year."

Specks of saliva dappled Mark's cheek. Disgusted, he jerked back. He wiped his face dry with the back of his hand, and as he did Slick pushed him hard and fast. Mark staggered backward, scrambling to keep his feet beneath him. The wasps were instantly enraged. The thrum was everywhere, an audible buzz, a tension that tightened every muscle and sharpened his vision and shredded the fragile control he'd clung to since Jake left town.

Slick smoothed his hair with the palm of his hand. He wore a self-satisfied smirk. He strode to the Neon and when he got there he kicked in the headlight that hadn't shattered in the accident. "Maybe you couldn't see me, what with the busted headlight." He looked at his Gucci loafer. "Glass on my shoe. Can't have that." He kicked the side of the Neon. A fresh dent appeared in the quarter panel. The glass pebbles on the toe of his shoe fell to the ground.

"That's how you want to play this?" Mark yelled, the wasps in complete control now. "That's what you wanna do? You wanna kick things?" He stomped toward the BMW and smashed one of the taillights. "How do you like 'dem apples?" He kicked in the opposite taillight. "How do you like that?" He marched around to the front of the vehicle and smashed both headlights. "And, that?"

Slick turned purple with rage. His mouth gaped open. "You know who you're fucking with?" he shouted. "I'm Gino Gianolo! Nobody treats a Gianolo like that. Nobody." He tugged back the lapel of his coat.

Mark saw the movement, knew exactly what it meant. "Open the trunk, Philip. Now," he yelled.

The trunk lid bobbed open.

Gino's hand came out from beneath his coat. He straight-armed a blued revolver, pointing it at Mark.

Instinctively, Mark ducked and rolled and the revolver boomed incredibly loud on the quiet street, and then he was back on his feet. He snatched a maple baseball bat out of the Neon's trunk. In a hazy, buzzing corner of his brain he remembered buying the Louisville Slugger the day before Jake left town because it was on sale for twenty percent off and felt good in his hands.

In a terrified falsetto, Phillip said out the Neon's open window, "Hey, guys…"

Gino cut him a quizzical sideways glance, the revolver in his hand hanging down beside his leg while Mark walked toward him, long steps that covered ground in a hurry. The bat still felt good, like an extension of his arm. He pointed it at his student and said, "Phillip, I told you to stay put."

Mark's voice snapped Gino's head around. His expression changed, like maybe seeing a driving instructor coming toward him instead of running away, was a huge surprise. His arm came up, the revolver enormous now that Mark was up close.

Mark swung from the waist. The Louisville Slugger gained speed as it swept through its arc, whispering in the humid Floridian afternoon. The sweet spot, right around the Major League Baseball endorsement, buried itself in Gino's stomach with a muffled whoomp.

Gino grunted heavily, folded in half and collapsed to his knees. He flopped onto his side with a surprised, airy huff. The revolver clattered to the ground. Long past caring about the consequences, Mark kicked the handgun away from Gino's twitching fingers, strode to the rear of the Beamer and swung the bat. The rear window disintegrated. He swung again. Both widows on the right side of the car shattered in a hail of safety glass. Crystals of glass sprinkled the street like rain drops from a spring shower.

Panting with exertion and adrenaline, he glanced at Gino.

The man had risen to his knees. He was bent over propping himself up with one hand, clutching his belly with the other. He gulped spasmodically for breath. Without warning, his back arched and he vomited. Thin, watery bile splashed on the ground, spattering the expensive Italian suit.

The retching sounds carried in the quiet neighborhood, cutting through Mark's rage, making him wince. The anger left him in a rush and his shoulders slumped.

Coughing, gulping, and snorting spasmodically for breath, Gino raised his head. Inadvertent tears leaked out the corners of his eyes. Stringy drool dripped from his mouth. He started a slow crawl toward the BMW.

Mark watched impassively, bouncing the Louisville Slugger in the palm of his hand. *What do you have in mind, Slick?* Then he saw the revolver. It hadn't gone under the car when he kicked it. The barest smile touched his lips. He walked toward Gino, narrowing the distance between them. Shaking his head, he said, "Leave it alone, my man."

With his eyes pinned on Mark, Gino blindly slapped the pavement, groping for the revolver. He found it. Struggled to a crouch. Stood up with a long, painful groan.

Mark waited, every nerve hot-wired. "Last warning. Don't do it." His voice was low and dangerous.

Swaying drunkenly, still bent at the waist, Gino raised the revolver and squinted down the stubby barrel, the muzzle carving Michelin-sized circles in the air at the end of his unsteady arm.

Mark decided he'd waited long enough, given this dumbass enough chances. The Louisville Slugger whistled another perfect arc through the air. It smashed Gino's shin with a crack Mark heard clearly on the quiet street.

Both Gino's legs went out from under him. He hit the ground on his back, his piercing screams as shrill as a gaggle of forty-something housewives at a high school reunion. After several seconds, the screams dissolved into moans. Lying on his side, slobber and tears wetting his cheek, Gino stupidly raised his arm a second time and jerked the trigger. Mark smashed Gino's tibia like it was piece of rotten wood, before the stray bullet knocked a mailbox off its pole on the other side of the street. A lawyer's promotional flyers fluttered across a heavily manicured lawn.

"I warned you." Mark swiveled, cut the BMW a glance and thought, something about the forty-thousand-dollar vehicle looked... inconsistent. He studied the car more intently. Nodded. One window remained intact. He swung the Louisville Slugger once more, and caved in the windshield with a home run swing. Then, doing his best to avoid the glass on the road, he walked toward the Neon. He dropped the bat in the trunk and climbed into the passenger seat.

Who was Gino Gianolo? The name rang a bell. He seemed to remember Jake talking about the Gianolo family. The lady Gianolo of course...

Sonja?

Sara?

Sofia maybe. Plus, Jake mentioned a couple of brothers, Gino and Paolo. That sounded right. Earlier in the day when they spoke, he had also mentioned a third Gianolo—Mario. And, Mario was somehow connected to this Mr. Blonde guy with whom Jake tangled. Mark kept connecting dots. The car crash with Gino Gianolo was most likely accidental. Only an insane person deliberately damages a luxury rental vehicle. However, the fact that Gino showed up in Tampa, on the same residential street at the same time as Mark, most definitely wasn't a coincidence. Mark guessed his younger brother might not have seen the last of Mr. Blonde.

In the distance, he heard the first shrill wail of an approaching siren. Protocol dictated he not leave the scene of an accident. He thought about it, and decided driving away was the least of his problems. Hanging around, talking to the cops, would finish off an already terrible day in the worst possible way. On top of which, he thought getting his student onto familiar ground was a good idea. The afternoon's events were a lot for a sixteen-year-old to absorb.

"Fuck it," Mark muttered. He fastened his seat belt. Said, "There was no coolant on the ground, Philip. I think the car will start."

Phillip stared at him catatonically out of eyes as wide as wagon wheels. His mouth hung open. Both hands clutched the top of the steering wheel, knuckles pale white, pimple brilliant crimson.

"Give it a try, would you?"

Still staring at him, Philip twisted the key. The Neon came to life. He slowly swung his head around and gawked at Gino Gianolo puddled on the ground beside his totaled luxury automobile. "That guy. He shot a gun at us. He cut us off."

Mark nodded. He swiped his hand across his forehead, looked at his sweaty fingers, and wiped them dry on his thigh. "You going to be okay?" The sirens were louder. Mark checked the side mirror. Still no sign of the cops, but they weren't far away. "We've got to get a hustle on, Phillip. You need me to drive?"

The kid's voice was faint. It wavered but he didn't hesitate. "I can do it."

Mark was oddly proud. "Okay. Excellent. You're a tough kid," he said. "Signal left. Take us back to the office."

Phillip did exactly as he was told.

Mark blinked. He brushed his hands through his crew cut and sighed in exasperation. "I shouldn't have to remind you to shoulder check, Philip."

CHAPTER 21

B Y THE TIME Jake saw the Deep Cove sign he'd already driven past it. It was set back from the road, hidden amongst the pines and poplars. He spiked the brakes, came to a stop, and waited on the gravel shoulder. When sporadic traffic passed, he cranked the Mustang into a tight U-turn and drove back to the narrow laneway.

The sign read, "Deep Cove. Tundra Air Float Base and Lodge." Below it, a second sign was nailed to the post. "Private Drive. Guests only."

"This is so exciting," Chloe said, squirming in the passenger seat like a kid on her way to a birthday party.

Jake looked at her and raised an eyebrow. The end of the road was in sight. He knew what his immediate future held. Chloe didn't. He said, "Why are you so excited?"

"Because we're finally here. I want to see what the place looks like."

He knew what she meant. It didn't matter if a person was coming or going, the end of a road trip was always exciting. He wanted to see Deep Cove in person as much as she did. Her enthusiasm was infectious and he grinned.

Fleetingly.

Chloe said, "Considering how far you've come, you don't seem too pumped."

"I am. I'm just…" This new position was vastly different from the airline job he held six weeks before. It was flying—Jake could hardly wait to get back in the cockpit—but the similarities ended there. No matter how proficient he was at World Ways, there was a whole new set of skills to learn for Tundra Air. His resume wouldn't mean a thing to his new peers. They'd want to see how well the airline boy performed in the bush, without paved runways, flight management computers, and air traffic controllers. What he did at World Ways wouldn't be considered real work. They'd want to see him load his own plane, fuel it, and work without the airline's infrastructure.

He frowned, and scratched the back of his head and tried to explain. "This is way different from what I was doing. And, the owner's a dick."

"Why do you say that?"

"He drinks too much. Then he gets yappy. Opinionated. I met him once in Montreal. He was shit-faced. Started running down my job. Airline flying in general."

"Seems like a strange way to act. Considering he just met you."

Jake didn't answer right away. He'd walked into a restaurant with Lawrence Stevenson's niece, Marie-Claude looking scrumptious in tight jeans and high boots—what she called her hooker boots—the heels clacking on the hardwood, the soles crushing the peanut husks her uncle was tossing on the floor where he waited. Stevenson's blurry, slightly out of focus eyes narrowed. Maybe he guessed by night's end his niece would be riding Jake the same way the wanna-be cowboys rode the mechanical bull in Outlaws, the country bar in which she worked, and didn't like the idea. His attitude didn't climb above unfriendly all night. Jake couldn't wait to get out of there.

Jake said, "My brother has an expression, 'Instant asshole,

just add alcohol.' I think booze brings his natural temperament to the surface."

"I heard a comedian say something about that once. Somebody said cocaine was wonderful, it intensified his personality, and the comedian asked, 'What if you're an asshole?'"

Jake laughed. "That's Lawrence Stevenson."

"Maybe he only acts that way when he's away from his business?"

"Let's hope."

Chloe said, "Your first impressions generally accurate?"

"Almost never. Which is good, I guess. I don't want to work for a guy who throws chairs around the office when he doesn't get what he wants."

He drove slowly, concentrating on the winding gravel road, trying to avoid potholes that would have swallowed the Mustang whole. A mixture of green spring weeds and dead brown grass ran down the middle where tires never rolled, sweeping the under carriage of the car. At the bottom of a slight valley, he idled through a small stream. In a month all the snow in the shady spots would have melted. The stream would be nothing more than scratches in the dirt but in mid-May the runoff still ran freely.

"However Lawrence acts, you'll be able to handle him, Jake."

Surprised, he glanced at her. She flashed him a quick smile, the shy look he'd only seen once before. He appreciated her comment more because of it. "Thanks Chloe. Listen, we're only stopping for a minute. Long enough to let him know I made it. He doesn't know I have company. I'd appreciate it if—"

"I'll behave."

"I know. What I was going to say, I'd appreciate it if you'd wait in the car. Lawrence said the cabins are going through a spring refurbishing, some shit like that. They smell like paint. We won't be staying overnight. I'll take two minutes. Re-introduce myself.

Then we can find a hotel in town." *And, I'll drop you wherever it is you want to go and the strangest relationship in history will end.*

She didn't look at him or answer.

They rounded a slight bend and Tundra Air's lodge and float plane base unfolded in front of them. He pulled into a crushed gravel parking lot meant for a fleet of Ford Excursions and Chevy Suburbans. He shut the Mustang off and climbed out. Bent at the waist, with one hand on the door and the other on the roof of the Mustang, he leaned into the car. "I'll be right back."

Chloe nodded once, her jaw locked in a rigid frown. She slid the pendant of her necklace back and forth in quick, jerky motions.

Jake closed his eyes and suppressed a sigh. What did he do this time? It was on the tip of his tongue to ask. He held back. Why did it matter she was angry? Why did he care? Little pouts like this, snits like he'd seen before they crossed the border, were the exact reason he avoided long-term relationships. Over the last couple of days, he and Chloe had moved from open hostility to cautious friendship, but her mood was as fickle as the weather. If this was going to be his reaction whenever it changed, he preferred to see her on the next plane out of town.

He straightened, shook his head and slapped the top of the car once.

A door at the side of the lodge opened. Lawrence Stevenson stepped onto the porch. "Made it, huh?" Both hands were stuffed into the front pockets of faded, oversized jeans. One-half of his shirt was un-tucked. A shock of black hair stuck up on the side of his head like he hadn't bothered combing it after crawling out of bed.

Jake decided to worry about Chloe later. For now, he needed to make a good impression on his new boss. He nodded. "Yeah," and extended his hand. "You have a nice spot here."

Stevenson, reluctantly it seemed to Jake, pulled one hand out of his pocket. "Thanks. What the hell happened to your face?"

Jake mentally kicked himself for not thinking about that beforehand. He'd forgotten he looked like a Mob hit man had beat him senseless. His face was healing, the purple bruises turning yellow. It looked far worse than he felt. "It's kind of a long story."

Stevenson waited with an inquiring look on his face.

Behind Jake a car door opened and slammed shut with a heavy, solid clang. His heart dropped. He pressed his lips into a thin, frustrated line. Obviously, it was Chloe. Nobody slammed a door like her. He turned slowly, wondering what kind of new hell she was going to put him through.

She'd slipped on some jeans, covering her B.U.M. shorts. The flip-flops were gone, replaced with new sneakers. Most of her loose red curls were stuffed into his Yankees cap, but a few dangled out at the sides and back. He knew it was her attempt to dress down. He thought the new look was as sexy as bare legs and copper toenails. She couldn't hide her smile or her nice high cheekbones.

"Hi. I'm Chloe Sheridan," she said, walking with long, confident steps in Jake and Stevenson's direction. She extended her hand, just like Jake did, giving Stevenson no choice but to shake. "You have an absolutely beautiful spot here."

"What happened to your face?" Stevenson looked back and forth between the two of them. "Both of you. You look like you've been in a fight." His hard gaze settled on Jake. "The hell is going on?"

Chloe made a face and rolled her eyes. "Oh this?" She sighed. "We were in a car accident."

Stevenson glanced with skepticism at the Mustang.

Chloe giggled. "No. Not Jake's precious Mustang." Using Jake's line from a few days before she added, "Sadly, my Cavalier was totaled."

"I see. And, who are you?"

"An old friend of Jake's. We've been through a lot together."

Jake wanted to grin but the timing was inappropriate. Instead, he shook his head slightly and wiped a hand down his face.

"I've never seen this part of the world," Chloe continued. "I'm a big city girl," she giggled some more and touched Stevenson's arm. "I came along for the ride, is all."

Stevenson said, "Chloe?" He raised his eyebrows.

She nodded. "Yes. Chloe."

"Can you give us a minute, please?" He faced Jake. "Let's walk."

Without waiting for an answer, he swiveled and strode along the porch toward the front of the lodge. His hands, tight angry fists, swung at his sides.

Here it comes, Jake thought. Five minutes on the job and thanks to Chloe he was already facing a fight. He glared at her. She smiled back, eyes wide with innocence. "What?" she mouthed, palms raised.

The porch stretched along the right hand side of the lodge. It wrapped around the front of the building, widening into a balcony that overlooked the lake. The water glistened blue and cold. Winter ice still clung stubbornly to the shoreline in the shadows of overhanging trees. Jake saw a Cessna one-eighty-five tied to one of the docks. The de Havilland Beaver was nowhere to be seen. A second dock, meant for the fishing boats, Jake guessed, was empty.

Stevenson sat at a patio table, waiting with his arms crossed over his chest. He stared out at the lake with his forehead stitched into an angry frown. He kicked a second chair in Jake's direction. Pointed. "Sit. Who is she? Why the hell did you show up with a lady in tow? I thought you were seeing my niece. Marie-Claude, in case you don't remember her name. The person who got you this job."

Jake bristled. With effort, he bit back an angry retort. He flopped into the chair, and took his time getting comfortable while the hot surge of anger cooled and he figured out the best way to answer the barrage of questions. One thing was certain.

He couldn't answer truthfully. How do you tell a new employer that you stopped in Chicago for a night of rodeo sex with a hot-blooded Italian, got side tracked by a girl locked in the trunk of a car, got attacked by a Mob hit man, and escaped in a hail of gunfire? Particularly when Chloe already lied and said they were in a car accident?

There was no way.

"First things first, Lawrence," Jake said. "I'm not a Border Collie. 'Sit' and, 'Roll over' aren't going to fly." If he didn't stand up for himself on day one, Stevenson would walk all over him for the rest of the summer. He pressed on quickly, getting in front of what he guessed was the root of Stevenson's irritation—the man agreed to hire him on Marie-Claude's insistence and Jake knew Stevenson would fire his ass in a heartbeat if he thought Jake mistreated her. "I spoke to Marie-Claude a couple of days ago. We're as solid as we ever were. She likes to hear about the trip, what the drive was like from Florida. I like to keep her updated." Jake didn't elaborate further. His relationship with Marie-Claude was his business.

He continued, "As for this," he pointed at his bruised and battered face. "I have friends in Chicago. A couple of brothers named Gino and Paolo. I stopped to see them." He was lying on the fly now, sticking to vestiges of truth in case Stevenson asked him about it at a different time. "Gino and Chloe are close. The four of us went out for supper. Someone blew through a red light and hit us."

He felt beads of nervous sweat forming between his shoulder blades. He had the insane urge to laugh out loud. The situation was ludicrous. "Gino wasn't hurt. He went right back to work. Chloe was told to take a month off."

"What's she do?"

Jake panicked. The first thing that popped into his head was, "flight attendant," which made sense considering his job, then he thought "architect." He completely forgot about her background in interior design and for some reason blurted out, "Dental hygienist."

Stevenson didn't comment. He stared out at the lake for a minute. He nodded, seemingly satisfied with the answer. "That makes sense. She's pretty bashed up. You don't want someone looks like that leaning into your face. Six inches away."

"That's true." Jake bit the inside of his cheek to keep the earlier chuckle in check.

"She's not planning on staying, is she? Not gonna hang around and be a distraction?"

If she stays, she'll definitely be a distraction, Jake thought, remembering his reaction to her little pout in the car. He shook his head. "As far as I know she's flying out to Thunder Bay. Connecting to Chicago from there."

Stevenson pushed himself out of the patio chair. The metal legs scraped across the wooden balcony with an echoing rattle. He gestured for Jake to lead the way back to the parking lot.

Jake was several steps in front of Stevenson when he rounded the corner, in time to see Chloe sprinting down the porch, away from him. She came to a sliding halt, spun and dropped him a slow, deliberate wink. Half a second later Stevenson rounded the corner. Chloe's hands were clasped behind her back and she was scuffing the toe of her sneaker through the gravel and staring at the sky like she'd been waiting there the entire time.

"Jake tells me you got some time off work?" Stevenson said.

Chloe nodded without hesitation. She even managed to look somewhat annoyed. "Yep. People are nervous enough in a dentist's chair. They don't want to see my beat-up mug staring them in the face. I got a month off. Two weeks actually, but they tacked them onto my annual vacation time."

Jake choked back a smile. She covered well! But it was time to get Stevenson away from the story and thinking about something else. "Those the guest cabins?" he asked, pointing to several cabins spread out in the trees on the left side of the bay.

"One, and two." Stevenson pointed to the other side of the bay. "Three, four, and five are over there. Yours is behind the lodge."

Four of the cabins were easy to spot. "Where's number five?"

"Right out there on the point."

"I see a cabin on that little island."

"That's cabin five. But it's not an island. The bay hooks to the left. Makes the point at the end of the bay look like an island. Most of the You-Alls like cabin five. It's got a great view on two sides and it's isolated from the other cabins. They can party it up without bothering the other guests.

"Let's go inside. Discuss what we're going to do tomorrow. Then you can head off to the hotel."

Jake said, "Where's the Beaver?"

"The other pilot, Dennis, he's gone with it. He's at one of the outpost camps getting it ready for the first batch of tourists."

Chloe hadn't interrupted in three, four minutes, some kind of record, so Jake wasn't surprised when she said, "Can we have a tour of the lodge before we go? I'd love a tour." She smiled her most engaging smile and Jake couldn't believe it. Stevenson seemed to melt.

A dopey smile crossed his face. "Sure." He still had his hands in his pockets.

Chloe grabbled his arm in both hands. She looked over her shoulder at Jake with a cocky grin on her face. "This is so exciting."

Shaking his head, Jake followed them. He liked it when she grabbed his arm when they walked. He wasn't crazy seeing her do it with Stevenson.

They entered the lodge through the side door Stevenson had exited earlier, into a large common area. Daylight poured in through windows on either side of the French doors. A variety of armchairs and sofas on area rugs were arranged to face a big screen television tuned to CNN, the volume on mute. Bookcases lined one wall. The shelves were cluttered with secondhand best sellers.

A long table with benches on either side sat just past the living area. A swinging door led into the kitchen and another led into an office. A counter divided the office in two. One half was devoted to racks of clothing advertising, "Fly-in-fishing at Tundra Air." On the other side was an area for pilots to flight plan and a staircase leading upstairs.

"What's up there?" Chloe asked.

"One washroom. Two bedrooms. One bedroom is for the cook. The other is for the hostess. They both have to be up early. Earlier than the pilots and the guests. Mid-summer, when it's the busiest, the planes are in the air the moment the sun rises. Jake and Dennis, as well as all the guests have to be fed and watered by that time."

"Where's the cook?"

"He's in town picking up supplies. Him and the hostess are seasonal employees. I usually have two full-time pilots. Dennis has been here a couple of years. The other pilot quit this spring. Went to a regional airline." There was a knot of anger in Stevenson's voice.

Jake smiled. That was how aviation worked. A pilot was always looking for the next airplane. When it came to airplanes and pilots, size mattered. He was surprised Stevenson hadn't accepted that undeniable fact of aviation life.

"What's the hostess do?"

"At mealtime she's a waitress. During the day, when there aren't too many people around, she's a janitor responsible for keeping the lodge clean. The guests keep their cabin clean. When they leave the hostess makes sure the cabin is ready for the next batch of You-Alls."

Chloe looked at Jake with a questioning expression. She silently mouthed, "You-Alls?"

Jake shrugged. He suspected the term meant "Americans."

Stevenson was still talking. "The hostess tallies up their bills. Sells them souvenirs. Answers phones during the day." He hiked his shoulders. "A Jack of all trades, really. A hostess works hard. The compensation in tips is worth it."

"Is the hostess in town with the cook?"

"No. I haven't—"

With immediate realization, Jake saw where the conversation was heading. Obviously, Chloe did too. She cut a second glance at Jake, an expression of complete epiphany on her face.

"We should get going," Jake said quickly. He grabbed Chloe's hand. "Right now."

"—hired one yet," Stevenson finished saying.

Chloe beamed. "I could be your hostess," she said in her shy voice.

Stevenson didn't say anything right away, clearly the only one of the three who hadn't seen this coming. He furrowed his brow and eventually said, "Have you ever waitressed?"

Jake said, "No. She hasn't."

"Do you have a problem cleaning up after other people? Sometimes really sloppy people?"

"Yes, she does," Jake said, thinking about the Doritos, Chloe telling him she wasn't a waitress or a maid.

"Oh, Jake. I was a waitress at TGIFs when I was nineteen. Remember? As for cleaning, I do that every day. I clean people's teeth. That's pretty personal. What do you think, Lawrence?" She played with her hair, twisting a red curl around her index finger, like Jake had seen her do over and over again.

Still frowning in thought, Stevenson, said, "I don't think so, Chloe. You'll be back at work in four weeks. Tourist season doesn't end until Labor Day. I need a hostess until the end of September."

Chloe's face fell.

"Sorry it won't work out, Chloe," Jake said. He took a couple of steps toward the door, tugging her by the hand. "We really should be going. When's the next flight out of town?"

"What if I made a call?" Chloe said. "Stretched my time off?"

"Don't bother unless you can stretch it until the end of September."

"Can I let you know tomorrow?"

"I guess that'll work," Stevenson said. "Jake starts tomorrow. Come back with him. But only if you can arrange the time off."

CHAPTER 22

PAOLO GIANOLO THOUGHT phoning every Weatherly in the Tampa phonebook would be the hard part of the day. Turned out it was easy. He shone on the phone. When nobody could see him, he was as gregarious as his brother wanted to be. He didn't get his defensive back up like he routinely did in face-to-face situations, when his hideously scarred face was the first thing people saw.

In less than twenty minutes, he reached the correct Weatherly.

"Good morning, Ma'am," he said. Old folks liked that, the more formal greeting the word Ma'am implied.

"Yes?" she answered, in a wavering old woman's voice.

Paolo guessed an old lady wouldn't know who the Rolling Stones were so he said, "My name is Keith Richards. I'm a friend of Jake's. From World Ways." When he was lying Paolo liked to include a smattering of common knowledge, for credibility's sake. "I was wondering, is he home today?"

"No. I'm sorry. He's not."

Right away he recognized the loneliness in her voice. Unexpected sympathy twisted his heart. Oftentimes he felt lonely himself, with Gino always hogging the spotlight. "That's too bad," he said, without having to put unhappiness in his tone. "What about Mark? Maybe I could leave a message with him?"

"Oh dear. I'm sorry. His car isn't in the driveway. I think he's at work."

She was probably right, being it was the middle of the day and all. He and Gino were counting on it. Paolo manufactured a short laugh. "I'm zero for two. Do you know when Jake will be home? That way I can call back." He held his breath, halfway expecting her to ask why he hadn't called Jake directly, which would have been a reasonable question, and one for which he had an answer. "I called and left a message on his machine. And, and I tried his cell phone, but no luck there. I'm only in town for a short time, so touching base with him sooner than later is important..." But, Mrs. Weatherly didn't ask so Paolo stuck to his first script and said, "We talked about getting together, you know? Maybe heading out on the town."

It was all about bringing the right tone. A little courtesy here. A little teasing there. Sympathetic or not, he didn't feel the least bit bad about pumping her for information. Lying to her. Far as he was concerned, he was doing her a favor, breaking up the monotony of her day.

"You boys."

He heard the smile in her voice and imagined her shaking her head.

"I don't know how long he'll be gone. Sometimes I hear him and Mark chatting when Jake is washing his black car. Sometimes they help me with the yard work and they talk about their days. You know World Ways went bankrupt, I imagine? Jake told me a lady friend in Montreal found him a flying job. Marie-Claude Lefevre. I don't think I'm saying it correctly. They have funny names, don't they? She's a student at McGill. She must be smart." Mrs. Weatherly's voice became disapproving. "I don't know how she keeps her grades up working in a country music bar all night."

Paolo hurriedly scribbled everything down while the old lady prattled on. Unless he'd gotten seriously lost on the drive north, Harris wasn't working in Montreal. Clearly Mrs. Weatherly had fucked up that part of the story. Still, there was a boatload of information in what she was saying. One tidbit or another would pan out.

There was another certainty. They wouldn't have to look too far to find a country bar in Montreal. If Marie-Claude lived in Calgary, finding her would have been a big problem, all the redneck bars out there, but Montreal was filled with wannabe Euro trash. If there were more country bars in Montreal than he could count on one hand, Paolo would be surprised.

"A new job? Good for him," Paolo said. "I've probably taken up enough of your time, Ma'am. I better get going."

There was a long sigh. "Oh, I'm not doing too much this morning."

"No? How come? It's a beautiful day. You should be out in your garden. I bet you've got a dog, maybe a cat that would like to go for a walk?" Getting someone to talk wasn't the least bit tricky. Find common ground then pretend you're interested, something Gino never figured out. The fuck was he thinking, chatting up a flight attendant with a line like, "Have you tried the Pinot Noir?" If Paolo hadn't been so convinced the Boeing was one bump away from cart-wheeling out of the sky, he might have laughed at his brother's awful pick up attempt.

"… can't take my cats for a walk. I have three. I'm going out later to buy flea collars…"

Paolo grunted occasional agreements and tapped his teeth with the eraser on the end of the pencil, listening with half an ear in case Mrs. Weatherly dropped anything else of interest into their conversation. He shook his head and suppressed a chuckle. Even on a good day there was no chance Gino was getting anywhere with a flight attendant using a line like, "Have you tried the Pinot Noir?"

If he wanted to flirt instead of get lucky, that was different. But he still needed to come up with something stronger than, "Have you tried the Pinot Noir?" If he wanted to use wine as a common starting point, fine. Ask her if she flies into San Fran, if she's ever gone on a Napa Valley wine tour. Or, to the South of France. Or, if she says she didn't drink, bust out a lie. Say something like, "My sister don't drink either. She stays healthy. Runs marathons." Pretty soon you find something the lady is interested in. After that it's simple. Maintain eye contact, let her do all the talking, and pretend to be interested.

Just like he was pretending to be interested in the old lady's cats and azaleas. If it hadn't been pets and flowers, it would have been needlepoint and grandchildren. He took a shot with the cats and got lucky.

It wasn't difficult.

When Mrs. Weatherly finally wound down, Paolo thanked her several times, hung up and climbed into the rented Corvette. He spent the next hour searching for the old lady's house. When he found it, he was confident he had the right place. The cats sitting on the window ledge, the azaleas in the window box, and the baby blue New Yorker in the driveway gave it away. He orbited the block a couple of times in expanding circles, getting to know the lay of the land in case she noticed him and decided there was a stalker in the neighborhood. If she were to call the cops and he needed to make a run for it, he didn't want to swing into a cul-de-sac with the Federales up his ass.

He didn't bump into any dead ends and discovered his best escape route, no more than a block and a half away. It was some kind of traffic artery. Two lanes, both directions, one side of the street residential, the other side a strip mall full of stores with unrecognizable names and security bars:

Rainy Day Video.

Stardust Disc Jockeys.

Sunshine State Convenience.

Sunset Pita's and Subs.

Oddly out of place was Honest Ed's Pre-owned Vehicles.

If Sunshine State Convenience sold liquor, and Paolo was sure it did, the only thing missing from this particular piece of Floridian hell was a hardware store. Food, entertainment, and transportation. All the bases were covered.

He made his way back to Mrs. Weatherly's. When he was parked in the shade of a palm tree opposite her bungalow, he reclined the Corvette's seat. He wondered if Gino had managed to track down Mark Harris. He glanced at the dashboard clock. The better part of the day gone and Gino hadn't checked in once? Paolo could have called his brother himself, but that wasn't happening. He was still pissed off, the way Gino continued to point out they were twins, then soaked up the attention while people like the overly made-up flight attendant tried disguising her horror at the lines burnt into his face.

Nope. The pretty boy could phone him.

Paolo squirmed in his seat and drummed his fingers on the armrest. He glanced at the clock. Exactly seven minutes had passed since he parked. Talking to the old lady wasn't difficult. Finding her place hadn't been hard either. The real problem was the waiting; nothing was happening. The world wasn't even passing by, not a single vehicle in the entire seven minutes. He tapped the radio's scan button, searching for something, anything, that would hold his attention. He'd never had the patience for stakeouts, not now nor years ago when he was doing B&Es as a teen. The harder he worked at not being bored, the slower the clock ticked. It might have been a law written down somewhere. He thought one day he'd look that up—why was it when you were bored, time slowed down?

But where? Where did a guy look up that kind of stuff?

Not in a skin mag or a comic book. He knew that for sure,

because the only thing he ever read had to include either Batman or naked women. He was anxiously waiting for one of the Dark Knight's babes, Cat Woman, Poison Ivy, maybe Vicky Vale, it didn't matter who, to show up between the covers of a men's magazine. That was called "synergy" and Paolo liked the concept. He had yet to see an article explaining why time stalled when you were trading stares with three cats.

His stomach rumbled. His throat was as dry as old cracked asphalt. Ignoring those physiological nuisances wasn't a huge issue. A bigger problem had developed. He hadn't bothered using a restroom before he parked. He had to piss and that was something he couldn't ignore.

Paolo scanned the sleepy neighborhood. Palm trees. Bushes. White picket fences. The old lady's cats wouldn't care if he ducked behind a hedge. They might have been statues, the way they sat on the windowsill without blinking. But, if everyone who lived on the street was as old as Mrs. Weatherly, they probably spent their mornings staring out the windows sipping Earl Grey. Just like the cats. That would be all he needed... The cops showing up, waiting a respectful distance away while he drained the snake, then charging him with indecent exposure when he finished shaking off the dew.

Maybe if he just whipped up the street to the convenience store? He could take care of the hunger problem and the bathroom problem at the same time.

The more Paolo thought about it, the more he liked the idea. He'd be back on Mrs. Weatherly's curb inside fifteen minutes. No way he'd miss Harris in that short of time. The guy was at work. If he came home while Paolo was at the store, there'd be a second vehicle parked in the driveway beside the baby blue New Yorker, and Paolo wouldn't have missed a thing.

Paolo re-set the driver's seat and flashed up the 'Vette. Two minutes later, he pulled into the Sunshine State Convenience store parking lot. Thirty seconds after that, he sauntered through the front doors, shoulders rolling, heavy boot heels thumping on the floor. Maybe some beef jerky and a Coke…

The clerk leaning on his forearms behind the counter, an old black man with steel wool hair shaved tight to his head, looked up from a crossword puzzle and tracked Paolo with his eyes.

Paolo eyeballed him right back. It didn't usually take more than a glance before a person dropped their eyes. He liked to think it was his intimidating, hard-as-nails glare; he suspected it was because nobody could stand looking at the lines burnt into his face.

The old spook's gaze dropped right on schedule.

After a couple of minutes in the washroom, Paolo grabbed a Coke out of one of the refrigerators lining the rear wall. He spent some time chugging the soda and browsing through the tourist shit in the store—t-shirts hanging on the walls, postcards, seashells, beach towels and, inexplicably, necklaces with flip-flop pendants. Who needed that kind of crap? He strolled over to the magazine stand by way of the beef jerky rack, loudly belching Coca-Cola along the way.

The clerk's head snapped up. He pinned his eyes on Paolo's, forehead creased, an annoyed look on his face, maybe adding up the price of the soda and the bag of Teriyaki jerky Paolo was dipping into while he flipped through the magazines on the top shelf.

Paolo sent back a scornful gaze then dropped his eyes to the centerfold. Out of the corner of his eye he saw the clerk still staring angrily in his direction. Paolo decided to ignore him. For now. If the clerk said something, made an issue out of him eating and reading, he'd react. Show the man who he was dealing with. For now, though, there was no reason to create extra problems.

CHAPTER 23

FLIPPING THROUGH THE top shelf magazines was one thing. Melvin understood the need to catch a glimpse of the centerfold, just so you knew what you were buying. But most guys wouldn't spend too much time with it right out in the open. This thug though, he'd been messing up the men's mags for fifteen minutes, casual with his slicked-back hair, not at all like his ratty Harley shirt and camo cargo pants. Drinking a Coke and eating jerky he hadn't paid for. Meanwhile, all the little subscription cards were falling out of the magazines, raining pornographic confetti onto the scuffed toes of his combat boots.

When the thug dropped a *Penthouse* into the women's lifestyle section, Melvin narrowed his eyes. It was good business selling men's magazines, but he didn't want one of his elderly customers picking one up, instead of the *Home and Garden* they were reaching for. He secured his pencil above his ear. The crossword lay forgotten on the counter. "Hey, pal," he said. "Can you read?" He pointed to the sign above the magazine rack: black Magic Marker on white photocopy paper. "Read the magazines AFTER you buy them."

The thug leaned back far enough to study the entire sign. He faced Melvin with a nonchalant look on his scarred face, held up a *Swank*, and said, "'Course I can read. What do you think I'm doing here?" He hiked his shoulders, showing Melvin he was cool.

A baby blue New Yorker pulled into the Sunshine State Convenience parking lot.

Melvin barely glanced out the window. He knew the car. He knew the driver. Mrs. Edith Weatherly was a regular. A sweet old lady. Not much of a driver. Her land yacht slammed into the side of the only other vehicle in the parking lot. A Corvette.

A screeching, rending of metal pierced the air, and simultaneously the 'Vette's alarm went off, the horn bleating every two seconds. Melvin raised an eyebrow briefly as paint and fiberglass splintered. He turned his attention back to the thug in his store. For Melvin the excitement was over. Sideswipes, rear-enders, T-bones, he saw them all in his parking lot, and damn, all car alarms did was give thieves a sporting chance.

The thug straightened instantly, the man's cool vaporizing. "My car!" He dropped the *Swank* and when he spun around and sprinted for the door he planted a heavy boot heel on top of Miss June and all her glory, and tore the poor girl right off her staples.

Melvin's anger flared. "You're gonna pay for that," he shouted, rounding the counter fast. "Five ninety-five. Plus, the jerky and the soda."

The thug slowed long enough to yank the front of his shirt up, showing Melvin the butt of a semi-automatic pistol stuffed in his waistband. "Step off, man." His face was a snarl of teeth and rage. "I could pop you right now. I'm Paolo Gianolo!"

Melvin came to a sliding halt, holding his hands open, palms up near his shoulders. "Hey, pal," he said soothingly, "take it easy." He took a cautious step backward. A chill ran up and down his spine at the same time as an angry flush surged up his neck and warmed his face. He sucked a deep, calming breath through his teeth. Crazies with guns were in the store all the time. Giving them space was the best way to deal with them, but damn, he hated rolling over in his own place.

Gianolo swiveled and resumed his sprint. A couple of steps away from the front door, and still moving fast, he grabbed the top corner of the newspaper rack and yanked. Perhaps he was trying to prove he could mess with anything he wanted. Maybe he was a destructive individual. Either way, the rack teetered drunkenly for a brief moment then toppled, scattering newspapers all over the floor.

The tentative grip Melvin had on his temper disappeared. His vision blurred until all he could see was the memory of another time when foreigners were pointing guns at him. The Vietnam flashback held him in its grasp for all of a second before he shook it off and dove behind the counter. When he resurfaced, he held a Remington twelve-gauge shotgun.

He'd modified the shotgun with a few choice parts he mail-ordered from Cabela's. A custom pistol grip made the shotgun easy to handle. A red, glow-dot sight improved accuracy. The last time he used it, he blew apart a rack of Lays chips and Mountain Dew. Fucking Cubs fans all trying to steal bobble head Sammy Sosa's after the Cubs pummeled the Marlins in their own house, and Sosa hadn't even homered that night. Buckshot and soda had sprayed all over his store, like a five-year-old boy pissing into wind.

He racked the pump, chambering a round of Federal Barnes Expander Sabot Slug, put his head down and, screaming like a banshee, hurtled out the front door into the parking lot.

Mrs. Weatherly studied the crumpled front fender of her New Yorker. With one hand on her hip, the other covering her mouth, she shook her head and muttered, "Oh dear."

Gianolo danced in an incoherent rage, pointing at his Corvette with one hand and gesturing wildly with the other.

Jacked up on adrenaline and flashing back to Khe Sanh, Melvin started shooting. The first round punctured the Corvette's engine block. The car bled black oil and green coolant. The second slug tore up hoses. Red brake fluid joined the expanding rainbow puddle on the asphalt beneath the Corvette. Round three ripped through the dashboard, turning plastic into shrapnel, and snapping wires. With a final, mournful shriek, the alarm went silent.

A moment of shocked calm followed.

Gianolo said, quietly, sort of amazed, "You shot my car." Then he went nuclear. Veins bulged and glowed purple. Spit flew. His eyes, as big and black as Goodyear tires, gleamed maniacally. "You shot my fucking car!" He pulled his shirt up and palmed the nine in his waistband.

Mrs. Weatherly's arm flashed out, an indistinct blur that belied her age, delivering Gianolo a stinging slap, and she told him she wouldn't tolerate coarse language, no matter what the circumstances. Six fleas moved from her lamb's wool sweater onto his black Harley shirt. With a startled expression, Gianolo rubbed his cheek. For a moment, he seemed to completely forget the Glock in his free hand.

Melvin grinned at the thug's surprise. He turned his attention to the old lady. "Were you looking for anything special today, Mrs. Weatherly?" he asked gently, while he thumbed fresh Federals into the Remington. She usually needed something for her cats, and Melvin believed in helping his regulars. Particularly the older folks. It was important to show respect for his elders, a sentiment the younger generation, kids like Gianolo, needed to embrace.

"Yes, Melvin. I need catnip and flea collars."

"You'll find both on aisle three, ma'am. The opposite end from the Metamucil." He nodded at her encouragingly. "You go on in. I'll need a minute out here."

Mrs. Weatherly started a slow and steady shuffle, aiming for the entrance to the convenience store.

Gianolo was suddenly back in the game. The pistol in his hand rose. He took aim at Melvin. The barrel wavered. He swung it around and pointed it at Mrs. Weatherly's rounded back.

"Hey, pal," Melvin said.

Gianolo's eyes flicked in Melvin's direction. The barrel of the nine followed.

"Yeah, you." Melvin squeezed the trigger. The Remington roared. The muzzle kicked skyward. Melvin compensated and jacked another round into the chamber, just in case.

The Federal Barnes expander slug tore through Gianolo's arm like the Storm of the Century through Tampa's Whispering Palms trailer park, leaving a similar swath of carnage in its wake. It entered the size of a dime and exited the size of a pie plate, tearing skin, ripping flesh, and shattering bone. All that kept the arm from falling off at the elbow was a tenacious, one-inch flap of skin. The force of the blow spun him around in a dizzy pirouette. He flung his arms out, possibly searching for balance and the dogged shred of skin let go. The severed arm hurtled into space like an off balance Frisbee. A second later it landed with a splat on the Sunshine State Convenience store parking lot, still clutching the Glock. It did a lazy half circle, trailing a pinwheel of smoke from the shredded remains of the Harley sleeve it was clothed in, and finally came to rest.

In the second before Gianolo started screaming, Mrs. Weatherly said, "Oh dear." She disappeared into the store without a backward glance.

"You shot my arm off!"

Melvin nodded, a big smile on his face. "Yeah. These Federal slugs, they work good, huh? Not near as messy as buckshot. I'll never use that stuff again." He pointed to the cell phone on Gianolo's belt. "You mind?"

When Gianolo shook his head, Melvin unclipped the phone, flipped it open and dialed 911. While he waited for the operator to answer he looked at Gianolo and said, "They're doing amazing things with prosthetics these days."

Gianolo sputtered and stammered.

Melvin raised a finger, interrupting him. "Hang on." Into the phone he said, "Hi, Cindy. It's me."

"Hi Sugar. How're things today?"

"Good. Good day. Little hot for me."

Between gum chomps Cindy said, "What's your emergency, Shug?"

"I had to shoot a guy in my parking lot."

Cindy sighed long and hard. "You gotta stop doing that, Melvin."

"I didn't have a choice. He was waving a big automatic at me." With his index finger he swiped at some dust on the Remington's barrel. He glanced at Gianolo and winked. "I was afraid for my life."

Gianolo's mouth dropped open. He stared at Melvin with a look of incredible shock glued on his face.

"Don't be telling me," Cindy said. "Save it for the cops. You need a hearse or an ambulance?"

"An ambulance be fine."

"Okay. They're on the way. You enjoy the rest of the day."

Melvin disconnected. He squinted in concentration at the thug. "Now, what was I saying?" He snapped his fingers. "Oh yeah. They can probably make you a new arm out of Carbon Fibre. Or Kevlar."

Gianolo turned an unhealthy shade of gray and passed out.

"What'd I say?" Melvin asked, thinking the time had come to wrap a tourniquet around Gianolo's bleeding stump.

A new voice spoke. "Uhm, are you still open?"

Surprised, Melvin looked up. A crowd of curious onlookers surrounded him, including a teen on roller blades, and a family of four dressed in identical aloha wear, all of them beaming at each other and agreeing the parking lot firefight beat the Indiana Jones Epic Stunt Spectacular hands down.

"Because I could really go for a Raspberry Slurpee."

Melvin smiled. Regular gunfire wasn't good for business, although the occasional shooting definitely was. "I tell you what," he said, looking at the skater boy. "Give me your bandanna and the Raspberry Slurpee is on the house."

"Cool."

Melvin wrapped the bandanna around Gianolo's arm. He let the smile widen. Cops, paramedics, curious onlookers… it would be a lucrative afternoon.

CHAPTER 24

"HE SHOT YOU?"

"He shot at me," Mark corrected.

Jake's knees weakened. He planted a steadying hand on the counter and pressed the phone tightly to his ear with the other. His voice rose. "He fucking shot you?"

"Twice. But he missed," Mark said calmly. "So it was no big deal."

"Oh shit, Mark," Jake answered, so relieved that the words rushed out in heavy exhalation. He dropped onto the sofa in front of the big screen, preparing himself for the next, obvious question. A nervous ripple ran up and down his body. "What did he want?" He figured he already knew the answer.

"The subject didn't come up."

Chloe poked her head around the corner, wearing the Yankees cap and a concerned look. "Who got shot?"

Jake ignored her. Another concern had popped into his head. If Mark didn't end up in jail—and despite his present composure Jake couldn't imagine a scenario that allowed him to remain free—his brother was on the fast track to the key-cutting kiosk at Home Depot. How he didn't end up behind bars after the JC Penny episode remained a mystery. He used up another life after the fiasco with the condo contractor. This incident with Gino had to be strike three. Jake took a deep breath, preparing himself for the bad news. "What about your job?"

Mark started laughing.

Annoyed at the unreasonable reaction, Jake snapped, "What?"

"I'm sorry, Junior. But this is too good. Behind closed doors, management reprimanded me for leaving the scene of an accident. Then they flung the doors open and publicly commended me!" Still chuckling, he said, "How great is that?"

The twisted Medusa's knot of nerves in Jake's belly loosened slightly. "What are you talking about?"

"Turns out Phillip's father is a state judge of some stature. Phillip told him how Gino cut us off, attacked us with the gun. Built up the road rage angle, as far as I can tell. He told Daddy-dearest how I defended us with the baseball bat. I don't know exactly what he said. Next thing I know, the cops backed off."

The feeling of relief was instant and overwhelming. Jake wiped his free hand down his face. He blew out a noisy breath. "I don't know how you keep doing that. Getting away with stuff like that."

"Me neither." The levity left Mark's voice. "The question you've got to ask yourself is, why was Gino in Tampa?"

Perhaps the overly protective twins were searching for him on Sofia's behalf although that made very little sense. Jake thought the more logical answer was the twins were working for Mr. Blonde. He said hesitantly, "Could be a couple of different reasons, I guess."

As usual Mark didn't mince words. "He's not Mr. Blonde's advance team, is he?"

Jake stiffened on the couch then forced himself to relax. He scratched a spot over his ear. "I don't know. Maybe. Probably. The entire bunch are whack jobs. No kidding. I'll ask Chloe. See what she thinks. She knows them better than me."

"Good enough. You find out, let me know. How's she doing?"

Jake glanced at Chloe on the other side of the room, pretending to be hard at work, the tips of her ears quivering she was listening so hard. A cleaning rag was stuffed in her back pocket of her jeans and a bottle of Fantastic dangled from its trigger in the front pocket. He looked away and dropped his voice so she wouldn't get the idea he was talking about her. "Good," Jake said. "Things have changed."

"What do you mean?"

"Not now."

"Okay, Junior. You take care. Keep your eyes open."

"I'll do that," Jake said and disconnected.

Chloe immediately stopped pretending to dust the bookshelf. "Who got shot? Was that Mark?"

One thing that hadn't changed was her nosiness.

"You don't have the slightest concept of 'private conversation,' do you?" Jake's tone was light.

"Did he get shot?"

"Nobody ever told you it's impolite to listen in on people's conversations?"

"Is he all right?"

"I mean, you could at least pretend you weren't listening."

She stamped her foot. "Ja–ke!"

Jake shook his head. Grinned. "Mark's fine. He's always fine. Gino Gianolo showed up in Tampa."

"Paolo too?"

"Mark didn't mention him."

"Gino doesn't go anywhere without Paolo. What else did he say?"

"He was in a car accident. He thinks Gino cut him off on purpose," Jake said. Knowing Chloe would harangue him with questions, he told her the rest of Mark's story, finishing with, "He was wondering if maybe they were looking for us. On Mr. Blonde's behalf?"

Chloe flopped onto the sofa beside him, nodding. "They were

in Tampa for one reason. Because Mario sent them. He sent them because you're the only link he has to me. Mario needs to find me before Dalrymple knows I'm gone." Her face grew chalky, her eyes haunted. "I'm surprised he doesn't know already."

"Oh," was all Jake could manage.

"I know what's going on. I just don't know what to do about it." She found his hand. Wound her fingers through his.

He kept his eyes pinned on the television in front of him, in case the surprise he felt showed up in his face. He tightened his grip slightly. Her hand was small and rough, the painted fingernails chipped. Cleaning supplies and twelve-hour work days had destroyed her manicure. He didn't care. In the three days since Chloe talked herself into a job, she had become more than a passing moment in his life. Now that she was employed, she'd exchanged a portion of her blasé attitude for seriousness. She tackled every task Stevenson gave her with vigor. Jake was strangely proud of her.

Releasing her hand, he stood, walked around the sofa, then sat down beside her again. He scratched his head and looked at her, the nice high cheekbones, the curls of red hair dangling down the side of her face from beneath his Yankees cap. Her cap now, he decided. "This is going to be complicated," he said, and it wasn't just the Gianolos and Mr. Blonde he was thinking about.

A smile momentarily tugged the corners of her mouth. Jake thought she may have guessed what he was thinking. He stood and circled the sofa a second time. This time he didn't sit. "I gotta go for a run. Give this some thought. Figure out what we should do."

"Jake? Did your brother tell Gino anything? Is there any way the Gianolos can find us?"

"No." Jake thought for a moment. He shook his head. "No. Mark knows I'm in Sioux River. He has my cell phone number. That's it. No address. I don't think he even knows the name of this place. I can't think of one thing that would lead the Gianolos here."

Chloe seemed satisfied. She nodded. "You mind if I come with you?" she asked timidly. "I'm almost done."

Jake hid his surprise. Coming from Chloe it was a strange and amusing request. A sarcastic reply automatically rose to his lips. He pushed it away. "Sure thing, Chloe. I'll wait."

PART 2
LATE SUMMER THROUGH LATE AUTUMN
2005

WHEN THE GUARD told him he had two visitors, Mario Gianolo let the anger simmering under the surface come to a full-fledged boil. He sent the twins out of town in late May with a simple task. Find a connection to Jake Harris. Then they dropped off the face of the planet. No visits. No calls. Nothing.

He straight-armed the door and strode into the visitor's room, moving easily in orange, government-issue coveralls that fit a whole lot better than when he was jailed almost four months before. His beach-ball belly had lost some of its robustness after three squares a day of crappy prison food. His hands swung in tight, angry fists at his side. No contact of any kind, not even a carrier pigeon, and now they'd shown up and he was going to make sure they…

His step faltered. He blinked. Gaped at his brothers. What the hell? The anger evaporated, replaced with astonishment. One thing seemed clear—he didn't need to ask where they'd been. Convalescing in a hospital or hiding under a porch licking their wounds was the clear and obvious answer.

Gino stood opposite the table, leaning awkwardly on an aluminum crutch, what looked like a cast on his leg. His entire leg.

From ankle to groin. And Paolo, there was something wrong with his arm. It looked almost like…

Mario steadied himself with his hands on the back of the chair. After a second or two, eyes moving from brother to brother, he pulled the chair out and sat down, too confused to know what to say. He threaded his fingers together and placed the knot squarely on the table in front of him. He desperately wanted to rip each of them a new one, but evidently something had gone terribly wrong in Florida and now the situation demanded delicacy.

Avoiding his gaze, Paolo sat down opposite him. One arm dangled at his side. The other, the one with a shiny stainless steel claw poking out the sleeve of his black leather jacket, clanked loudly in the room when he planted it on the table and leaned his weight into it.

Gino remained standing like a schoolboy in front of the principal, hands clasped together in front of him, eyes downcast. The white cast bulged out of the split seam of his pants. He scuffed the floor with the foot of his good leg.

Mario cut questioning eyes back and forth, from brother to brother. The silence stretched, pressing heavily on his shoulders. When it became clear neither twin would say the first word, Mario settled his glare on Gino. "What did you find out in Tampa? Anything at all? You find Chloe?"

Gino shook his head. "Sweet fuck all. I didn't find either of them. I met the brother. Mark Harris. We didn't get a chance to talk before…" His voice faded into nothing. His gaze returned to the floor. He shook his head and in a barely audible mumble, repeated weakly, "Sweet fuck all."

Mario looked at Paolo. "What about you?"

"I spoke to the landlady. She told me about a girl in Montreal, a friend I gather. She set Harris up with a new job."

Mario tossed his head back, and pinched the bridge of his

nose. He sighed wearily. It was thin. Nothing but smoke. Was it worth following up?

No.

Then again, what else was there? There were no other choices. He fished a package of Camels out of the breast pocket of his coveralls. Tapping the package on the edge of the table, he shook out a cigarette. He lit it and dropped the match into an overflowing ashtray. Smoke rose, adding another layer of grime to the tarnished walls of the visitor's room. A move was afoot to ban smoking in the visitor's room and confine it to special outdoor zones. It hadn't happened yet. Mario guessed there'd be a riot the day it became regulation. The bitching in prison that went on about "our rights" was ironic even to Mario. With the cigarette burning between his fingers, Mario pointed. "Sit down."

Gino ran nervous fingers through his hair. "It's easier to stand."

"What happened to your leg?"

"I was in an accident."

"Obviously. Car?"

"Not exactly."

Mario eyed Gino. He drummed his fingers on the table. Gino refused to volunteer anything else. Eventually Mario said, "Gino. Look at me. The fuck happened to your leg?"

Gino flashed him a quick embarrassed glance. He couldn't hold Mario's eye. He sighed heavily. His face was the color of an over-ripe tomato. "Well, Mario, you see, Mark Harris looks like a geek. He's a driving instructor. He had this baseball bat in the trunk of his—"

Mario's free hand shot up, palm open. It was clear Harris fucked Gino up with a baseball bat. He didn't need to hear the details. "Stop right there," he said. "I've changed my mind. I don't wanna hear it." There was another long pause. "You tell Harris the geek driving instructor who you are?"

Gino hung his head. He nodded miserably.

Mario clenched his back teeth. He switched his gaze to Paolo. Voice taut, he said, "The fuck happened to your arm?"

Paolo held up his right arm, showed Mario the stainless steel prosthetic. The pincher claw plucked at the lapel of his leather jacket, like a lobster would the rim of a pot, just before it got dunked into boiling water. "Well, Mario, you see, there was this little old lady—"

Mario raised his hand once more. Smoke twisted lazily toward the ceiling from the Camel smoldering between his fingers. "Stop. Stop. Please tell me you didn't use the family name too."

The look on Paolo's face said it all.

"What I tell you and Gino about that?" Mario didn't wait for an answer. "You guys run around getting beat up by geek driving instructors and little old ladies. Then for some reason you make sure everybody knows about it." He shook his head and waved both hands in the air in exasperation. "It's... It's fucking..." Words failed him. He shook his head. "I don't know what it is."

"Astounding?" Paolo asked

"Yes. It's astounding. And, it's not good for the family reputation. Word gets around. Every time something like this happens, you're considered more of a Disney character. Might as well wear big floppy shoes and a red ball nose. You know what there're calling us? The guys in the other Outfits? They're calling us the Fruity O's."

Gino squinted at Mario obviously trying to figure out the reference.

"Like the breakfast cereal," Mario explained tiredly. "But not the name brand stuff, Fruit Loops. No. We're the stuff on the bottom shelf, the Fruity O's. Let me say this again, so you both understand. Stop using the family name. Nobody is scared of us. Every time I see you two, someone's beaten you senseless. I'm tempted to change your names. Start calling you Black," his gaze switched to Paolo, "and you're gonna be Blue."

Gino suddenly looked furious, Paolo resigned.

Mario violently stubbed out the Camel and studied his crippled brothers. Gino propped himself up with the aluminum crutch. His angry expression carved deep furrows into his forehead and between his eyes. Paolo stroked his fingers down the burn lines in his face and rhythmically opened and closed the pincher on his new claw arm, like a fish out of water sucking its last breath, which was about how Mario felt…

Chloe Sheridan had vanished. At best, Gino would walk with a limp for the rest of his life. Every day, Paolo looked more like a science experiment gone awry. As for himself, he was facing a dime for attempted manslaughter. Bullshit of course. How a random bullet hitting a random vehicle constituted attempted manslaughter was a mystery.

His lawyer said, "You shoot a vehicle with a young mommy and an infant inside, the stakes go up in a hurry." In the end though, he guessed Mario would only get a couple of months for dangerous use of a firearm.

Mario washed both hands down his face, feeling the stubble the cheap prison razors left behind. It was time to face facts. None of them had any idea where to find Chloe. Any thought of staying ahead of Dalrymple was virtually gone. As he saw it, he had three choices. He could explain the situation to the crazy-man. He could pretend like it never happened. Or, he could follow the smoky shred of hope Paolo mentioned earlier. Option one and two were non-starters. He'd already considered and dismissed them in May because of the danger they meant to the family. All that remained was option three.

Mario said, "Paolo, tell me exactly what the landlady said. Is there any chance we can find this Montreal girlfriend?"

Paolo's face wrinkled in concentration. "Well, apparently she knew about a flying job. She called Harris after World Ways filed Chapter 11. A week or so later he went to Montreal for work, is what the old bag said. I think she had it screwed up. No way he was working in Montreal when you saw him here in—"

Gino looked confused. "Why not?"

"Look at a fucking map," Paolo snapped. "Anyway, the girl's name is Marie-Claude Lefevre. She's a student at McGill. She moonlights at a country and western bar." He paused. "That's it."

"How old is the landlady?" Mario said. "She firing on every plug?"

"She's still got her driver's license," Paolo answered, shifting uneasily in his chair. "When I…" He paused, visibly fortifying himself. His face turned a bright, embarrassed crimson. "When I talked to her, she was very aware. She told me everything she knew. As she saw it."

It wasn't much. Just a breeze over dying embers. Smoke. Mario closed his eyes and tossed his head back, needing silence to think it out. He tended to agree with Paolo's analysis. Harris wasn't in Montreal. A person didn't drive from Florida to Montreal via Chicago, eight-hundred and fifty miles out of his way, for a sport fuck. He might make that kind of detour if he was in a committed relationship, but (as much as Mario hated to acknowledge it), faithful and steady wasn't the way his sister rolled.

"Okay you two. Listen up. Both of you pack your bags. Get on an airplane and get to Montreal. Find this Marie-Claude Lefevre person. Find out about the job she set Harris up with."

Paolo's shoulders slumped. The resigned look on his face deepened.

Gino shook his head. "No way I'm going to Montreal."

"Yes, Gino, you are."

Gino raised his eyes. He stared at Mario without blinking. Still shaking his head slowly and deliberately, he said, "No. I'm not. I'm done with this. Look at us." He cut a sideways glance at his brother. "Look at Paolo." For once Gino's voice held a trace of sympathy. Gone was the condescension and mocking tone to which Mario had become accustomed. "You say Dalrymple will come after us. Hurt us. Maybe kill us? Bullshit. Chloe's gone, what? Three months now? He doesn't know she's gone or he doesn't care. Either way, what's he gonna do after three months? Fuck us up worse than this?" He shook his head. "I don't think so. The three of us have already suffered enough chasing her."

Mario said nothing, enjoying a warm feeling of pride. He wasn't used to Gino standing up like this. It seemed his pretty boy brother had grown some stones after the smack down in Tampa. Which didn't change the fact that he was going to Montreal. Mario just needed to come up with a fresh way of convincing him. He pushed himself back in his plastic chair, laced his hands together and rested them on his belly. He raised his eyebrows, said, "You done?"

Gino didn't drop his eyes or look away. "Yeah."

"How's your leg feeling?"

Clearly not expecting the question, a surprised sort of expression covered Gino's face. "It hurts. All the time."

Mario nodded. He shook another cigarette out of the package. "I imagine it's worse in cramped places, huh? When you can't stretch out. Like in an airplane?"

"Yeah."

Mario nodded again in commiseration. "I get that. Jake's brother, he fucked you up good with that baseball bat, didn't he?"

Gino only nodded this time, his face long, his large dark eyes watery like he was a moment away from crying. In normal circumstances, Mario would have told him to get ahold of himself, quit acting like a child. But not today. He couldn't risk putting Gino's back up.

Mario sucked on the Camel until it seemed his face would cave in. He exhausted the smoke from his mouth and nostrils in three mighty geysers and thought about what he'd say next. "It's not over, Gino. I want to tell you something about Eric Dalrymple. Mr. fucking Blonde. That crazy-man—"

"Why's he called Mr. Blonde?" Paolo asked. "Something I always wondered."

Mario said, "What I heard, he was a big fan of the psycho in *Reservoir Dogs*. The guy the other mobsters didn't like?"

Paolo shrugged. "I never saw it."

Mario continued, "Anyway, he's been around for as long as I can remember. Good luck isn't the reason he became a Lieutenant for the Outfit. He has a resume. After his initiation, when he killed the cop, he started collecting. You know how it goes. Someone borrows money at twenty percent. The vig is another twenty percent a week, and let's face it, a guy borrows from the Outfit, it's a last resort. Paying the money back isn't foremost in his mind. Anyway, when the guy misses the deadline it was Dalrymple's job to collect."

"I've heard all this before, Mario."

Mario held up his hand. "Patience, Gino. You may have heard the stories, muttered 'bullshit' under your breath, but you've never dealt with the guy. I'm gonna tell you the facts." He picked up the thread of his story. "Dalrymple's first check-in was a gentle reminder. Gentle because Dalrymple doesn't really want the guy to pay right away. He has too much fun on subsequent visits."

"What do you mean?"

"The second visit meant a beating. Dalrymple and his roll of nickels. He'd explain how the guy was still on the hook for the debt, hang a thumping on him, and return in a week. Usually the third visit entailed a bunch of broken bones."

Paolo crossed his stainless arm and his flesh arm over his chest. His face changed from resignation to interest. Mario was pleased to see it. The twins needed to pay attention. They didn't know Dalrymple like he did, so they didn't appreciate the serious situation the family was in, although it looked like Paolo was getting an idea. By the time Mario was finished he hoped Gino would get it too.

Mario continued, focusing most of his attention on Gino.

"What happens this one time, you two were just kids, Dalrymple was in his late teens, he pays a fellow named Wayne Cameron a visit. Friendly as can be he tells Cameron he'll be back in a week. Which he is. Of course Cameron expects him. Somewhere he managed to round up five friends and a .38. The gun was a good idea because other than violent, Dalrymple is unpredictable. You never know what he's gonna do, although in this case, it was obvious. He asks Cameron where the money is, plus the vig. He's looking at the ceiling, doing the math in his head and pulling out the roll of nickels all at the same time. He's got a happy grin on his face. He knows Cameron don't have the cash.

"About that time Cameron's five friends boil out of closets and other rooms and out from under a desk. They take Dalrymple down. Cameron pulls out the rusty Saturday Night Special and blows a hole in Dalrymple's right hand. Tells him that's as close to having the money in his hand as he's ever going to get."

Mario studied the glowing end of his cigarette, grimaced like he didn't have a taste for it anymore, and stubbed it out. He shook his head once. "I liked Wayne," he said quietly. Louder he said, "What Cameron should have done, he should have shot him in the face. Twice. Instead he got cute."

He shifted. The chair was as comfortable as molded concrete but that wasn't the reason he was squirming. It was what he had to say next, the part that cemented Dalrymple's reputation, that made him uncomfortable, and would ultimately convince Gino to go to Montreal.

"As you can imagine," he continued, nervously flipping his cigarette package from end to end on the table in front of him, "Dalrymple was plenty embarrassed. When his hand healed, him and a couple of fellas went Wayne Cameron hunting. Dalrymple dragged Cameron's ass out of his car on his way home from a beer run. Took him out to a construction site. Then he went to work with a baseball bat. Like Jake's brother did to you. Difference was,

Dalrymple didn't smoke the guy a couple of times then walk away. He made a sport out of it. For the money and the vig. But mostly because he was embarrassed.

"When Cameron was all busted up, nothing but blood and flesh, Dalrymple kicked him into a ditch. Cameron was looking up at him, begging and crying but he couldn't move 'cause of all the busted bones. That's when Dalrymple started shoveling dirt on him. With each shovel of dirt, he tells Cameron what he's gonna do to his wife. How he's gonna work her over with a pair of pliers and a knife. He didn't stop there. He went on about how he'd ass fuck Cameron's sister and burn her with a blowtorch. How he was gonna drag Cameron's chocolate Lab along the highway behind his car. Pretty soon, Cameron's almost all buried, except for his face peering out of a two-foot hole, and Dalrymple says, "We're done here. Now I'm gonna go visit your wife." Then he started shoveling dirt onto Cameron's face."

Gino's face was a long pale mask. His hand rose to his neck and he slowly, automatically, adjusted his tie. He didn't say anything. Mario gave him time to think about poor Wayne Cameron getting buried alive in a construction site in the Chicago suburbs.

Eventually Paolo asked, "Did Dalrymple go after the wife?"

Mario said, "Oh yeah. She died in a house fire. The sister was raped and burnt. She ended up committing suicide. None of it was ever pinned on Dalrymple officially. It didn't have to be. The people who mattered knew the enforcer was back in business."

"What happened to the dog?"

"What?"

"The chocolate Lab. Cameron's dog," Paolo said. "What happened to it?"

Mario closed his eyes, pinched the bridge of his nose. "Dalrymple adopted the dog. By all accounts they got along great. A lab is too stupid to know his master is a psycho. As far as I know, the poor mutt died of old age. Okay?"

Paolo looked relieved. "Oh. Well, that's good."

Mario opened his eyes. Leaned forward. When he spoke the urgency in his voice was not feigned. "Gino. You and Paolo have to go to Montreal. You have to find this Marie-Claude bitch. She's the last chance we have of figuring out what happened to Chloe. I don't know why the Outfit wants her dead. I don't know why Dalrymple decided to chip her, instead of popping her. Probably 'cause he's a sick mother-fucker, but the job was given to me, and it didn't get done.

"Is this as serious as Wayne Cameron not paying off his gambling debt?" Mario did a palms up, showing he didn't know. "Probably not. Who knows? If Chloe were going to spill the Outfit's dirty little secrets, seems to me she would have done it already. We would have heard. Those sort of thing aren't easy to keep quiet.

"One thing I do know. If we take care of Chloe, Dalrymple won't be waking Sofia up with a knife and a blowtorch. Or coming after you and Paolo with a baseball bat. Personally I think our last chance is in Montreal."

Gino sighed. "Okay. I'm going to Montreal. What am I supposed to do when I get there?"

"Track down Marie-Claude. Make her tell you where Jake Harris is."

Gino nodded.

"And, Gino? I want a phone call from you every night. Something else. Don't split up. I don't know how a driving instructor and an old lady got the better of you both. But together I'm confident you and Paolo can handle a cocktail waitress."

"Confident" might have been too strong a word. "Hopeful" was more accurate, but for the time being, the twins' self-esteem had suffered enough. Mario didn't want to drag it down any further.

CHAPTER 26

A COUPLE OF DAYS later the prison's public address system blared, "Visitor for Mario Gianolo."

Prone on his bunk, Mario's eyes flicked from the *Newsweek* he was reading to the speaker in the ceiling. He let the magazine fall open on his chest, wondering who'd be visiting him with the twins out of town. Maybe Sofia? Hopefully not. He told her to make herself scarce. He couldn't think of anyone else.

He rolled off the bunk and, filled with curiosity, marched toward the visitor's room. When he entered the room he paused, wishing he could turn around and walk right back out.

It was too late.

Eric Dalrymple sat at the table, his coal black hair contrasting oddly with his pale face. His suit coat hung neatly over the back of his chair. His white T-shirt was tight across his chest and around his biceps. He smiled glacially.

Mario's insides froze momentarily. Then a surprising calm washed over him, like the waters of a pond early in the morning, instead of a storm-whipped sea. Dalrymple was as frightening as he'd always been, but this moment of confrontation was inevitable. Now it had arrived Mario found himself glad the wait was over. He saw the future clearly. There was only one thing he needed to do to prevent a world of hurt from falling upon his family. He had to keep Dalrymple away from his siblings. He needed to buy time. How much depended entirely on what Dalrymple already knew.

Dalrymple dropped the Ray-Bans he was fiddling with and stuck his hand out, gesturing to the chair opposite him. "Have a seat."

Mario nodded once. Taking his time, making sure Dalrymple knew he was sitting down because he chose to, not because he'd been ordered to, he pulled the chair away from the table and settled himself with a quiet grunt. He fished a package of Camels out of his breast pocket. Tapped the package on the table. Shook a cigarette free.

"Don't light up, Mario," Dalrymple said threateningly, his always dangerous voice laced with hint of unease.

Or what? Mario looked the man in the eye, struck the match and held it to the end of his cigarette.

Dalrymple's cheeks flamed angry red. He wrinkled his face with disgust and turned his head away from the smoke leaching out of Mario's nose and mouth. Glanced around the room. "You want to tell me how you ended up here?"

"Nope."

"You're not going to say the words, huh?" Dalrymple shrugged. "That's all right. I put my ear to the ground. Asked a few questions. Put two and two together. I know what happened." His voice grew angry. "I give you one simple fucking job and you screw it up. You're shooting people thirty minutes after I leave your place? Your two fuck-wit brothers disappear. The next time anyone sees them, they're both sporting broken bones and Florida tans. I was hoping you'd step up. Take responsibility."

Mario thought about Jake Harris walking into his office, the man all beat up, how he wanted to call the cops, how he heard the cell phone ringing in the trunk, how he rescued Chloe before driving away in his shiny black Mustang.

"Fuck you, Eric," Mario said. Knowing his breath would stink like an ashtray, he leaned into Dalrymple's face. "Fuck you. None of this would have happened if you just shot the bitch. But no. You gotta get cute and chip her. I'm the only person who did anything right, trying to find her."

The crazy-man jerked back, his face stony. "Far as I can tell, you did diddly-shit," he snapped. He gave his head a rapid, quarter turn. There was a series of sickening pops and clicks. "The fuck-wits did all the work."

There was no way to answer that so Mario didn't say anything.

Dalrymple said through clenched teeth, "Remember that day in your office, back when I gave you this simple task? You pulled a gun on me." He bent forward, eyes burning with barely contained murder. "You think you can pull a gun on me and get away with it?" His voice rose. "You honestly believe you can tell me to 'fuck off' and get away with it," he looked around the visitor's room and waved an arm, "because you're safe in here?"

Two guards at the door straightened up, suddenly paying closer attention.

When Dalrymple spoke again there was a forced calm in his voice. "Well you are wrong, my greasy, wop friend. I'm going to ask one question. If I think you're telling me the truth, you bought yourself some time. If I think you're lying, well, you figure it out. So, here goes. After Chloe Sheridan escaped, why'd you send the fuck-wits to Florida?"

Mario rocked back in his chair, balancing on the two back legs. Eyes closed, he pinched the bridge of his nose. Dalrymple seemed to know everything. He knew what happened at the wreckers. He knew about Chloe's subsequent escape. And, he knew the twins went to Florida. The only thing he didn't know was why they went to the sunshine state.

His breath caught.

There was something else.

Dalrymple, Mr. fucking Blonde, didn't know where Gino and Paolo were right now.

Mario bit back a grin. He shifted his weight and the chair came down on all four legs with a thump. He could buy several days. Enough time to alert the twins. All he had to do was tell Dalrymple exactly why his brothers went to Tampa and make no reference to their present trip to Montreal. To this point, Mario thought he'd done a decent job of keeping the crazy-man angry and unbalanced. If he kept it up, kept Dalrymple thinking about something else and made him focus his attention on Florida, he'd buy the twins the time they'd need to disappear.

"That day, Eric," Mario said, putting heavy emphasis on the name, "when you screwed up and didn't kill Chloe? That wasn't your only mistake. You shouldn't have assaulted the guy driving the Mustang. He's the one Chloe escaped with. I don't know where they went but he came from Florida. Jake Harris. He's a pilot. Him and his brother rent from an elderly lady named Mrs. Weatherly. The reason I know all this? Harris was sport fucking Sofia. I sent the twins to Florida because if they can find Harris, they should be able to find Chloe."

Dalrymple stared at him for several long seconds. He nodded. "I believe you. Means you bought your sister and the fuck-wits some time." He pushed himself away from the table, stood and shrugged into his sport coat. Dropping the Wayfarers into his breast pocket, he swiveled and walked away. He paused after three steps.

Mario raised his eyebrows inquiringly.

"Meant to ask. Where are the fuck-wits now?"

The question wasn't unexpected and there'd been time to come up with a reasonable answer. Mario didn't blink or hesitate. "Both of 'em are a little angry with me. Seem to think it's my fault they got all broken up in Florida. They haven't been by and I don't know where they are."

Dalrymple nodded. "The screwing around is over. It's time to wrap this thing up. And, Mario? That last little bit of trash talk? That wasn't smart. I know people in here. The weeks coming up you're gonna learn how body orifices can be used for more than the purpose they were intended."

Mario gave the crazy-man a dismissive, whatever wave. He needed to speak with Sofia. And, he needed to speak to the twins. There was no longer any point in them hunting down Marie-Claude Lefevre. What was important now was putting distance between them and Dalrymple.

CHAPTER 27

MARIE-CLAUDE LEFEVRE WOVE her way expertly through the throng in the nightclub. She turned on a flirty, five-hundred-watt smile when she was mixing shooters for a crowd of big tippers and turned it off afterward, until she met her next customer.

A successful night in Outlaws was all about remembering who tipped big, and making sure they didn't wait too long until she returned with more drinks. That meant keeping an eye on the tables, watching to see who left and waiting to see who took their place. It wasn't easy. Outlaws attracted a clone-like crowd, everybody dressed in denim jeans and satin shirts. But she'd honed the skill quickly, so when a guy wearing an expensive Italian suit, really *wearing* the suit, walked in, Marie-Claude noticed.

Tall. Broad shoulders. Flowing, stylishly cut hair. There was a certain confidence in the way he walked, despite an obvious limp and an aluminum crutch, which made her mildly curious because she didn't see a cast on his leg. She adjusted a twenty-six of Kahlua in the holster on one hip, and twenty-six of Mezcal in the holster on the other hip, then wound through the crowd toward him.

As she got closer and fewer people walked between her and his table, she realized the Suit had company, someone she hadn't noticed, although she wasn't sure why. A black leather jacket wasn't unusual in Outlaws. Camo cargo pants definitely were. She wondered if this fellow was as good looking as the Suit, but when he sat down his back was to her and she couldn't tell.

The Suit spotted her. He raised an arm and waved.

Up close, he was better looking than she first thought. Nice certainly, but attractive men in Outlaws were as common as dirt and experience had made Marie-Claude cautious. More than any other revelers in the night club, the studs seemed to think their good looks and generous tips meant they'd get somewhere with her. One look at her Daisy Dukes and cowboy boots and they grew stupid.

She turned on her smile and prepared to trade innuendo and giggle at inane jokes—simple friendliness wasn't enough for the big tips—and by the end of the night she'd have a couple of hundred bucks in her jeans. Exhausting, yes, but after a few busy nights she'd have enough money to pay for another month of rent, or tuition, or textbooks.

"Shooters, guys?" she said, reaching for a couple of shot glasses stored in the bullet loops of the bandoleers crisscrossing her chest.

Before the Suit answered, his companion swung around and faced her.

Marie-Claude felt her smile slip. Sucking a startled breath in through her teeth, she tried not to recoil. The guy's face was a mess. A cross hatch of scars. The skin surrounding the parallel scars was tight and sharp, like the seams in the hem of the other one's trousers. He pushed a coaster around the table with the tip of a stainless steel claw extending out the sleeve of his leather jacket.

For a moment Marie-Claude was speechless.

"What?" His eyes were mean slits, his chin thrust forward.

Knowing he caught her staring, she flushed and hoped her embarrassment wasn't evident. "Shooters?"

"Are you Marie-Claude Lefevre?" the Suit asked, enunciating

every syllable, instead of turning her name into the beautiful musical note it was.

Marie-Claude narrowed her gaze. The guy obviously couldn't speak French. That didn't bother her. What did put a pea under her mattress was a complete stranger knowing her name. "Who's asking? How do you know my name?"

He placed his palm, fingers spread, on his chest. "My name is Gino Gianolo." His voice was oily smooth. He paused a beat and waited, as if she should recognize his name. When she didn't respond, Gino nodded at his hideous companion. "This is my twin brother, Paolo."

Paolo shot an irritated glare at his brother. Gino continued to smile. But now it looked like a huge effort. Suddenly he wasn't as good looking as she first thought. Those big black eyes glared mean rather than mysterious.

"Twins," she said. "Right. Do you want a drink?"

"We'd like—" Gino dropped the sentence with a start. He pulled a cell phone out of a case on his belt. After glancing at the phone's little window, he made an annoyed face and shook his head. Turning to Paolo he said, "Mario. Third time today. Call him later?"

Paolo nodded.

Marie-Claude tugged one of the bandoleers higher up on her shoulder. She tapped her foot while they carried on this little conference, waiting longer than she normally did for an indecisive customer, in hopes they'd tell her how they knew her name.

"We'd like to talk to you about—"

"I'm not here to socialize. If you don't want a drink…" She started to turn away.

"—Jake Harris."

Marie-Claude paused mid-step. "You guy's friends of Jake's?"

Gino shook his head. "No."

Simultaneously Paolo said, "Yeah. We are."

"We want to know where he is," Gino finished.

Marie-Claude laughed. "Right. Like I'm going to tell you. You can't even agree if you know him." She walked away, shaking her head. She and Jake talked semi-regularly. She'd give him a call in a day or two. See what he knew about these two circus sideshows. In the meantime, she debated whether giving the bouncers a heads-up was a worthwhile idea. The Gianolos looked weird but they hadn't threatened her. They were polite, putting a big effort into it, actually. When she walked away, neither tried to stop her. Still, they made her a little uneasy.

She scanned the bar until she spotted one of the bouncers, a mountain of a man stroking his goatee and keeping a wary eye on the crowd. She bee-lined toward him. "Hey, Tony," she said, leaning in and speaking loudly over the bar music. "Watch out for those two." She pointed at the Gianolos. The "twins" were staring in her direction so she gave them a wide smile and a little finger wave. "Something's not right about them."

The bouncer, already the size of a skyscraper, seemed to inflate. His eyes, rimmed with thick black eyeliner, narrowed. He cracked his knuckles. "You want them out of here, MC?"

She put a calming hand on his hairless arm, his bicep the size of a bowling ball under her fingers. Marie-Claude tried to ignore the image that popped into her mind, Tony, bare assed, strolling around the YMCA locker room waiting for Neat to shrivel all the hair on his body like worms in the sun.

"'Cuz, if you want them out of here, they're gone." Tony's voice was close to pleading. Under the club's black lights, his bald head glowed like a snow cone. The gold hoop in his right ear glinted. He proudly showed her the hoop's twin once. It dangled from his left nipple, not the kind of body decoration Marie-Claude would have chosen, but fair enough. What made her shudder was the skull tattooed on his chest, the skull wearing a toothy leer and a fedora at a jaunty angle, the second gold hoop an integral part of the artwork.

Marie-Claude thought for a few more seconds. The bouncers treated the waitresses in Outlaws like younger sisters. Handing out an ass kicking was considered a perk of the job but she wouldn't feel right turning him loose on the Gianolo brothers for looking like circus sideshows. "Not yet, babe."

"All right." He sounded disappointed but his tone quickly lightened. "You change your mind, though," he tapped his chest with his index finger, "come and find me. Just say the word."

"I will. Maybe let Peter know too, huh?" She shot him a wink over her shoulder, and worked her way back into the crowd.

It took her twenty minutes to wind her way through the bar back to the Gianolos. "You both still here, huh?" she said. "Do you want drinks this time?"

"You know I got a headache waiting for you," Gino snapped, with no attempt at civility. "I don't want a drink. I wanna know where Jake Harris is. You're going to tell me."

Marie-Claude straightened. Her curiosity changed to instant annoyance. She tilted her head and said slowly, "Did you just threaten me?"

Paolo patted the air with a calming, steel claw. "No, no, no. He was just—"

"Look at it any way you want, cupcake." Gino looked around the bar, searching for and finding the speakers. He gave them an evil glare. "Son-of-a-bitch it's loud in here."

Cupcake? "There is no way I'm talking to you about Jake. Or anything else for that matter. In fact, you two weirdoes are leaving. Now." She stood even taller, and swiveled her head, searching until she caught Tony's eye. She nodded. The bouncer smiled wide, waved at a friend, and the two of them headed in her direction.

Paolo gave his brother an angry glare then turned to Mari-Claude. "This boyfriend you're so busy protecting? He got himself on the wrong side of some very angry people." He spoke rapidly, flicking his eyes back and forth from her face to the two bouncers pushing their way through the crowd, like a cow catcher on the front of a train.

"Jake's not my boyfriend."

Paolo hiked his shoulders. "Don't matter to me what you call him. Me and Gino, we've gotta talk to him. Warn him. Because we're much nicer than the guy he pissed off." He tried an unsuccessful smile.

Marie-Claude thought fast without changing her expression. After hours of suggestive remarks, months of ass-grabbing hands, and three years of university psychology classes, her bullshit instinct was honed. She sensed truth in what Paolo said. With one hand wrapped around the neck of the Mezcal bottle in the holster at her hip, she studied the twins, wondering about the best course of action.

How did they know her name? How did they know Jake? And, what kind of trouble was coming after him? She nodded briefly and hooked an index finger at them. "Follow me. I'll take my break."

Triumphant grins crossed their faces.

Marie-Claude's fuse burnt a little shorter.

When she passed Tony and Peter, she jerked her thumb at the twins and whispered, "I really need to ask them a couple of questions." She glanced at her watch. "Give me four minutes. If they haven't answered by then, they won't. Then you can toss them out of here—"

Tony nodded.

"—as roughly as you like."

His smile grew.

Marie-Claude headed for the ladies' change room. She threw a glance back, making sure the twins were following. They were a couple of steps behind, Paolo walking slowly, Gino limping along with his crutch. Both men were locked in a staring contest with Tony and Peter. Testosterone hung in the air as thick as rush hour smog. Then, as if working a checklist—How to Get Beat in Ten Easy Steps—Gino said, "You don't want to keep eyeballing us like that. Fucking queer."

Marie-Claude's stride broke and she thought, *There goes any chance I have of talking to them.* Admirably, Tony and Peter showed restraint. She wasn't sure how or why, other than they were giving her the four minutes she wanted. After that, well, she needn't have bothered telling Tony to toss them as violently as he wanted. He probably would have done it anyway. The "queer" comment simply sealed the deal.

She pushed her way into the ladies' change room, holding the door open until a moment before Paolo grabbed at it with his metal claw, then she flipped it closed. It slammed hard in his face, shutting out the din of the bar and a muffled curse that made her laugh.

After the clamor and energy of the club, the dressing room quiet was an oasis. She blinked away a film of cigarette smoke. She unbuckled the alcohol holsters and placed them on the counter. The bandoleers of shooter glasses came next. With the bottles, glasses, bandoleers and holsters gone she felt thirty pounds lighter. She blew out a noisy sigh of relief, enjoying the relative quiet.

The door burst open. Two angry Gianolos strode into the room, Gino leading the way.

"Fucking bitch," Paolo said. He rubbed his forehead. "The door hit me on the head."

"I'm a bitch? He threatens me and you call me a bitch?" Marie-Claude shook her head. "Tell me about Jake. You've got four minutes."

Paolo flipped the bolt on the change room door. "We got as long as we need."

Marie-Claude stiffened. Her pulse accelerated. She had chosen the dressing room to avoid having to yell questions over the music. Big mistake.

Gino pulled open his coat. Planted his fists on his hips. "I wanna know where Jake Harris is. One way or another, you're going to tell me."

"Screw you," Marie-Claude said, sounding braver than she felt. "I want to know how you know my name."

Lightning fast, Gino slapped her face.

The sound was a whip crack in the change room. Marie-Claude's head snapped back and her cheek burned with pain and humiliation. Blood flavored her tongue. She blinked away sudden tears of shock.

"I'll ask once more. Where's Jake Harris? We know you set him up with a job. Tell me where."

Marie-Claude rubbed her cheek slowly. The two or three minutes she'd have to wait before Tony and Peter stormed the door seemed an hour away. "I'll say it once more too. Screw you." She grabbed her shirt at the opening above her breasts and tugged. Buttons flew.

The twins gawked.

She undid the top button of her Daisy Dukes and unzipped enough for the twins to see white lace panties. Then she screamed. Really put some effort into it, until the sound filled the dressing room and both Gianolos winced. When the scream died, she said calmly, "I suggest you get out of here."

Gino furrowed his brow in confusion. "The fuck are you doing?"

Paolo faced the door. "She's making it look like we grabbed her."

"He's smart. You should pay attention. Maybe learn something." She pointed to the dressing room door. "Get out. In a hurry, if I were you." She screamed a second time.

The door flew open.

Marie-Claude peeked at her watch. The scream worked. Tony and Peter were early. Standing one behind the other, they more than filled the doorway. Tony pocketed a key. He looked at her open shorts, the torn shirt, and the fresh sprinkling of tears she'd managed to squeeze out, and she actually saw the steroids kick in. Like Las Vegas neon at dusk, the bouncers' faces turned a glowing scarlet. Veins along their hairless arms swelled ropy blue. Their eyes bulged brilliant white.

With an animalistic growl of rage, Tony seized Paolo and quickly wrapped him in a headlock.

Paolo started screaming. He thrashed and beat the air in a hopeless attempt to get away. "Let me go, you cocksucker," he bawled.

Tony raised his eyebrows. "When you say it like that, it sounds dirty. Like an insult." He flexed. His bicep swelled like a balloon filling with helium, blotting over Paolo's eyes. Paolo's face immediately turned a shiny shade of eggplant. His howls became shrill. "I can't see, you fucking ass jockey." He continued flailing his arms like a turkey trying to fly. When he couldn't free himself he changed tactics and tried prying Tony's arm away from his neck. The tip of the claw and all five fingers were no match for the vice-like grip the bouncer had on his head and neck.

Meanwhile, Peter grabbed Gino's arm and in a slick move, twisted it behind his back and tugged it north to a point high up between his shoulder blades. Gino yowled in rage and pain. Then Peter body slammed Gino into a wall. The aluminum crutch clattered on the floor. Gino's knees buckled. For a slice of a second he teetered drunkenly then collapsed. She heard an audible pop as he fell and Gino's shrieks increased to an inhuman pitch and then faded to whimpers. Peter let go of Gino's arm. It dropped and hung like spaghetti, loose in the sleeve of his sport coat. His eyes were wet, his face gray. He slurred, "You son-of-a-bitch. I'm a Gianolo. You can't get away with this."

Marie-Claude sat on the edge of the dressing table and laughed until her face hurt. Some of her laughter was simple stress release but more enjoyable was seeing two tough guys get abused by a couple of gay-as-Santa's-elves bouncers. It was like watching a Bugs Bunny cartoon. When her laughter subsided to giggles, she dried her eyes on the sleeves of her torn cowboy shirt. In a quiet second between screams, she said, "Get 'em out of here, guys."

Tony, with Paolo still clamped under his arm in an unbreakable headlock, walked his captive toward the door, Paolo bent at the waist, arms stretched out for balance. His mouth pulsed open and closed as he sucked in shallow, bird-like breaths. Peter crouched, wrapped his arms around Gino's chest beneath his arms, and lifted him upright. He held on tight and dragged him backward toward the door, Gino's heels scuffing across the floor. He held his dislocated arm tightly across his chest with his good arm, and whimpered with every step Peter took.

Marie-Claude straightened, held up her index finger and said, "You know what? Hang on a sec."

The crowd of four paused. The bouncers looked at her with questioning expressions. Held captive like they were, the Gianolos were obliged to look too. Paolo stared up at her out of two panicked eyes. Gino, mumbling incoherent obscenities, blinked rapidly, clearing his eyes of water. Marie-Claude smiled at him, winked, and slugged him with all her strength on the point of his nose.

There was a second audible pop and once again, Gino shrieked. His eyes poured water. His free hand flew to his face, cupping his bloody nose as his face turned white. His dislocated arm, no longer supported, fell. His eyes rolled up into his skull and his chin dropped down on his chest.

"You shouldn't hit girls," Marie-Claude said. "Asshole."

The dressing room door swung closed, leaving her alone. Gianolo's face wasn't as soft as it looked. In the mirror, she saw herself grimacing in pain. It hurt, slugging someone in the nose. It had been worth it though. She shook her hand, trying to relieve some of the ache and the grimace changed into a smile.

She fastened her shorts and put on a new shirt then she draped the bandoleers over each shoulder and buckled the alcohol holsters around her waist. Jake was a nice guy. Not serious enough for her, but sweet and generous. She didn't want to see him hurt. By the time Tony and Peter were done with the Gianolos, neither she nor Jake would have to worry about them again. But who was the other individual they had mentioned, the not-as-nice-guy Jake had pissed off? What had Jake gotten himself into? She would definitely call him and warn him, and maybe ask him what was happening.

CHAPTER 28

ERIC DALRYMPLE DRAPED his coat over the passenger seat headrest. He brushed a hand down the fabric, smoothing it until it hung to his satisfaction. Finished taking care of his jacket, he looked out the window of his rented Dodge Charger and scowled. Plain and simple, Florida was a disease. Cancer. Or Lupus. Something horrible anyway. He didn't plan on spending a minute longer than he needed to in Tampa, and he certainly didn't want his six hundred and fifty dollar Kenneth Cole jacket getting sweaty or wrinkled in the waves of heat radiating off the asphalt road.

His gaze drifted across the street to the well-maintained brick bungalow. It was time to get some answers.

Taking a deep breath, he steeled himself against the heat and opened the car door. It was like opening an oven, a blast furnace, every bit as bad as he expected. Breathing was difficult in the thin, hot air. Moving quickly, he crossed the street and strode up the walk. Sweat beads popped on his scalp. At the top of three short stairs, he raised his hand to knock.

A curtain beside the door shifted. He looked and saw two brilliant lemon eyes staring back at him out of a tiny, hairy face. Great. A rat with hair. Another reason to get in and out as fast as possible.

He wondered why he hadn't expected cats and taken a Claritin—with a name like Edith Weatherly and a baby blue New Yorker, crumpled fender and all, sitting in the driveway, there could be no doubt the person who lived here was a cat lover.

He rapped his knuckles on the door. After twenty or thirty seconds, he raised his fist to knock a second time. Hearing footsteps, he lowered his arm. A moment later, the door opened as far as the security chain allowed.

An elderly lady peered up at him with shrewd, bright eyes. "Yes?"

"Morning, Ma'am," Mr. Blonde said. "Was wondering if Jake was home?"

The eyes sharpened. "No."

To Mr. Blonde's amazement, the door slammed shut. The security chain rattled and he heard the lock snap closed.

One thing about the elderly. They moved slowly, but they often didn't think that way. Not until the end anyway, when they ended up in diapers in a "retirement" home. Until that happened their experience was a commodity. Mr. Blonde respected and admired it. He didn't know what he'd done to make Mrs. Weatherly suspicious but something had definitely raised the wispy blue hairs on the back of her neck.

It didn't matter.

He glanced quickly over each shoulder. There wasn't a soul in sight. Raising his foot, he kicked the door hard just above the knob. The doorjamb splintered and cracked. He kicked it again. The chain snapped and the door swung open. A shrill, short scream echoed in the foyer. The old lady staggered, flung an arm out searching in vain for balance then tumbled awkwardly onto the tiled floor.

Mr. Blonde stepped into the house. He pushed the door shut behind him with the toe of his shoe.

She lay on the floor near his feet moaning. Tears wet her

wrinkled cheeks. Ignoring her, Mr. Blonde glanced around the foyer searching for signs of another habitant.

Flowered wallpaper. Lace doilies. There was an antique telephone on the foyer table, a round white dial set into black Bakelite. He spotted a huge Grandfather clock in the sitting room. Every rhythmic tick was as loud as a sniper's rifle. A row of sensible old lady shoes with wide flat heels was lined up neatly on a mat near the door. Her home was marginally cooler than the great outdoors, but the air conditioning was not turned down to what he considered a comfortable level. Always amazed him, people who had air conditioning and didn't set it for sixty-eight. The stench of cat piss tickled his nose. He felt a sneeze coming on.

Convinced no one except an old woman lived in this house, he squatted beside her and studied her with interest but not concern. "You all right, Ma'am?" Her flowered dress had rucked up past her knees. Flesh-colored stockings were inching down her shins, bunching at her ankles and baring mottled legs. Grimacing, he looked away. He had no issue with blemishes and wrinkles as a by-product of age. It was his sense of organization that took offense. He liked smooth and even. Straight lines. Symmetry.

She shook her head once. "My hip. I think my hip's broken."

Mr. Blonde nodded. She reminded him of his own mother, although most old ladies did. "You're Mrs. Weatherly, right?"

"Yes."

He said, "Good. I'm not going to…" The unsightly blue veins on her legs stretched north and south like interstates on a map. He didn't want to look but they were distracting. "Let me fix your dress for you." He pulled the hemline down, arranging it neatly over her calves and shins. Satisfied, he rocked back on his haunches. "I'm not going to stay long. So, here's how it's going to go."

While he spoke, he pulled on a thin pair of latex gloves, working them down into the crevices between his fingers. When they were comfortable, he grabbed the phone off the hallway table. Up close, he realized it wasn't an antique at all. The numbers were actually push buttons, designed to look like a rotary dial.

New or old, it had some weight to it. He held it up, made sure she got a good look at it. Balancing it on one knee and resting his other arm across the opposite thigh, he said, "I'm going to ask one question. If you don't answer, or I think you're lying, I'm going to cave your head in with this telephone."

The old lady's eyes widened with fear.

"On the other hand, if you answer and I believe you're telling me the truth, I'm going to dial 911. Get some medics to look at your hip. All right? Sound fair?"

It wasn't the smartest play. Bouncing her head off the floor several times made a lot more sense, but offing an old lady didn't sit well. She reminded him too much of his mother. Looking at Mrs. Weatherly, he actually heard his mother asking with concern, "How's your job, Eric?" She would shake her head with disbelief. "I just don't know how you make a living selling computers."

Mrs. Weatherly nodded vigorously and stopped with a whimper when her body shifted.

"Okay, here goes. Where can I find Jake Harris?"

She answered immediately, in her quivering old lady voice. "A young lady in Montreal arranged a job for him. That's where he went. I told Keith Richards this already. Marie-Claude Lefevre."

Mr. Blonde froze. Keith Richards? There had to be more than one Keith Richards in the world, right? The Rolling Stones guitarist didn't have exclusive rights to the name. "Anything else?" he asked.

"She's a waitress in a country music bar."

Mr. Blonde rolled his hand, prompting her.

"That's it."

"You sure?"

She nodded, the movement slow and deliberate this time.

He studied her face. Her jaw was tight with pain and he saw

fear in her eyes, but she stared back at him without blinking. That, more than anything else, convinced him she had nothing left to tell. Old folks had life figured out. They knew every day was worth living. At the same time, they accepted the fact that death wasn't far away. It was inescapable. So, if they'd done everything to hold it off, and it was still coming, it made sense to accept it. Her expression said, "It's out of my hands. I've done all I can."

He swiped the back of his hand across his forehead and glanced at his wrist for black dye. Seeing none, he wiped his wrist dry on his T-shirt. There were extra shirts in his suitcase. The one he was wearing would go into the garbage before the end of the day. No chance it was getting re-packed in a suitcase with all his clean clothes.

In the sitting room the Grandfather clock banged away, letting him know time was wasting. He bounced the Bakelite telephone up and down on his thigh. What to do, what to do? His sixth sense, the one that kept him a step ahead of trouble all these years, poked him.

Keith Richards?

Montreal?

Deep inside he realized this Florida trip was unnecessary. Mario Gianolo was screwing him. Again. He just couldn't figure out how.

Yet.

A cat, a different one from the fur-ball he saw in the window, walked around the corner, its tail curled into a fiddlehead over its back. It glanced at him with haughty indifference. Mewing, it rubbed and arched across the old lady's leg and padded into the kitchen.

Mr. Blonde sneezed. Sniffing, he glared at the cat. It was time to finish this thing. "All right, Ma'am," he said. "You did good. Just hang on. I'll call 911."

He dialed, placed the phone on the floor near her head and

handed her the receiver. Planting a hand on each knee, he shoved himself upright. Moving quickly, he walked out of the house into the afternoon heat, pulling the splintered door shut behind him.

Mrs. Weatherly didn't know everything. But she wasn't the only lead he had in Tampa. There was another person with whom he could speak. Seeing as he was in town anyway. He'd just find some place cool, McDonald's, maybe eat a late lunch, and wait there until the workday ended. With any kind of luck, he'd be on a plane to Montreal before eight PM.

CHAPTER 29

JAKE RAN EASILY while Chloe played twenty questions about the phone call he received the previous evening. Normally he kept the pace brisk. It was the only way to control her incessant talking, and as much as he enjoyed her company, he still needed the silent exertion of his run to clear his head. Today the weight of Marie-Claude's phone call seemed to press on her. He sensed Chloe needed to talk rather than just chatter.

"How did they know to go to Montreal? You said Mark didn't tell them anything."

"He didn't. The only thing I can think of, Paolo spoke to Mrs. Weatherly. You said Gino and him are always together. We know Gino tried to talk to Mark. I bet Paolo was at Mrs. Weatherly's at the same time."

"Your landlady," Chloe said with conviction. "Gotta be." Her tone changed. "And, she told them to go Montreal? Why not right to Sioux River?"

"I don't know. She couldn't wrap her head around a cocktail waitress in Montreal arranging a job for me in Sioux River. She was more concerned about Marie-Claude spending all night in a bar and all day in school."

For the next couple of minutes, they jogged without saying

anything. The only sound was the wind rustling the leaves and their rhythmic breathing. Jake glanced at Chloe running beside him. The determined look on her face impressed him somehow. Very few days went by that she didn't join him for an afternoon run. They'd started slowly. She adapted quickly. Now they ran for ten minutes straight and took one-minute walk breaks. Soon she wouldn't need the walks. She'd even started asking him about ten K races.

"We won't be seeing the Gianolo boys again," Jake said, interrupting a chickadee's cheerful, autumn song. "Marie-Claude told me they got on the wrong side of a couple of bouncers in the bar where she works. The bouncers put them both in the hospital. Apparently they'll be there for a long time."

"Why did this Marie-Claude person get you a job?" It was an innocent enough question, but the flat, devoid-of-emotion tone, loaded it with complications.

"We're old friends," Jake said shortly.

"Girlfriend?"

He hesitated. He could say, "yes," but that would raise a whole bunch of new questions, like, "How long did you go out?" and "How did you meet?" If he answered, "no" it was obvious the kind of relationship he and Marie-Claude used to share. He didn't want to discuss either option. What he wanted to do was drop the entire subject. Unfortunately, he didn't feel they'd reached the end of the conversation and as little as he wanted to discuss the nature of past relationships, he refused to pretend people who were important to him didn't exist. He couldn't see an easy way out of the corner he was painted into. "She wasn't really a girlfriend."

"A casual fuck?"

"Chloe—"

"It's fine, Jake," she said, her voice letting him know it wasn't. "You go ahead. I need to catch my breath."

Intuitively he realized she needed a minute or two without him nearby. He pressed his lips together into a tight line and picked up his pace. What was with her attitude? They weren't a couple. Neither serious nor casual. They hadn't shared even a single moment of intimacy. Not that the thought hadn't entered his mind. She looked good sitting on the dock late in the afternoon, soaking up the sun in her B.U.M. shorts. Throw a gentle breeze off the lake and her nipples popped through the fabric of her bikini like diamonds…

Jake's frown turned into a smile.

A short scream pierced the afternoon.

Fear seized him by the throat, shortening his breath. He swiveled and broke into a sprint back down the trail. A bear, maybe? Mr. Blonde? Shit, he shouldn't have left her. He rounded the corner, still accelerating. Charged down the hill, taking huge, dangerous steps. He leapt over rocks and sticks on the path, his breath loud in his ears.

Chloe sat on the path clutching her leg while blood welled out of her scraped knee. The Yankees cap lay a few feet away.

He slowed, stopped, and crouched beside her, panting with his hands on his knees.

Her eyes were moist but she wasn't crying.

"I hate running."

"I know," Jake said, pushing her hands aside. "Let's take a look." He brushed the dirt and sand away from her cuts with the tail of his shirt. "We'll need to go back to the lodge and get this cleaned up, but I think you'll live. Just to be sure though…" He bent over and kissed her knee. "Better?"

"Yes."

"What happened?"

Her pale face blushed pink. "Jake, I was being a… I was trying to catch up to you and I was running too fast." She glanced around. "I tripped on that stupid root." She pointed to a root bulging out of the trail.

He didn't say anything right away. "Running hills is hard, isn't it?"

She nodded.

"Can I suggest something?"

She looked at him with an arched eyebrow, a look that said, "no," but after a brief hesitation, she nodded a second time.

"When you run a hill, stand up straight. Pretend someone is pulling you up with a string attached to your chest. It's easier that way." Still crouching beside her, he said, "When you want to go faster, you know, to catch up with someone—"

"Or get away from someone."

"That too," Jake said ignoring her sarcasm. "Pump your arms, shorten your stride, and turn your legs over faster."

"Okay. Jake, I shouldn't have…" She looked away and bit her lip. Then, "It's not my place to judge, considering my last job—"

"Listen, Chloe. We both have histories. Stuff maybe we don't want to talk about, right?" He thought about how she still wouldn't tell him what she'd done to annoy the Outfit. "Some things are just that. History. Best left there. Other things might be relevant. Depending on what happens, maybe one day we gotta discuss them."

"What do you mean, 'depending on what happens?'"

"Chloe, I don't—"

"Oh come on. You were doing so well."

Jake looked into the bush as the heat of embarrassment climbed up his neck and warmed his ears. "Shit. Depending on if we… If something between you and…" He sighed heavily and scratched his neck with irritation. "All right. Depending on if we decide to spend a little more time together, like a couple. All right? Are you happy? Can we go now?"

Chloe giggled. "I guess that's as good as it's going to get, huh?" She looked at her bloody knee then in both directions, up and down the trail. "No. I don't wanna move. I hurt all over."

Jake's demeanor changed instantly. "Tell me where. Are you injured? Other than your knee, I mean?"

"I'm fine."

"So you're not hurt? You're just complaining?"

She stuck her tongue out at him. "Go away."

"Are you hurt here?" he asked and kissed the spot on her back where her arm, running top and shoulder all met.

"Go away."

"What about here," he said, lifting up her ponytail and kissing her neck. "Mmmmm. Salty."

"Go away, Homer."

"What about here?" He kissed the top of her ear.

She looked at him, her expression soft. Nibbling the corner of her lower lip, she brushed a tendril of sweaty red curls away from her face.

His breath caught in the back of his throat. He leaned in, focusing on her lips. Closer…

And, knelt on a rock.

A sharp edge jabbed into his knee. He slammed his eyes shut, jerked back, and bounded to his feet. Hopping in circles, bent over swiping at his leg, he yelled, "Shit. Shit. Shit! Oh man that hurts."

Chloe rose to her feet, laughing. "The walking wounded. Let's go back." She grabbed his hand. Side-by-side they limped toward the lodge. "I'm glad Gino and Paolo aren't going to bother us anymore. But I was never really worried about those two."

"Mr. Blonde, right?

"If the Gianolos were smart enough to find us through your landlady, he definitely is."

"He won't find out from Mark," Jake said. It would take more than a freak with a bad dye job and a shitty attitude to force Mark into saying something he didn't want to say.

"You should call him. Warn him. Get him to talk to Mrs. Weatherly."

"I'll call him tonight. Giving him a heads up is a good idea. I think you're right about that."

CHAPTER 30

MARK FLIPPED THE front door shut, twisting the knob, automatically locking himself in. He slid the security chain into its slot. Blew out a heavy sigh. What was it about hospitals that made everyone mute? Mrs. Weatherly often wandered down to the basement suite he shared with Jake, usually with a plate of cookies, and the two of them talked effortlessly. Or, more accurately, he ate the cookies while the old duck rattled on about her azaleas and the cats.

He tossed his keys on the hallway table and walked into the kitchen.

In the hospital he had nothing to say. The hour he spent with her felt like twenty-four. Long silences. Incoherent ramblings. In her defense she was still doped up on Demerol. The doctor said it would help with the pain of the surgery he'd performed to repair her shattered hip.

The only thing about their conversation that made sense was that she was worried about her cats. Mark promised to walk upstairs and check on them. He'd water her flowers at the same time.

In the kitchen, he yanked the refrigerator door open. He searched for a beer. Knowing he wouldn't find one he grabbed a Coke instead. A real one. All the sugar, calories, and caffeine. He made a face. This was living. An old woman, three cats, and a soda for supper. Real vices were a whole lot more fun.

Well, there was always ESPN.

He ambled into the living room. Just as he was about to flop his ass down on the couch and throw his feet up on the table, the doorbell rang.

"Bloody hell," Mark muttered. He took a slug of the Cola and walked to the front door. He opened it as far as the security chain would allow and peered around the edge.

Then slammed the door hard.

I need a weapon right now!

A loud crash filled the hallway. The front door shook on its hinges. It banged a second time. And, a third in rapid succession. The wood splintered. The frame held.

Searching for a weapon, Mark's eyes flicked around the hallway, settling on his golf bag. He snatched a Callaway three wood out of the bag, raised it over his right shoulder and waited. Two brawls in a week without stepping into a bar! Maybe he was living right after all. He was amped. Excited. He took a deep breath, forcing himself to stay calm and concentrate.

The front door thudded a final time. The jam around the handle cracked. Chunks of wood fell on the floor. The security chain links stretched. Pulled apart. Landed with metallic clinks on the linoleum. The door swung open, banging against the wall.

Mark had never met the man, never even seen him. Jake's description was enough. The person filling the doorframe could be no other than Mr. Blonde, the guy Jake referred to as the Freak.

Grinning slightly, with adrenaline drying his mouth and roaring in his ears like surf at the beach, Mark stepped forward with the three wood raised.

The crazed smile on Mr. Blonde's face quickly changed to shock. His glance cut to the head of the golf club. He shrunk away from it, raising a defensive arm.

Mark swung the club in an overhand arc, transferring his weight evenly from his rear foot to his front as the head of the club rose. On the links it would have been a two-twenty drive at least. It felt right. Smooth and easy. It would end this fight before it began. It was going to end any thought Mr. Blonde ever had about hassling his little brother.

The club reached the apex of its arc, Mark putting every muscle in his back, shoulders, and arms into it, the club sweeping across the top, slicing down…

Something grabbed the head of the club. Mark staggered, his perfect balance gone. A pop. Clanging metal. Hot light-bulb glass rained down. Slivers of glass sprinkled his neck and the top of his head. He caught a sickening whiff of burnt hair and imagined he heard sizzles as freckles of skin on his scalp burned. The pain was undeniable.

The chandelier swung back and forth in a squeaking arc.

Knowing he couldn't waste time with distractions like burning flesh, Mark jerked the club past the chain holding the light fixture. Most of the strength and momentum were gone from his swing. Hopefully, there'd be enough left.

The head of the club hit Mr. Blonde on the upper cheek with a soggy thump. Blood spattered the wall. He staggered sideways, cursing, and dropped to his knees. His hand flew to his face. Blood seeped from between his fingers.

This guy is tough, Mark thought. Anyone else is unconscious on the floor. No big deal though. Hit him one more time and the fight is finished.

Unwilling to risk tangling the club in the chandelier a second time, and with no room in the narrow hallway to swing sideways, he tossed it behind him.

Mr. Blonde lurched to his feet, swaying, shaking his head. A glazed expression in his eyes. Blood dripped from his cheek to his shoulder.

Mark drove his fist into the Freak's face. Pain from the impact rocked up his arm. He ignored it.

Moaning, Mr. Blonde fell to his knees again.

Mark re-cocked his fist. Mr. Blonde assaulted his brother. Tied Chloe up with duct tape and tossed her in the trunk of a car. Those were only the incidents Mark knew about. He also knew if the Freak had done it twice, he'd done it a dozen times. He was a bully. And, there was nothing better than dropping a bully like the sack of shit he was. Mark stepped into him, put his entire body into it and smashed his fist into Mr. Blonde's face a second time.

Mr. Blonde teetered over onto his back with a heavy, wet grunt and lay still.

Panting, Mark stepped back. He kept a wary eye on his assailant and shook his arm. Already his fist had started to numb. He'd need to wrap it in ice if he wanted his fingers to work in the morning.

First priority, the cops.

He glanced around, searching for his cell phone, trying to remember where he left it. It was nowhere in sight. Which meant he'd have to use a landline, the phone in the living room. He frowned. He didn't like the idea of turning his back and leaving Mr. Blonde alone. The guy was incredibly strong and resilient.

But there wasn't any choice.

Keeping Mr. Blonde in sight, Mark back-stepped into the living room.

The Freak's foot convulsed.

Mark paused, tensed.

The Freak lay still.

Mark stepped back.

Onto the head of the three wood.

His ankle rolled. He stumbled as white-hot agony lanced up his calf. Flinging an arm out, he grabbed the wall for support. Too late. He crashed to the floor in a heap, his ankle sending waves of pain through his foot and up his leg. He gritted his teeth, forcing himself to forget it. This wasn't the time to be flopping around on the floor. He pushed himself up the wall. Gingerly placed his bad foot on the floor and transferred a pound or two of weight onto it.

Agony seared as high as his knee. He involuntarily closed his eyes and cried out.

An animalistic roar filled the air. Mark's eyes popped open.

Mr. Blonde dove at him, tackling him around the waist. Their combined weight carried them backward into the living room, onto the coffee table. Magazines went airborne. The soda fell off the table and rolled toward the wall leaving a foaming, hissing trail. The table skidded across the floor, all four legs making loud scraping sounds. It slammed into the wall and dumped the two men onto the floor.

Legs and fists flew.

Mark felt the punches in a muted, offhand way, knowing they'd hurt far more tomorrow than they did right now. He hammered his own fist into every free spot he found. It was a street fight now, where anything went and when Mr. Blonde opened himself up, Mark punched him in the groin.

Hot breath blasted him in the face. Mr. Blonde went limp. Curled into the fetal position, retching and drooling. Black dye leached out of his hairline, shading his forehead.

Twisting away, Mark rose to his feet. He limped for the front door. There was only one choice. Get out of the house, call the cops from someplace else, someplace safe where he didn't have to fight anymore. His ankle was too much of a disability with someone as powerful as Mr. Blonde. He wiped a hand down his sweaty face. Backing away didn't feel right, but it was the wisest choice.

Two hands wrapped around his good leg and yanked.

Unable to support himself on his injured foot, Mark fell.

The hallway table rushed toward him.

He raised his hands to push it out of the way. He wasn't fast enough. His chin slammed into the corner of the table.

His universe went black. A second or two later the darkness brightened. Pinpoints of light flashed in his eyes like a meteor shower. For a moment, he was unsure what happened, his memory blurred by watery eyes, and an indescribable ache in his ankle and jaw.

A shadow washed across his face. He tensed. Squinted up at Mr. Blonde. And remembered. He rolled over with only one clear thought. *Get up, get out.*

Mr. Blonde swayed, but remained on his feet. He twisted his head in a quarter turn. There were a couple of noisy clicks. Drops of blood rained off his pulverized cheek, sprinkling Mark's arm and chest.

Mr. Blonde clutched the Callaway three wood.

Mark drove his suddenly clammy hands into the floor and pushed himself away.

Mr. Blonde staggered a step, pacing him. He raised the golf club. His pulverized lips, teeth slick with blood, twisted into a macabre smile. "You fucked with the wrong guy," he said, the words slurred almost beyond recognition.

Mark grinned. Got shot at in Afghanistan and didn't get dead. Played in Tampa traffic and didn't get dead. And, now a stupid hallway table is going punch my lights out, and that just doesn't seem right.

The head of the club dropped.

Time slowed down and became an errant ray of sunlight that for an instant managed to cut through the overcast, before extinguishing forever. Basking in that light Mark thought about Jake, the two of them and the fun they had when they were young. Baseball and go-carts. Sneaking into movies. Stealing their dad's beer. Kid shit. He remembered protecting him years ago in the school yard, how he liked to fight, liked the crazy shit, as Jake used to say, how Jake was always the smart one.

They'd made a pretty good team, Mark thought. He lived a pretty a good life, no question about it.

He remembered Jake getting his pilot's license, how he near burst with pride when Jake landed the World Ways job, Junior standing there in his navy blue uniform, what he disdainfully called his costume, but the kid always so careful with his tunic with the bright yellow stripes on the sleeves and his pilot's hat with its special spot on the shelf. When the kid gave up part of his salary, Mark thought anyone would have been lucky to have him as a brother. There were no words.

He thought of how pleased Jake was with his shiny black Mustang, and the last thought Mark had was regret because he really wanted to meet Chloe, the girl Jake spoke about in a different tone of voice than he'd ever used before.

Jake's voice rang clearly in his mind, the boy asking what they were going to do today, the teen rambling on about flying, the man talking about Chloe in that tone, and Mark smiled happily, because he knew Jake was happy.

The errant ray of sunlight disappeared.

The head of the club swooped down and Mark didn't think of anything else.

CHAPTER 31

"TEN BUCKS?" ERIC Dalrymple said. "To listen to this crap music?"

The bouncer looked at him from beneath a Stetson large enough to shade Wyoming, the brim creased down hiding his eyes. He shrugged. Crossed his arms over his massive chest. His flat, uninterested gaze flicked to something on the wall behind Mr. Blonde. "Your choice."

Mr. Blonde considered making an issue out of the cover charge. He hesitated. For a second he felt something unusual, something that was difficult to identify.

What?

Not fear, certainly. Wariness maybe?

He licked his lips and swallowed. The fuck was going on? He couldn't remember a time when someone made him "wary." Except, the bouncer, who had biceps the size of hams and shoulders as wide across as an axe handle, made Mark Harris look small and Harris had handed him his ass on a plate, so maybe wary (or at the very least, cautious), was the correct emotion.

He needed to toughen up. Remember who he was. He could blame this uncomfortable feeling, this vague sick feeling in the pit of his belly, on lack of sleep and too much coffee. Two hours after he caved Mark Harris' head in with the three wood, he was on a plane bound for JFK. After landing, he immediately caught a connector flight from JFK to Burlington, Vermont. In Burlington he rented a car. Drove from there to Montreal, customs far less of a hassle at a road crossing in the middle of nowhere than at one of Canada's largest international airports. He reached out to a contact he had in La Belle Ville and purchased a new handgun. Paid three times what it would have cost anywhere else, but he didn't have much choice. Then he worked the phone book until he found Outlaws.

All and all, a long twenty-four hours when catnaps accounted for his only rest.

He straightened his spine and squared his shoulders and fished ten bucks out of his wallet. He handed it over with a scowl. The bouncer grabbed the bill but Mr. Blonde kept it pinched between his thumb and forefinger. "Where can I find Marie-Claude?"

The bouncer tensed. All the seams of his too-small T-shirt stretched. He turned his attention from the money to Mr. Blonde, his face hardening beneath his goatee.

Jumpy or not, getting into something with the Tim McGraw look-a-like was a waste of time. Mr. Blonde released the bill with a sigh. Muffled bass thumped through twin oak doors. He scowled. The nightclub would surely test his patience even further. He pushed through the double doors into the club.

The place vibrated with high-strung energy. The music, no longer muted by the doors, thrummed through his body like an extra heart. Colored lights splashed on fake fog making it look like fireworks were going off inside the club. The dance floor moved like swells on the ocean, all the sheeple in the place gyrating to some ridiculous song about saving a horse and riding a cowboy. He suppressed a shudder. The club reeked of spilled beer, stale alcohol, and too many sweaty people in too small an area.

He limped toward the first waitress he saw, a beauty wearing tiny denim shorts and a huge jeweled belt buckle. She stood behind an aluminum tub filled to the brim with ice cubes and cans of beer.

"I'm looking for Marie-Claude."

"What are you drinking, handsome?"

Mr. Blonde gritted his teeth. The forty minutes he was about to spend in Outlaws was something else for which Jake Harris would pay… along with the broken cheekbone and busted blood vessels in his eye that tinted everything a feminine shade of pink. And, he wasn't sure if it was possible, but he thought maybe his balls were bruised. They ached liked slow death, the pain radiating up and down the inside of his left leg.

His fingers strayed to the pomegranate-sized bruise on the side of his face. Knowing he looked far from handsome, he said, "Don't piss in my pocket and tell me it's raining, sweetheart." He glanced from the tub-tramp to the trough she stood behind. "Give me a Bud."

She bent over and fished a beer out of the trough, displaying what had to be five thousand dollars' worth of cleavage. He handed over another ten spot, not expecting to see any change in return. He wasn't disappointed.

"See the cute blonde over there? The shooter girl? That's Marie-Claude."

Mr. Blonde nodded his thanks. Clutching his beer, he walked over to Marie- Claude. He sipped his beer and waited, watching her as she snaked two shooter glasses out of the loops of the bandoleer she wore, and quickly and efficiently mixed the drinks. After the customers paid and she'd re-stowed the bottles in the holsters around her waist, he tapped her on the shoulder.

"Hi," he said. He fingered the Band-Aid on his cheek. The heat in the club made it itch. "Can you please tell me where Jake Harris is?"

Even in the dimly lit bar he saw Marie-Claude's face turn white. She rose up on her toes and waved an arm in the air.

Two enormous-looking biker types with angry faces straightened, puffed out their chests, and strode toward him with a gymguy don't-mess-with-me gait.

"Get out of here," she said. "Don't come back. If you do, you'll be joining your two buddies in intensive care."

Mr. Blonde's rage was instant and extreme. He ground his teeth so hard his jaw ached. The delicate pink haze turned a glowing angry red. There was no doubt she was referring to the Gianolo twins, which meant, as he suspected, the trip to Florida was a complete waste of time. It was time to make a call. Mario's days of being a bitch were finished. His days of being dead, shanked in the yard were about to begin.

Taking a deep breath, he forced himself to calm down. He placed the nearly full Budweiser on a table, glanced quickly at the bouncers and raised both hands in surrender. Clearly he wouldn't find out what he needed to know from Marie-Claude before they arrived. He cut his gaze back to the waitress, memorizing her face. He needed to make sure he recognized her the next time he saw her, when the costume she wore, the bandoleers, Daisy Dukes, and cowboy shirt, were gone.

Swiveling, Mr. Blonde strode for the exit.

CHAPTER 32

LATE SEPTEMBER IN Montreal, the nights were growing colder. Mr. Blonde shivered and blew warm air through one fist then the other. He raised miniature binoculars to his face, careful not to press them too tightly to his damaged eye, and studied the faces emptying out of Outlaws.

Three hours he'd been sitting there, slouched low in the seat of his rental car, waiting for Marie-Claude Lefevre. At first it was just a steady stream of patrons leaving the bar—drunks staggering off in different directions, affectionate couples getting into taxi-cabs, borderline hysterical partiers heading off to after-hours clubs—but the flow had shrunk to a trickle. Mr. Blonde guessed his wait was about over. He fingered the roll of nickels in his pocket. He doubted it would take much persuasion to get Marie-Claude talking but he wasn't planning on fucking about. His patience with the entire Gianolo, Sheridan situation had disappeared with summer's warm weather.

When a couple of bouncers finally escorted Marie-Claude out of the club, he almost missed her. She was virtually unrecognizable from the shooter girl he met earlier. Her hair was pulled off her face in a tight ponytail. She wore a leather coat, cinched at the waist, collar turned up against the evening chill. The ridiculous short shorts were gone. Now she wore what looked like chinos, except all the pockets were on the outside, that sloppy look youngsters found fashionable. There were sneakers on her feet, instead of the equally ridiculous cowboy boots.

He rolled the car window down and listened intently and caught the tail end of their conversation, Marie-Claude telling the bouncers not to worry, the guy was a nut and she'd be fine.

Mr. Blonde smiled.

She stood on her tiptoes and kissed each bouncer's cheek. "Thanks, guys," she said. "See you tomorrow." With a McGill University backpack slung over her shoulder, she pivoted and walked away. After a couple of steps she did a pirouette, gave the bouncers a little finger dance, then continued down the street.

Mr. Blonde dropped the binoculars on the passenger seat. He pulled thin latex gloves on and worked them down into the area between his fingers, tracking Marie-Claude with his eyes until she reached a yellow two-door Saturn. She got in and a moment later the car came to life. When she pulled onto the main road, he started his own vehicle and eased onto the road behind her. He kept his distance. He didn't want his headlights making her jittery. A short drive later, she turned onto a quiet residential street. A random scattering of porch lights did little to cut the darkness. The stars were invisible behind a canopy of trees and the tiny sickle of moon was too far away to make a difference. He let her pull ahead until her taillights became nothing more than red dots in the distance. Headlights might not have made her jittery on a main road but they certainly would have done so on an empty residential street.

When the intensity of the red dots flared briefly then blinked out, a hot surge of adrenaline flooded Mr. Blonde's body. She'd parked. The time was now. Answers. He forced his hands to relax on the steering wheel and kept a sedate speed. Three or four seconds later he passed the Saturn parked on the right hand curb, Marie-Claude waiting at the rear bumper before crossing the road.

He drove by without turning to look at her, but he watched in the rear view mirror as she started across the street. Instantly, hand over hand, he cranked the rental car into a tight U-turn. Moving quickly, with precision, he killed the engine and the headlights and jumped out of the car.

For a moment she stared at him with a confused expression. Her look quickly changed to recognition. She flashed a glance at a house on the far side of the street. After half a step in that direction, she changed her mind, spun and bolted for her car. One hand dove into her pack, going for the cell phone, Mr. Blonde guessed. With the other arm she aimed a key chain at the Saturn.

The Saturn's horn blared and the lights strobed.

Mr. Blonde ground his teeth and cursed. It seemed every piece-of-shit car, including turn of the century Saturns, came equipped with security systems and panic alarms. The only good thing— they weren't uncommon and nobody paid attention when they activated. He loped toward her, each step sending a sharp twinge of pain from his groin down his left leg. The hard soles of his dress shoes sent stabs of pain into his heels. His breath came out it in wraith-like clouds that disappeared as quickly as he exhaled.

Marie-Claude was much faster than him. She reached the Saturn, and pulled the door open and wheeled around it and dove into the driver's seat, all in one liquid motion.

The horn continued to bleat every two seconds. The flashing lights looked like those of a cop's car. The whole fucked up (and rapidly getting worse) situation reminded Mr. Blonde of his gang initiation all those years ago.

He lunged, caught the edge of the car door with the tips of his fingers as she started to close it. He yanked it out of her hand. Marie-Claude shrieked in what sounded like surprise. He reached into the car and grabbed her by an arm and pulled her toward him.

She shrieked a second time and swung her free arm, her fist with the keys between her fingers. He jerked backward... too late. Her knuckles caught him high on the cheekbone under his eye, the blow not powerful but the keys dug in and he roared and recoiled with pain, surprise, and anger. The keychain fell to the street with a metallic jangle. He crouched and scooped them up and stabbed at the buttons until the alarm silenced. Panting, he glanced over each shoulder. Still no neighborhood lights on, nobody out late walking the dog. He touched his cheek and his fingers came away sticky and damp. He looked into the car. Again, he was surprised at her speed. In the three or four seconds it had taken him to cancel the alarm and study the neighborhood, she'd scrambled across the center console toward the passenger door.

He hooked his fingers into the waistband of her pants and towed her back.

"Let go of me, you bastard," Marie-Claude screamed. She rolled over, broke his grip and lashed out with her feet. The soft soul of her sneaker scraped up his arm and he jerked away and she stopped shrieking and went for the passenger door once more.

He thrust the upper half of his body into the car and knelt on the driver's seat. With his hand wrapped around the roll of nickels, he slugged her in the kidneys, a quick violent jab. She collapsed with a shrill yelp. He backed out of the car, hustled around to the passenger side, opened the door and grabbed a fistful of her leather jacket. He dragged her out of the car and when he let go of her coat, she dropped limp and groaning.

"Dumb bitch," Mr. Blonde said, panting heavily. "All you had to do was answer one question."

Marie-Claude slowly pushed herself up right, groaning and wincing with each slow and awkward movement. She leaned back, propping herself against the Saturn's quarter panel, legs splayed on the street.

Mr. Blonde watched her. He'd popped a couple mutts in the

past, guys who could have followed her example instead of wasting energy howling and blubbering. He admired her character, which wouldn't change what he was about to do.

He knelt down, hands on his knees, so they were eye to eye. "We've never met so you wouldn't know but when I ask a question, I expect to be answered promptly." He seized her right arm and stretched it out and held it in place so that her palm lay across the Saturn's door jam. With his free hand he grabbed the car door…

… and slammed it closed across the middle of her hand.

Her scream was piercingly shrill. And, short-lived. Her face dissolved into tears and agony. She flopped sideways and lay prone on the street with one arm stretched out as though for balance. The other arm was bent so her damaged hand lay on her chest in an expanding pool of blood. Her breath came in short, panicky huffs.

While he waited for her to recover, Mr. Blonde studied the neighborhood. Crouched deep in the shadows beside the Saturn, he was reasonably sure he and the girl were invisible. Still, caution was an instinct and he couldn't help himself. He grabbed a handful of hair and lifted her head toward him. "I have a question for you. Understand?"

Nothing.

"Answer me." He shook her head like a puppy shakes a chew toy. "Nod. Grunt. Whatever. I don't care. Let me know you hear what I'm saying."

Her head moved fractionally, up and down in his hand.

"Good. Now that we understand each other, you know I'm not fucking around, I'm going to ask one question. You're going to answer me, aren't you?"

Another weak nod.

"Where is Jake Harris?"

She didn't answer immediately and he tightened his grip.

She whimpered, then whispered, "Up north. Sioux River. Near Thunder Bay."

"What's he doing there?"

A confused look crossed her face. "Flying, of course."

Now it was Mr. Blonde's turn to be confused. "Who's flying around way up there?"

"Tourists. You know. Fisherman. Hunters."

Still mystified, Mr. Blonde rocked back on his heels. People were all kinds of crazy. Why pay good money to get gnawed on by bugs in the Canadian wilderness, miles from decent bathroom facilities? The idea was baffling. "How far away is Sioux River?"

"I don't know." Her voice was shrill and wobbly. "Twelve hundred miles?"

A long way then. He'd have to fly. He wasn't about to spend three or four days driving on shit roads, nothing but potholes and frost heaves. He nodded. He had all the answers he needed. With a quick sharp flick, he slammed Marie-Claude's head into the side of the car. There was a sick, dull thump. Her eyes rolled back in her skull until all that showed was white. With a near-silent moan, she went limp, and sagged unconscious on the street. Mr. Blonde reached inside his coat and wrapped his hand around the rubber grip of the revolver under his arm.

He hesitated.

No suppressor.

A slamming car door in a quiet neighborhood wouldn't wake anyone. Her scream may have. A gunshot surely would. Someone would toss the covers back, pad over to the window and nosy eyes would peek around the edge of a bedroom curtain. He didn't need that. He rotated his head quickly, in a tight quarter twitch. With a chorus of clicks and pops the adrenaline bled away. He gently stroked the cut and growing bruise on his cheekbone where she'd slugged him with the keys. Beating her to death was an option.

He grimaced. It was just so messy. Blood and skull and hair

all over the butt of his gun. Splatter everywhere. His t-shirt was disposable. After all this exertion, he'd worked up a sweat. With no time and no laundry facilities, it was going in the garbage. He wasn't about to toss his Kenneth Cole jacket.

Splatter wasn't the only reason of course, if he was being completely honest. Killing someone with her kind of spirit didn't sit well. Coming from a cocktail waitress, it was unexpected. He admired it the same way he admired the old lady in Florida, the way Mrs. Weatherly slammed the door in his face. After another second or two of careful thought, Mr. Blonde grabbed Marie-Claude by the hair again, and slammed her head into the side of the car a second time.

He left it at that. If she woke up, and that was a big if, she'd have a hell of a headache and presumably be in no condition to provide the cops with a statement or sit down with a sketch artist. He stood and limping slightly, with blood drizzling down his cheek, he walked back to the car. First chance he got he'd ditch the revolver, turn in the rental car and catch a flight to Thunder Bay. Then on to Sioux River, wherever the fuck that was.

Before driving away, he pulled out his cell phone and made a call. He gave the person who answered very specific instructions about what he wanted couriered to the Sioux River airport. Then he slipped the car in gear and drove away, thinking about Chloe Sheridan.

Chloe was too smart by half, but not smart enough to act stupid when the Boss told her to leave the room and close the door behind her. Dalrymple couldn't wait to talk to her. She'd tell him if she'd passed on any of the Boss's little secrets. He'd use Jake Harris as a tool, make sure she was one hundred percent forthcoming. With any kind of luck this ridiculous cross-country chase would be over inside the next twenty-four hours.

CHAPTER 33

J AKE WATCHED THE ambulance drive away in a whirl of red and white lights, glad the Navajo was parked for the night and the medical evacuation was over. A long afternoon was coming to an end. He massaged the back of his neck and blew out a noisy breath. "Ready to call it a night, Dennis?"

"Damn straight," his first officer answered.

Side by side they headed toward an idling half-ton with a "Tundra Air" graphic stenciled along the length of the box. Jake opened the passenger door, said, "Hey Lawrence," without looking into the truck.

"Hey yourself."

Surprised, he looked across the bench seat into Chloe's eyes. "This is a nice change," he said with smile. He climbed in and slid over until he was sitting beside her. Dennis followed, slamming the door behind him. "Why are you picking us up? Where's Lawrence?"

Chloe slipped the truck into gear and drove out of the parking lot, leaning forward over the steering wheel with lips pursed and her forehead furrowed in concentration. Without taking her eyes off the road she said, "He flew to Thunder Bay after you guys left."

She spoke quickly, with a forced precision. "He's catching the first flight to Montreal in the morning."

"Why?"

"His niece is in the hospital."

Jake stiffened. "What happened in—"

"It's Lawrence, Jake. He's not going to say much. Marie-Claude was assaulted coming home from work." Chloe hiked her shoulders. "That's all he said."

Unable to voice his real concern, Jake didn't answer right away. Finally, he said tentatively, "Assaulted?"

"Beat up," Chloe said. She patted his leg reassuringly, left her hand resting on his thigh rather than putting it back on the steering wheel where it belonged. "I think she has a concussion. That's all."

Jake started. All thoughts of Marie-Claude momentarily disappeared. The warmth and weight of her hand on his leg was nice. Arousing. Lately everything about Chloe revved him up. Her constant chatter didn't grind him anymore. Little things he used to find merely interesting had become the sexiest things in the world, like the way she tugged on the loose red curls dangling by her cheeks. And, the images that randomly popped into his mind… Sometimes in his mind's eye she even wore clothes—a wet bathing suit a size too small, or thigh highs and the tall boots she bought in Chicago and nothing else. More than ever he wanted to run his hands up her legs, hook his fingers in the lacy waistband of her panties, and run his hands south again.

He shook his head slightly, chasing the image away. "I wonder if—"

Chloe's hand tightened on his thigh. "What about your guy?" she interrupted. He looked at her and she gave an almost imperceptible headshake. "What happened to him?"

"Our medivac?" Dennis asked. He yawned into the back of his hand. "The guy's wife shot him. They were drinking. Playing with guns. He told her she was a terrible shot. He told her she couldn't hit the side of a barn." Dennis laughed. "When he said she probably couldn't hit him, she—"

"She shot him?"

"Damn straight. What's going on in the lodge tonight?"

"A bunch of hunters showed up. Eight guys from Atlanta. I gave them cabin five. They haven't left the lodge since they got there. They've got me running my tail off." She let go of Jake's thigh and put her hand back on the steering wheel. "They're tipping huge. One guy, Cliff Nelson? He's tipping me with shots of Remy Martin. He's a pompous ass, but easy to impress."

A slight grin creased Jake's face. Several shots of Remy explained Chloe's careful driving and precisely delivered sentences. With her hands back at ten and two, Jake was able to think clearly again. Marie-Claude's assault came at a strange time, too close on the heels of the Gianolo's visit to Montreal for comfort. He pressed his lips together tightly and scratched the back of his neck in irritation. Was Mr. Blonde responsible? Or was he being paranoid? Maybe the assault was a terrible, random event. After all, Montreal was a long way from Chicago. There was no reason to assume Mr. Blonde made the trip, except... The Gianolo twins flew to Montreal and Dalrymple was far smarter and more dangerous than they were. With the twins in the hospital indefinitely, it made perfect sense for Mr. Blonde to pick up the chase.

Deep inside Jake knew he wasn't being paranoid.

Chloe said, "You know how much a bottle of Remy is? The cheap stuff? Four hundred and fifty bucks a bottle. These guys are drinking shots and chasing them with cans of Labatt Blue." She shook her head with clear disbelief. "It tastes like liquid gold. Doesn't burn at all. The good stuff, it's like fifteen hundred."

"How are you feeling, Chloe?" Jake asked, knowing shots had a way of sneaking up on a person. "You want me to drive?"

"Would you?"

"I don't mind."

She pulled over and they switched seats. When they were back on the road with Chloe slouched between Jake and Dennis, her head propped up on the back of the seat, she said, "There's two charters tomorrow. The Beaver will be gone all day. It leaves early. Seven AM. The other trip, Charlie Cariboo needs a ride into town. That one leaves at eight. Back by noon."

Dennis asked, "Care what you do, Jake?"

Jake wove around potholes, taking the road to the lodge slowly to save their backs and to avoid any nocturnal critters that ventured onto the road. He shook his head. "Not really."

"I'm bagged. I'm going straight to bed. I can get up early and take the Beaver."

"Fine with me," Jake said, parking behind the lodge. "I'll pick up Charlie."

Dennis bailed out. "That's it for me. See you tomorrow."

Chloe grabbed Jake's hand and dragged him toward the lodge. "Come on Jake. I gotta get back at it."

They entered a bedlam of noise. On a portable stereo turned way up, Shania Twain yodeled about getting someone good, while a muted baseball game played on the big screen television. Balls on the pool table clacked. Above it all a mixture of voices and curses filled the lodge. A thin blue haze hung between the rafters. The acrid odor of American cigarettes made Jake's nose twitch. When the hunters saw Chloe they all yelled and waved. One of the hunters said, "Who's the stiff, Chloe?" His voice carried above the din.

"Cliff, this is Jake. He's one of the pilots."

Without looking at Jake, Cliff said, "Does Jake play cards?" He twisted a diamond-studded pinkie ring in half circles around his finger.

Chloe raised her eyebrows. "Do you, Jake?"

"Sure. I'll play a hand or two. What are we playing for?"

Cliff laughed noisily, his mirth filled with condescension.

"What do you call cash up here in the Canadian bush, Jake? Eh?" Grinning, he looked around and soaked up the other hunter's chuckles. He polished the pinkie ring on his shirt.

"If you-all are playing for money, I'll pass," Jake said, turning the "you-all" into a deep, southern drawl. "I'm not much of a poker player."

The hunter's chuckles changed into laughs. Cliff's grin vanished.

One of the card players said, "Let the pilot play for free, Cliff."

"No way, Jerry. He has to pay to play." Cliff paused. "Tell you what. The next five hands we'll make the max bet five bucks. How's that sound, Junior? Think you can afford that?"

Jake forced a smile. "I'll get a loan," he said flatly. He didn't appreciate Cliff using the nickname Mark had given him. Which reminded him, he needed to phone Mark, warn him about Mr. Blonde. He'd called the previous night but so far Mark hadn't got back to him. Not unusual, but Jake felt a sense of urgency and didn't want to wait. He checked his watch. Too late to call tonight, but tomorrow after he landed…

He pulled a chair away from the table and sat down. Cliff dealt him into the poker game.

Jake tried to concentrate on the cards. Instead his eyes strayed to Chloe, watching her as she worked the room. She giggled at their jokes. The snack bowl was never empty and the only beer cans on the table were full. Occasionally one of the hunters touched her arm or elbow, looking for a little extra attention. She never allowed the hand to linger, but the man always ended up with a goofy sort of smile on his face before she moved away. Every now and then one of the hunters tipped her a five. Cliff got louder by the Blue. With every hand he won, he hollered, "Have one on me, Chlo-ee," and poured some of the liquid gold Remy into a shot glass.

The crowd gradually thinned as the evening grew later. One by one the hunters drifted out of the lodge toward cabin five. The volume on the stereo dropped. After losing eighty bucks, Jake said, "I'm out." With two hands on the edge of the table, he pushed himself back and moved to the couch, suddenly feeling too tired to make it out of the lodge to his cabin. He yawned and stretched his arms across the top of the sofa. His eye lids drooped. The background chatter faded into darkness.

When two small, warm hands landed on his shoulders, his eyes popped open. The television and stereo were off now, the babble of drunken hunters silent. Most of the lights in the lodge were dark.

He looked up.

Chloe stood over him, smiling. Her face glowed beautiful in the remaining lights of the lodge. She moistened her lips with the tip of her tongue and massaged his shoulders and neck. Jake was instantly awake, knowing something was going on, wondering where it would lead. "That's nice," he said.

She increased the pressure, digging her fingers into his shoulders, kneading the back of his neck. "You like?" Her voice was soft.

"I do."

"I'm a little drunk, Jake," she said enunciating every word clearly.

"Is that right?"

"Yes. I'm sorry about your friend. Marie-Claude."

He reached up and grabbed one of her hands. Holding it gave him pleasant head-to-toe tingles. "Thanks, Chloe."

She crouched. The side of her face pressed against his. Soft tendrils of hair tickled his cheek. This time when she spoke her voice was near his ear. Her breath smelled like spicy, four-hun-dred-and-fifty-dollar Cognac. "You don't think it was Dalrymple, do you?"

His stomach tied itself into a knot and the pleasant feeling disappeared. He shifted on the sofa. Keeping the anxiety out of his voice he said, "I kind of do. I think the Gianolos found out what they needed to know in Tampa. I think they ran into a wall in Montreal, so Mr. Blonde went there with his own brand of charm."

"I think so too. Earlier, in the truck? I didn't want to get into it with Dennis sitting there. What are we going to do?"

Jake hiked his shoulders, trying to show less concern than he felt. "What's he gonna do? Come to Sioux River and knife us in our sleep? Shoot us in front of a crowd of tourists?"

"Maybe we should go to the police."

"And, tell them what?"

She didn't answer immediately. The silence stretched. When she finally spoke, her voice was as thin as consommé. "I'm scared, Jake. He was going to kill me. He's killed other people."

He tightened his grip on her hand. "You know that for sure? That he's killed people?"

She nodded. "People more important than us."

"You didn't want to talk to the police before. What changed?"

She didn't answer the question. Instead she made a statement. "You think I'm nosy when it comes to other people's conversations."

At a different time, when the mood was less serious, he might have given her a sarcastic answer. Tonight though, he played it safe and made a noncommittal grunt.

"That's okay. You don't have to say." She sighed. Once again she remained silent for several seconds. Finally, she said, "A month before you and I met, I overheard the Boss and Dalrymple talking. I don't know… maybe the Boss just got tired of me. Usually though, when a guy wants a new girlfriend, he doesn't lock the old one in the trunk of a car. I'm pretty sure I wasn't supposed to hear what I heard."

"That's not proof."

"I know. We've been through that. The police won't lock him up based on what I overheard. What I was thinking though, if Marie-Claude can identify him, the cops will *have* to arrest him. If she can't identify him, I can point them in his direction. Either way, they're looking at him. Then, when I tell them everything I over-heard, they'll have lots of new information for their investigation."

"What investigation?"

"You might have missed this on the news, not being from Chicago. Or, maybe you didn't make the connection. Anyway, a thirty-eight foot Bertram went on a fishing charter, a corporate retreat kind of thing. There were twelve guests on the boat. Some elected officials, a couple of city employees, a property developer. A lawyer. They were honest people, according to the media. None of them had been accused of being corrupt or taking kickbacks. Not yet. The boat never came back. Nothing was found except a little bit of debris. But, Lake Michigan is big and deep, so I guess that's not too surprising."

"What happened?"

"I overheard the planning, is all. And, who was involved, of course."

Jake nodded. He said nothing. He thought it over and quickly decided Chloe was right. Her idea made sense. Mr. Blonde wasn't going away and more people were getting hurt. They had to slow him down, or stop him somehow. He said, "Listen Chloe, I never thought—"

He felt moisture between their cheeks. Surprised, Jake pulled back and looked at her. Her eyes were wide. Scared. Brimming with tears. Her chin quivered.

She blinked rapidly. "What a wimp."

Jake wiped the tears away with the tips of his fingers. "You're not a wimp," he said quietly. "I never thought he'd find us up here. It looks like he will. I think going to the cops is the best choice. But right now it's late. I'm whipped. All those Remy shots, you're probably not thinking too clearly either. Any decisions can wait until tomorrow morning. Montreal is over a thousand miles from here. If it was Dalrymple, and he actually figured out where we are, and he decides to come to Sioux River—"

"Oh, he's coming."

"—he won't show up tonight. We have some time."

"I want to go to the police soon, Jake."

"Tomorrow. As soon as I land. We can go together. That soon enough?"

His attitude seemed to buoy her. She nodded. "Okay." Most of the waver was gone from her voice. The tears had dried up as well.

For several seconds it was quiet. He said, "Mark didn't call back, did he?"

"No. But it's only been a day since you phoned him."

"I'll give him another try tomorrow."

She reached over his shoulder and pressed her hand, palm open, on his chest. A finger found its way between the buttons of his shirt and traced tiny circles.

Unwilling to break the spell, he remained motionless.

"I've never had a job. This hostess gig isn't the best, but you know what? I don't mind. I could do without cleaning bathrooms. Why do men pee everywhere but the toilet?"

Jake shook his head slightly. "They have decals that look like flies on the urinals in the Amsterdam airport. Something to aim at."

"I think I'd like a real job. You know? Something where people respected my work."

"Not interior design anymore?"

She sighed. "No. It's fun but it's pointless. I want something that makes a difference and matters."

"What do you have in mind?"

"Health care, I think."

"Where did that come from?"

"I'm good with people." She said nothing for several seconds. "In a week or two, when hunting season ends and the snow starts, I'll be done here. What are we going to do then?"

Jake shook his head again, slowly for a different reason this time. There was a lot to answer in that one simple question. Her job would end and his wouldn't. They had Mr. Blonde to consider. And, she said, "we." Inadvertent or not, she was looking ahead, wondering about her future, wondering if it included him. He wasn't sure how to answer her question. Eventually he said, "Think about what you want to do. If I can, I'll help you figure out how to make it happen."

"Okay. Um, Jake? I'm going upstairs." She ran the tip of her tongue along the edge of his ear. "If you want, maybe you could come upstairs too." She stood and dragged her fingers lightly across his shoulders and neck when she passed behind him, walking toward the staircase with the careful, self-conscious gait of someone who's had too much to drink.

For a moment Jake thought his heart would stop. He watched her go with his breath caught high in his chest. He pressed his palms together, held them near his lips and blew a calming breath between them. When he dropped them he was amused to see them shaking. The unease of a few minutes ago was gone. These new trembles came from anticipation and excitement. Mouth dry with desire, he pushed himself off the sofa.

At the bottom of the stairs he paused, listening as a new classic drifted out of the open door at the top. *Lost Together*. She picked a sappy song to be sure, but it was a great song and the band was just right. Older. Recognizable. A band with a library of songs that took him back to days with Mark. Blue Rodeo. More Mark's era than his, but when he trailed around after his big brother like a tail on a dog, he was happy to listen to whatever Mark put on the stereo. With a steadying hand on the banister he climbed the stairs. By the second riser all thoughts of Marie-Claude, Mr. Blonde, and Mark were gone. The only person on his mind was Chloe.

At the entrance to her bedroom, he paused.

She danced in a pool of moonlight, swaying without moving her feet, just swiveling her hips. She held her arms high, fingers near her ears. Eyes closed, she nibbled the corner of her lower lip. Her jeans, a tangle of denim, lay at the foot of the bed. She'd traded her shirt for a white cotton tank top. A filmy scrap of blue silk was the only thing covering her bottom half. The soft light colored her skin a delicious shade of caramel, and tinted her hair a deep, fiery crimson.

He inhaled sharply.

Her eyes fluttered open. "Jake," she murmured.

"Don't stop."

She kept dancing, looking at him past droopy eyelids the entire time. When the song ended she sashayed toward the bed.

Jake groaned aloud. The sound was low in his throat and came from an ancient place, deep inside. That image—Chloe beside the bed wearing a tiny blue thong, a white tank top, her hair hanging down in loose curls to the middle of her back—that image was with him and would fuel his fantasies for years to come.

She sat on the edge of the bed. With her feet flat on the floor, hands on her knees, she pushed her legs apart.

Jake's eyes dropped and he sought out the two sexy little hollows at the top, inside of each thigh, separated by the narrow ribbon of blue. He looked up, swallowing dryly.

Chloe winked and leaned back. Propping herself on her elbows, she crooked her index finger at him.

Abruptly she slipped and flopped back on the mattress. "Oopsy," she slurred.

A smile tugged at the corner of Jake's mouth. He looked at the ceiling, closed his eyes and shook his head. "Shit," he murmured, his voice filled with humor and regret. He took half a step in her direction, holding out both hands. "Come on, sexy girl. Give me your hands."

She reached for him.

When he had a firm grip, he pulled her upright into his arms. He kissed her neck and when she closed her eyes and purred, he brushed her eyelids with his lips. He spun her around so his back was to the bed. Supporting her wobbly body with one arm around her waist, he reached behind him, grabbed the covers and whipped the blankets back. Then he eased her onto the mattress.

She reached for him.

"Put your arms down, Chloe."

With unfocused eyes, she gave him an enquiring look and let her arms drop to her sides.

Jake pulled the blankets slowly back up, covering her inch by inch, wanting nothing more than to dive under them with her. He leaned down and kissed her forehead, the corners of her mouth and when she closed her eyes and sighed, he sloppily kissed the tip of her nose.

She scrunched up her nose, and wiped it dry with the back of her hand. "Ja–ke."

He laughed, stood, and scanned the room. He spotted a small garbage pail, which he placed near the head of her bed.

"I'm dizzy, Jake. I think I'm going to be sick."

"Open your eyes."

"I'm so sleepy."

"Do it."

When she did he nodded. "Good. Grab the top of the headboard. Hold on tight. Now, push your foot into the wall." He nodded again. "You can close your eyes now. But keep holding on. Let your body know the bed's not spinning."

"I don't feel good."

"Those Remy shots caught up with you, didn't they? If you need it, there's a pail near your head. Otherwise, hold on tight. Push with your foot. You'll fall asleep soon. You'll be okay." He chuckled. "Although tomorrow won't be a walk in the park."

"I gotta work tomorrow."

"It's quiet. Dennis and I know what's going on. Between the two of us we can figure out how to fly one trip each. The only guys in camp are those yahoos from Atlanta. They'll all be sleeping off hangovers in cabin five. You won't have to worry about them." He walked toward the bedroom door. "When you wake up tomorrow, roll over and go back to sleep. Good night, Chloe."

"Don't go."

She lay like a starfish across the single-sized mattress, so Jake sat on the floor. He stretched his legs out and propped himself up, back against the wall. He reached up and took her free hand. "I'm here. You just hang on."

Within moments she was snoring softly.

Jake slipped his hand out of hers and walked out of the room, pulling the door shut behind him. "So close," he muttered, shaking his head ruefully.

CHAPTER 34

SOMETHING WAS WRONG.

When the passenger service agent asked him if he preferred a window or an aisle, Mr. Blonde told her he didn't
care. As long as it was in first class. She smiled, said, "No problem
sir. You can have something in the front of the aircraft. Why don't
we go with an aisle seat?"

Walking down a long, indoor ramp with five other people,
Mr. Blonde's sixth sense poked him like a sharp stick. One of the
passengers, a kid who couldn't have been more than nineteen, was
dressed suspiciously like a pilot. Gold wings on the breast pocket
of his crisp white shirt. Four gold bars on his shoulder epaulettes.
This kid in the pilot costume acting like he knew what was going
on, and the only thought in Mr. Blonde's mind was, what kind of
an airplane am I getting on? Where's the jet-way? A second tingle
of apprehension stroked his spine.

The ramp ended at a set of stairs. At the bottom of the stairs,
the child-pilot stretched his arm across the door, holding it open.
All the passengers walked past him, out of the Thunder Bay airport
terminal toward...

The fuck was this?

The airplane was no bigger than a Chrysler.

Mr. Blonde's limping step broke. The wind whipped the tails of his sport coat into a frenzy around his waist. He looked at the young pilot. "What's that?"

"It's a Beech 99 sir." The pilot looked at him, started with obvious shock and quickly looked away.

It was his eye that scared the pilot, Mr. Blonde figured, the way it glowed crimson like that of a demon's in a science fiction movie. Or, it may have been the purple goose-egg on his cheek. Or, perhaps it was the scabbed over puncture wound from Marie-Claude's keys. He twitched his head a quarter turn. "I was expecting something bigger. A jet. Or a turboprop. Like a Dash 8."

"The 99 is a turboprop, sir." The pilot laughed. "I guess you've never been to Sioux River? There's barely enough people in the town for the fourteen seats on the Beech. It's certainly not big enough for a jet. Or a Dash. A 99 is as safe as either of those."

"She told me inside I'd get a first-class seat. On the aisle."

The pilot laughed a second time. He gestured at the plane. "Go ahead, please. At Superior Air Services every seat is first class. Every seat is window and an aisle."

Mr. Blonde snorted. "Yeah. Okay. I'm gonna need a rental car in Sioux River. Can you arrange that?"

The pilot laughed a third time.

Laugh once more, you little puke. Once more and I'll break your fucking neck.

"I can arrange a cab, if you want. There are no rental cars in Sioux River."

Large raindrops splattered the asphalt ramp like bugs on a windshield. With the child-pilot beside him, Mr. Blonde strode reluctantly toward the Beech, high stepping across the puddles, doing his best to keep his Rockports dry. Each step sent a twinge of pain from his groin to his leg. Almost three full days since he dealt with Mark Harris and if possible, the spot where the son-of-a-bitch punched him ached worse than it did before. "You old enough to drive this thing?"

The pilot didn't smile or laugh this time, Mr. Blonde noted with childish satisfaction. In fact, he appeared a little annoyed with the question.

"No sir," he answered, his voice flat and un-amused. He raised his eyebrows, managing to look shocked. "Even worse, the company gave me a million-dollar aircraft to fly without the appropriate training." He paused. His eyes furtively swiveled from side to side. He said in a stage whisper, "I haven't crashed in a week. But, don't tell anyone." Louder once again, he said, "Please climb aboard, sir. We have a schedule to keep."

Mr. Blonde squinted at him. The fuck did that mean? There were rules. Regulations. Even in the bush, pilots needed to know how to... He realized the pilot was being sarcastic and scowled, trying to decide if he needed to be angry or nervous. Settling on both, he climbed the steps at the rear of the plane.

Bent at the waist he looked down the length of the aircraft—a single row of seats on either side of a narrow aisle. Not even a partition separating the pilot from the passengers. He glanced at his boarding pass, searching for his seat assignment. There wasn't one. Suddenly he understood what the agent meant when she said he could have a seat in the front of the plane, and what the pilot meant when he said every seat was an aisle or a window. He rotated his head quickly and ground his teeth together.

Smart asses.

He chose a seat and buckled in using the tips of his fingers to fasten the seatbelt. A thin layer of age covered everything in the plane. The fabric smelled damp and grimy. Grimacing, he ripped open a lemon-scented Wet Ones and cleaned his hands.

A couple of minutes later the pilot pushed the throttles forward. The Beech accelerated. The faster it moved the harder Mr. Blonde gritted his teeth. He found himself tensing, fingers wrapped tightly around the armrests, pushing himself up off his seat slightly, somehow thinking the inch he held himself off the seat would be a sufficient cushion when the Beech smashed back on the ground.

Then they were airborne, not so much flying, as thrashing through the wind and rain toward Sioux River. The thin wall of the aircraft did nothing to muffle the shrill and deafening sound of the turbines on each wing. Thinking, formulating some kind of a plan in this kind of racket, was near impossible, but Mr. Blonde did his best.

The Boss had done some research for him while he was on the flight between Montreal and Thunder Bay. It turned out Tundra Air's tourist season was almost over. By early October the company entertained only the occasional hunting party. Except for the pilots, most the employees were seasonal and likely already gone for the winter. Which meant if Chloe had stayed in Sioux River all summer, which was unlikely—after all, who could stand having her around that long—she probably wouldn't be there now.

Mr. Blonde found the Band-Aid on his cheek and he fingered the bruise. His groin throbbed. If Chloe was gone, it almost didn't matter. He had personal reasons to re-introduce himself to Harris and after they became re-acquainted, the guy would beg to tell him where he saw Chloe last.

Eventually they landed in Sioux River. Mr. Blonde picked up his bag from beside the Beech 99 and hustled into the one-room terminal building.

"I had my fishing gear couriered," Mr. Blonde said to the agent at the Superior Air Services check in counter. "Has it arrived?" He didn't hold much hope. The tiny airplane, the one-room terminal building, the wart of a town he'd seen from the air all seemed backward and a great distance away from the big city life with which he was most familiar.

"It sure has, Mr. Dalrymple." The agent gave him a friendly

smile. "It was actually on the same plane as you. Let me just go get it."

Another thing working his last nerve—everyone at the airline was so helpful and cheerful. It was infuriating.

The agent returned with a long, black fishing rod case and a tackle box the size of a deep freeze. Mr. Blonde smiled. It took some calls, some organization but everything was coming together. "Thanks," he said and walked back outside.

A Caprice masquerading as a cab waited near the exit door. The vehicle was covered with dirt and rust and the rain blended both together into a muddy copper color. Mr. Blonde glanced in both directions. Perhaps there'd be another taxi, something cleaner, something that looked like it would actually make it off the airport property.

Of course there wasn't.

He hissed an exasperated breath through his teeth and climbed in, pushing the tackle box ahead of him on the seat and slamming the door behind him while the driver stowed his small carry-all and fishing rod in the trunk.

"Where ya to?" the driver asked, when he was sitting comfortably in the driver's seat.

"Tundra Air."

"You mean Deep Cove? The float base?"

"That's it."

"You got it." The cab driver pulled away. "You meeting people there?"

"Why?"

"Most you fellas from the States come up with ten friends."

"My friends arrived a couple of days back."

"Lotta tackle you got there?"

It sounded like a question and Mr. Blonde guessed the driver was curious about why he put the tackle box on the seat with him, instead of in the trunk with the rest of his gear. "I want to go through it. Make sure I have everything I need. I don't want to have to come back to town if I forgot something."

The driver nodded, his expression saying, "That makes sense, but..."

"You fellas all come up with huge tackle boxes. You got way too much stuff. Alls you really need is one lure, my friend. I tell everyone the same thing. An orange Wedding Band. That'll catch ya anything in the lake."

"I'd rather have some options. How far is it? Deep Cove, I mean."

"Twenty minutes."

"Any radio stations up here?"

"Sure." The driver switched on the radio. He tweaked the volume, raising it enough to hear over the rhythmic slap of the windshield wipers.

Mr. Blonde leaned back in his seat. He put the tackle box on his knees. Opened it. Rifled through it. He ignored an enormous variety of fishing gear and found the various parts of the nine-millimeter Glock that were dispersed throughout the tackle box. In several practiced movements, he put the pistol together, the metallic clicks indistinguishable over the radio, windshield wipers, and the Caprice's engine. Occasionally, he looked out the window and watched the scenery pass.

"You got everything, then?"

"Everything I need," Mr. Blonde answered.

When the cab pulled into the parking lot behind the lodge, Mr. Blonde took a moment to study the area before stepping out. Other than the car he was in, only two other vehicles occupied the parking lot. A half-ton Ford with "Tundra Air" stenciled on the side and a dusty black Mustang he recognized from Gianolo's Chicago wrecking yard.

A smile creased his face.

A couple of cabins lined each side of the bay. A hut stood

sentinel near the end of a dock that stretched into the lake like a finger pointing away from the lodge. A small boat bounced forlornly back and forth against tire bumpers. So far it looked like Chicago's intel was correct. The place seemed deserted.

He looked from the boat to the Mustang and his rudimentary plan solidified. Within a couple of hours, Harris wouldn't need his car anymore. It would make a fine getaway vehicle, save him from leaving town on that eggbeater of an airplane.

Mr. Blonde waited under the porch's overhang until the cab disappeared around the bend, before snaking the pistol out of the tackle box. He pulled the slide back and eased it forward quietly. He twisted the doorknob and stepped across the threshold into the lodge. Indistinguishable voices carried to him from a still hidden part of the building. His fingers tightened around the grip of the pistol. He heard a recognizable jingle then the familiar words, "This is CNN."

He shook his head slightly. Jumpy over voices on a television.

He walked deeper into the lodge, past a counter displaying Tundra Air caps and golf shirts. A muskellunge mounted on a slab of aged driftwood stared at him out of beady glass eyes. Mr. Blonde stared right back. "Fuck-wit fish," he muttered.

He walked past it into the main part of the lodge, the rubber soles of his shoes silent on the polished pine floor. The television flickered and chattered. Using the remote on the arm of the sofa, he muted the sound.

When he walked past the bay windows, the view caught his eye. Whitecaps, with tips like browned meringue, covered the slate gray lake. There was an island at the end of the bay, nothing more than a smear of green trees and orange leaves, partially obscured in rain and mist.

Shooting Harris and Chloe, dumping them in the lake was an obvious choice. Except the way the wind was blowing, they'd wash ashore in no time. The little island wasn't too far away. If he had a conversation with them out there, popped 'em both and drove away in Harris's Mustang, the island wouldn't be the first, or even second place the authorities searched. They'd look for the car first, assuming the couple eloped, something ridiculous like that. Eventually, when someone managed to convince the authorities the two were actually missing, they'd find the Mustang abandoned in a shopping mall parking lot.

Nodding, liking the plan so far, he rolled the eight ball the length of the table, into a cluster of balls at the opposite end. When they broke the clacks sounded like small arms fire. He looked past the pool table, through a small kitchen, and focused his attention on a staircase that led to the second floor.

Living quarters, maybe?

With a light tread he climbed the stairs. A riser from the top, he paused. Three doors, two partially open and one firmly closed, beckoned him. Standing to the side with his arm straight, he nudged the door directly in front of him open with the barrel of his Glock. The door squeaked on its hinge. He winced at the sound. His finger tightened on the trigger.

A bathroom. A white blouse, some kind of slippery fabric, hung on a hanger from the shower curtain rod. He shot a look at the vanity. Makeup and hair products cluttered the counter.

He looked through the open door into the room on his right. A deserted bedroom. A bare mattress on a box spring. A dresser with a lamp, the shade tilted sideways at an untidy angle. The closet door was open, nothing inside but four or five wire clothes hangers hooked forlornly on the bar.

He looked at the closed door to his left. A second bedroom he thought, no doubt in his mind that it was Chloe Sheridan's.

He reached for the doorknob.

CHAPTER 35

"WHERE'S THE BARF bag?"

Jake flicked a glance at his passenger. "Check the glove box," he yelled over the top of the engine noise.

The man in the seat beside Jake stared straight ahead out of twin black eyes. He didn't move. Flakes of dried blood stuck to a knot the size and color of an Easter egg on his temple. His lower lip was puffed to twice its normal size.

Jake's gaze returned to the view out the windshield. He frowned. Only four hundred feet remained between the airplane and the Canadian Shield granite. Sporadic raindrops pelted the fuselage and pebbled the windows. Fingers of stratus reached out of the overcast and plucked at the Cessna. The landscape and clouds blurred together like too much liquid in a watercolor wash. He eased the control column forward, descending another hundred feet into better visibility. A violent gust of wind snatched at the Cessna, tossing it from side to side. He rocked against his shoulder strap.

His passenger groaned.

With one hand tight on the controls, Jake leaned over and popped the tiny glove box open. "See if there's one in there."

"I'm gonna puke," he said, his accent thicker than normal, on account of his hangover, Jake guessed. The man's dark skin was chalky white, his lips wet. Pure Five Star rye oozed out of his pores. He slid a palm across his forehead and wiped it dry on his thigh. A greasy stain darkened his faded Levis.

"Reach up there, Charlie." Jake pointed to the right hand corner where the windshield and the ceiling met. "Pull that vent out. Let cold air blow on your face. You'll feel better."

Charlie tugged the vent out. A strong flow of cold air immediately filled the cabin. His expression switched from desperation to relief.

"What happened to your face?"

Charlie's mouth momentarily quirked into a gummy, toothless grin. "Had a party last night. My friend? He hit me with a log."

Jake chuckled. "Good party, was it?"

"Pretty good." The grin disappeared as fast as it came, the cold air reprieve already waning. The Native closed his eyes and white-knuckled the strap above his door like a drowning man clings to a life preserver.

Jake glanced at his watch. Ten minutes until they were on the water. He pressed his lips together. The way the wind was throwing the plane around there was no way they'd land in time. He felt bad for what he was about to say. He had no choice. "Charlie? You puke in here and all your stuff," he hooked his thumb over his shoulder at the cargo tied down behind the two front seats, "stays on board until you clean it up."

Charlie's eyes were clamped shut with concentration. "I know how it goes."

Hoping to distract him, Jake kept talking. "Why you coming to town on a day like today?"

Charlie looked at Jake with a smile, maybe his first all day. "My kid's birthday tomorrow. I'm going to the Northern. Get him some hockey equipment."

"How old is he?"

"Twelve. He loves hockey."

"Is he good?"

"Oh yeah." Despite the hangover and motion sickness, Charlie spoke proudly. "He's good. Maybe with some decent equipment he goes all the way."

"Like that kid from Rankin Inlet, huh? The one who went to the Nashville Predators?"

"Jordin Tootoo," Charlie said, shrugging. The proud smile didn't disappear. "I'd like to see it."

Jake nodded his agreement. "My brother, he's the expert. He loves sports. I'll tell him to keep his eyes open, watch for your boy."

The Cessna hit another air pocket. It seemed to freefall for a moment, before the propeller dragged it forward. That was too long for Charlie. An expression of extreme anxiety crossed his face. His hand scrambled through the glove box, the map pocket in the side of the door. Panting heavily, obviously desperate to get out of the plane, he reached behind him into the pouch on the back of his seat. He flung the life jacket aside and dropped the logbook and charts on the floor.

There was no Sic-Sac.

Cutting a frantic glance over his shoulder he managed to gasp, "I need my gear, Jake." He reached down and yanked the green rubber boot off his foot, the kind that usually come with yellow laces, except Charlie's laces were gone. He leaned over and simultaneously raised the rubber boot to his face. A second later his back arched, his shoulders rolled and he heaved what sounded like the better part of supper and the previous night's whiskey into the Wellington.

An oily layer of sweat instantly formed on Jake's forehead. His sinuses became hyper-sensitive. Like a ship in heavy seas, his stomach did a slow roll. He pulled his own vent open, diluting the acidic stench of fresh vomit and the oily, plastic odor for which Cessna interiors were infamous. Gritting his teeth, he concentrated on the attitude indicator and directional gyro. Stay level and on course for a few more miles. Then a half circle around the lake to get lined up into wind. They'd be on the water in no time.

Still bent over, with his face near the top of the boot, Charlie looked at Jake. "That feels better."

Jake nodded once. "Glad to hear it." He tried to ignore the slime and saliva on the Indian's chin, the Kentucky Fried Chicken chunks, some shit like that, dripping from the ends of the man's oily black hair.

He didn't have to worry about it for long.

Charlie crammed his face back into the Wellington. A fresh wave of flotsam splashed into the boot.

Shit, Jake thought. Now I need a distraction.

"Tundra base, from SCS," Jake called into the radio.

There was no response. Despite the turbulent ride, the noxious fumes, and his own vaguely upset stomach, Jake felt a flicker of amusement. He checked his watch. Almost noon. When he left to pick Charlie up, Chloe was in bed. He thought she might have rolled out by now. He tried again, "Base, from SCS."

Her voice suddenly filled Jake's headset speakers. "SCS, the wind is…" After a brief pause the radio crackled and Chloe recited the wind and altimeter setting.

"Check," Jake said, "Thanks."

There was no reply.

Not as sociable as she normally was on the radio. Too formal by half. Usually she said, "Welcome back, Jake," or something similar. With a heavyweight Remy Martin hangover, she must not have felt too affable. Still, cranky mood and all, he couldn't wait to see her. He wanted to touch her arm during their conversation and make sure the previous night wasn't random. He wanted to know that she was as distracted by him as he was by her.

Charlie removed his face from the rubber boot. It was like taking a cork out of a bottle. The smell of partially digested food and old alcohol filled the cabin. He wiped the back of his hand across his mouth, hawked and spit into the boot.

Jake's stomach lurched. Happy Chloe thoughts disappeared. It was time to land.

Four minutes later the back of the floats tugged on the water. The plane settled. A big spray of water washed past the side windows. After Jake docked the airplane, he stepped out of the Cessna onto the dock.

The wind gusted and blew. The rain slashed down in black, gray and white stripes. His denim jacket quickly turned Prussian blue. He glanced at the hut perched near the end of the dock, and from there to the dark windows of the lodge. The only tourists at the base were hidden away in cabin five. With Dennis and Stevenson out of town and no hunters waiting for a ride, the Tundra Air base felt deserted and forlorn. Shivering, Jake raised the collar of his fleece. It was a good time to be finished for the day.

After he tied the aircraft securely to the tire bumpers lining the dock, he said, "Here we are, Charlie. Cheated death again."

Charlie cautiously planted his feet, one in a green rubber boot, the other in a gray wool sock, on the float. He stepped up from the float to the dock, placing the vomit-filled boot beside him. "Thanks, Jake." His voice was filled with relief.

"Yeah. No problem. I'll pass over your gear." Jake walked toward the rear of the float and opened the tiny cargo door.

"I'll help." Charlie stepped back down.

Their combined weight pushed the back of the float deeper into the lake. Cold, gray waves broke over the top. Charlie quickly hopped back onto the dock, narrowly avoiding a soaking. "This is no good, Jake. I'm gonna get wet." He swung around, and snatched his boot off the dock.

Jake stared, curious. Then he realized what Charlie was going to do. He shouted, "Charlie! No!"

Too late.

Charlie thrust his foot into the boot. What seemed like nine gallons of vomit splashed over the rim. He said, "Man," in a mournful sort of way. He sat on the edge of the dock and pulled off the vomit boot. Holding it upside down, he drained what little residue was left into the lake. He tossed the boot aside and plunged his slimy leg, sock and all, into the water.

"You take it easy, Charlie. I'll get your gear." Jake unloaded the Cessna, piling the Indian's gear under the airplane's wing, out of the worst of the weather. When the last black garbage bag sat on the dock, he wiped a hand down his face. Trickles of water ran off his hair, gathered on the collar of his fleece and wound a cold trail down his back.

He glanced at the hut at the end of the dock hoping Chloe would poke her head out and wave. The window remained empty, the door shut. Jake scratched the back of his neck. Where was she? Perhaps she was keeping a low profile out of embarrassment? He shook his head slightly. Doubtful. He didn't think she'd be embarrassed about inviting him upstairs. They knew each other too well now, although the way they knew each other had changed. Widened. It was as though they'd lived together for several months in a two-story house, but never gone up to the second floor. Then one day they climbed the stairs. The house was the same. It remained familiar but there was a new unexplored dimension to it.

He told himself to quit acting like a high school kid. There was no reason to expect she'd get out of bed with a hangover on a day like today. It was time to look after his customer.

Charlie still sat on the edge of the dock, head hung low. His black hair obscured his face in greasy, wet tendrils. He swirled lazy figure eights in the lake with his foot, his bare toes poking out the end of his gray sock. Jake swallowed a laugh. He looked away fast, before Charlie caught him. It wasn't good business to laugh at your customers. Then again, it wasn't every day one of them puked last night's party into his rubber boot. Jake planned on getting some mileage out of the story. For sure Mark would laugh.

As humorous as it was, he also felt sorry for Charlie. Flying in bad weather with a whiskey hangover was like seeing someone get kicked in the groin. You laughed hysterically and felt the pain at the same time.

"Charlie, you finished washing up?"

"I guess."

"Let's go see if Chloe's got coffee brewing. Then you can go buy your boy his birthday present."

"Coffee sounds good." Charlie rose slowly to his feet. He stuffed his wet foot into the green Wellington with a grimace. "I need a cart for my stuff."

"There'll be one up there," Jake said, nodding at the hut. He bent at the waist, hoisted a black garbage bag in one hand and a jerry can in the other. "Wait under the wing out of the rain. I'll get it."

"Okay." Charlie's eyes narrowed. He gestured with his chin. When he spoke again there was an edge of tension in his voice. "What's going on, Jake?"

Furrowing his brow in a silent question, Jake followed Charlie's gaze. His breath caught in his throat. His insides froze.

Chloe walked down the dock with Mr. Blonde a step behind her. His face was stony, all business. Her face was drawn with fear.

CHAPTER 36

M R. BLONDE WALKED with a limp, one hand on Chloe's neck, directing her like a tiller on a ship. His other hand hung straight down, holding a pistol tight against his leg. A skinny black finger of dye dribbled out of his hairline down his cheek like a line from the tip of a Sharpie.

Jake placed the plastic bag and the jerry can on the dock and slowly straightened.

Chloe's eyes were wide. Her makeup ran in the rain, black mascara smudging a face white with fear. The wind tugged at curls of hair that weren't secure under the Yankees cap.

"What's going on?" Charlie asked a second time. His voice had come up an octave. He sounded alert, like the hangover had suddenly disappeared.

Jake kept his gaze riveted on Chloe. "Nothing, Charlie." Despite the rain and wind, itchy prickles of nervous sweat formed under his arms. His hands shook slightly at his sides. He balled them into tight fists. "Nothing is going on."

Mr. Blonde finally spoke. "Your car keys. Where are they?"

He wore the yellow slicker that normally hung from a nail on the back of the hut's door. It bunched tight under each arm, leaving most of his forearms exposed to the rain. A strip down the front of his suit where the slicker wasn't fastened was dappled with rain. The cream Band-Aid on his cheek shone brightly against a purple bruise. The man's left eye was crimson with broken blood vessels. He'd either tangled with a semi-truck or…

Jake decided he didn't want to see the other guy.

Charlie said, "Guy's got a gun."

Making an effort to stay composed, Jake nodded. "I see it." Answering Charlie but talking to Chloe, he said, "Just be cool. Nothing is going to happen."

Mr. Blonde raised an eyebrow, a look that said, "Really?" In a swift, smooth arc, he raised his arm. He squeezed the trigger. His arm snapped up with the recoil. The gunshot was deafening. Jake jerked with the suddenness of it. Hot blood splattered his cheek and he started a second time and shouted involuntarily.

Charlie Caribou dropped like an anvil, dead before he hit the dock. Rain pelted him, washing away the gore leaking from the fresh hole in his face.

For a moment, Jake stared uncomprehendingly at Charlie. The nausea from a few minutes ago rushed back. A feeling of deep hopelessness slammed him in the center of the chest. He raised his gaze. Mr. Blonde smiled back at him, that thin, scratch-in-granite smile that never reached his eyes.

"I'll ask again. Where are your car keys?" His gaze flicked to Charlie's corpse. "You don't tell me, that's as good a day as pretty little Chloe is going to have." A drop of water dripped from the tip of his nose. He raised both eyebrows enquiringly.

Numb with disbelief, Jake was unable to answer.

The Freak tightened his grip, driving his fingers deep into the hollow where Chloe's shoulder and neck met. Her mouth went wide and she shrieked once and dropped to one knee, desperately twisting under his grip.

The scream jolted Jake to life. He took three fast steps in their direction, not sure what he was going to do, just that he needed to stop the Freak from hurting her.

Mr. Blonde raised the pistol and shook his head. The unwavering black hole at the end of the barrel loomed huge. "The keys."

Jake slid to a halt. He raised both palms and lowered them, a calming gesture. "They're in the drawer under the phone," he said weakly. "In the lodge."

Mr. Blonde nodded once. "Put the redskin in the boat."

"Okay."

The fourteen-foot aluminum Lund bumped into the dock with each wave that slapped its side. A tangle of fishing line was trapped beneath one of the bench seats. Leaves and dirt clung to an empty Miller beer can floating aimlessly in an inch of pooled water. *The boat needs to be cleaned before the next group of tourists arrived,* Jake thought hazily. He squatted down and grabbed Charlie beneath each arm. The Native's vacant eyes stared up at him accusingly.

I'm sorry, Charlie.

He towed Charlie's body, the man's heels sliding on the slippery pine dock, toward the Lund. At the edge of the dock, he paused. It would have been easy to roll poor Charlie off the dock, let him fall into the boat. Jake couldn't bring himself to do it that way. Instead, he jumped into the boat first.

Feet spread wide for balance, he pulled Charlie into the boat so that he was holding the man's body upright when Charlie's feet slid off the dock. He eased the Indian onto the floor, propping his back against the middle bench, his feet up on the rear one. It seemed better that way, like Charlie wasn't just another piece of trash floating in the bottom of the boat.

Jake stepped toward the dock. The boat rocked. Charlie flopped sideways into the murky water. The beer can wedged itself between the side of the boat and his partially submerged face. His black hair floated on the water, writhing like a school of baby eels.

"Don't bother getting out," Mr. Blonde said. "We're going for a ride. You're driving." He shoved Chloe toward the boat. "You first. Center seat. Go."

Chloe stepped down, balancing herself with one hand on the edge of the dock. Jake grabbed her free hand, steadying her. She straddled the bench seat, sitting with her back against the side of the boat, as far away from Charlie's body as she could get. Her disbelieving stare alternated between Jake and the corpse. The beer can bobbed near her feet. She kicked it away. It clinked on the side of the rocking Lund.

Mr. Blonde looked at Charlie's corpse. "He looks better than your brother did the last time I saw him."

Jake cocked his head. *What did he just say?* It sounded like his brother was dead, but that was impossible. There was nobody on the planet as alive as Mark. He walked the knife's edge of control. Sometimes he fell, but he was bulletproof. Untouchable. He always regained his footing.

Very slowly, Jake scratched a spot behind his ear.

Chloe's gaze flashed from Charlie's body to Jake. It was pure grief. "Jake. I'm so sorry." The tears she worked so hard to contain finally fell.

Jake was aware they fell for him and Mark, not her. A glacial cold seeped through his body. Goosebumps bloomed on his arms. Was that why Mark hadn't called back? Did it explain the bruises and Mr. Blonde's bloody red eye? The limp?

He shook his head slightly, still not believing.

"Oh, it's true. I beat his ass to death. With a Callaway three wood. Nice club."

Jake thought of the golf bag full of clubs his brother left near the door to their basement apartment. His knees buckled. He staggered, fell and landed with a thump on the back seat of the boat. For a moment he couldn't breathe. His mouth opened and closed as he gulped spasmodically for air.

Chloe reached out and touched his arm. "Jake."

He looked from her face to her fingers on his arm and didn't see or feel her. He was aware of the rain pelting down, the wind slicing through his wet clothes like the blade of a knife. From a long way off, like he was talking at the far end of a tunnel, Jake heard Mr. Blonde curse.

The Freak was grimacing at the dirty water sloshing around in the bottom of the Lund. He stepped down, swearing louder this time, plucking the fabric of his pants at his thighs to keep the cuffs high above his ankles. Water, stained with Charlie's blood and old fish scales, slopped over the edge of his shiny black shoes. The muscles in his neck tightened into angry ropes. His face twisted in rage. His mouth moved.

Jake heard nothing but white noise. He squinted uncomprehendingly. Mark was dead. His brother went to Afghanistan and never for a moment did Jake believe he wouldn't make it home. And, all those times Mark talked about how his students were busy trying to kill him, Jake just laughed because how dangerous could they be?

Faster than a rattler, Mr. Blonde backhanded Chloe in the mouth.

She yelped and tumbled off the seat, landing with a small splash on the floor of the boat. Blood trickled from the corner of her mouth.

The scream jolted Jake back to the present. He flicked his eyes between Chloe and Mr. Blonde. He sucked in a steadying breath. *Concentrate.* When he didn't follow Mr. Blonde's orders, Chloe paid the price. Twice now. He wouldn't let it happen a third time. She needed him. He could think about Mark later, when Chloe was out of harm's way. For now, he needed to focus. The terrible emptiness spreading from the center of his stomach, slowed.

"I said start the boat," Mr. Blonde said. "We're going out to that little island." He pointed the barrel of his pistol like a long black index finger.

Jake was momentarily confused. He tugged the starter cord.

The little Mercury started on the second pull. Island? Then he remembered. He made the same mistake the day he arrived at Deep Cove, mistook the peninsula where cabin five sat at the end of the bay, for an island.

Rain danced on the surface of the lake, turning the afternoon into gray twilight, the edges soft in a hazy wet mist. Jake raked his fingers through his hair, plastering it to his head, away from his eyes. Water dribbled down his neck and found its way down his back. He shivered.

He twisted the grip on the Mercury's tiller all the way to the stop, operating the engine at full throttle. The Lund pushed slowly and steadily through the waves and wind toward the tip of the peninsula at the end of Deep Cove. With nothing to do but drive, the memories came like a fireworks show. Each fragment of light flared dazzlingly clear. He recognized them as the good days, the days he remembered as being more special than all the others.

Then the light extinguished, leaving an impenetrable black emptiness.

There'd be no more "frustrating walks," Mark telling him five putting a par four was unacceptable in a tone of voice that said, "Ten putting would be fine," because they were out there together, soaking up life, the heat of the sun, the smell of salt in the air, neither worrying about tomorrow. The two of them bullshitting all afternoon on the links, Mark telling exaggerated stories about the students who were trying to kill him, and Jake countering with lies of his own, parties in foreign cities with sexy young flight attendants.

He glanced at Chloe. She sat straddling the seat, shoulders rounded. Strings of hair dropped from the cap and hung listlessly alongside her cheeks. Her expression was empty, like she decided all hope was gone. Jake forced himself to straighten. He needed to give her hope. Needed to help her.

Like he helped Mark? The thought was brief and unbidden.

Jake considered it and dismissed it. The situations were entirely different. But it made him remember.

There'd be no more rushing around in the morning getting ready for work, Mark watching SportsCenter briefing him about things he considered important, "...and if anyone asks, Paul Tracy won from the pole in Vancouver. And, the Yankees beat Toronto in ten... Bloody hell, Jake, you should know this stuff. Talking the talk isn't good enough." And, as he walked out the door, Mark always losing the flippant attitude and telling him to fly safe in a way that assured Jake he was serious and concerned. Always the older brother. Always looking out for him, just like he did in the schoolyard when Jake was a child.

The tears were close to the surface now, narrowing his vision. Jake blinked several times. He told himself to think about Chloe. She needed him.

Near the end of Deep Cove, the peninsula narrowed to a spit of sand and gravel before widening like the dot on the top of an I. Jake aimed the boat at a dock sheltered in the narrows, recognizing the moment the Freak realized the peninsula didn't end in an island. His face hardened. He leaned forward in the boat and stared at the spit, scowling.

Jake said flatly, "Everybody thinks it's an island."

Mr. Blonde squinted at the sky. He twitched his head in a quick quarter turn and raised his index finger to his lips. After tapping several times, he said, "Park at the dock."

Jake idled into the dock at an angle. When he judged the time was right he twisted the throttle into neutral, letting the boat glide the final three feet.

"Neither of you move." Mr. Blonde rose to his feet. Swaying unsteadily in the rocking Lund, he stretched a hand out to the dock.

Jake's eyes widened. Anyone who spent time in a boat knew better than to stand up and grab for the dock. A person needed to stay seated, keep his center of gravity low, and wait for the boat and the dock to bump together. The Freak was probably still worrying about his shoes and clothes, and didn't want to kneel or crawl onto the dock.

Jake looked at Chloe, praying she'd do as he asked instead of asking her usual twenty questions. With his hand close to his chest, he pointed at her and mouthed, "Run."

A short, questioning look crossed her face. She nodded imperceptibly.

It was all Jake could hope for. An increased level of alertness.

Here we go. Show time.

He rolled his wrist on the tiller, switching the Mercury from neutral to reverse. The little engine roared. The prop churned the water into bubbling white foam. For a moment, as though surprising the forces of wind and water, the engine overcame the resistance. With a sudden jerk, the Lund's glide to the dock halted. The boat lunged backward.

With his weight out of the boat, over the lake, Mr. Blonde wobbled. His arms wind-milled for balance. The pistol fell out of his hand. It hit the side of the boat with a clatter, slid down the wet aluminum and came to a stop beneath the front seat.

"No!" His shins banged into the gunwale and he toppled over the side. He twisted in the air. His head missed the dock by mere inches. He hit the surface of the lake and a splash of frigid water fountained into the air. He disappeared beneath the waves.

Jake quickly twisted the grip in the opposite direction, driving the boat forward, straight at the spot Mr. Blonde fell, hoping to pin him under the water, force him to swim, or with luck, carve him up with the prop. He yelled, "Get ready."

Chloe was poised like a sprinter. She nodded.

The Lund hit the dock. She scrambled over the side of the boat, landing on the dock on her hands and knees. She leaped to her feet and hesitated, looking at Jake.

"Chloe, run! Go!"

For once she didn't argue and if he thought she ran fast that day in the wrecking yard it was nothing compared to how quickly she moved today.

Jake's eyes flicked from Chloe to the gun jammed between the forward seat and the side of the boat. *Grab it*, he thought. *End this the instant Mr. Blonde resurfaces.* He let go of the tiller and rose to a crouch, avoiding the mistake the Freak made. The Lund rocked. He paused, swaying from side to side, keeping his balance. He reached for the pistol.

A hollow thud echoed through the aluminum floor of the boat, vibrating the soles of Jake's shoes. The bow slewed sideways. He staggered. Fell. One knee slammed into the edge of the center seat with eye-watering force. Lightning bolts of pain radiated up and down his leg. He gasped.

Mr. Blonde rose out of the lake coughing and spitting water, pushing the boat out of his way. Lake water gushed out of the sleeves of the yellow slicker. Black dye ran from his hairline. It mixed with crimson blood leaching out of a cut across his forehead, the two fluids covering his face like a curtain. He washed both hands down his face, clearing his vision. He spotted Jake and roared with rage.

The pistol was at the other end of the boat, two bench seats away. Jake knew he'd never reach it with Mr. Blonde jerking the bow of the boat back and forth. He abandoned the idea and leapt for the dock. He landed on his stomach with a grunt, just managing to break his fall with his arms. Pain lanced into a palm. He jerked his arm back, a thick splinter of pine buried in his hand.

Mr. Blonde let go of the boat and grabbed Jake's foot. His grip was a manacle. He yanked, easily dragging Jake across the rain slick dock.

Jake rolled onto his back. He kicked hard, burying the flat of his foot squarely across Mr. Blonde's nose.

The Freak hollered. Both hands flew to his face.

Jake bounced to his feet and immediately dropped to all fours as a fresh barb of agony ripped through his knee. Panic shortened his breath. He shot a wide-eyed glance over his shoulder. Mr. Blonde wasn't looking his way. He was searching the bottom of the boat. For the pistol, Jake was certain.

A sudden flash of color caught his eye. His head snapped around in time to see Chloe disappear down the trail to the right of the dock. "No," he yelled, swinging his arm. "Other way." The wind and the rain carried his voice away. The woods swallowed her. Hands flat on the dock, he pushed himself to his feet. "Shit," he said as his injured knee sent warning spikes of pain to his brain. He couldn't run so he loped unsteadily down the dock.

He knew what Chloe was thinking. Cabin five was to the right, much closer than the lodge. It was filled with the hunters from Atlanta and there was safety in numbers. It seemed like a good idea, except Jake didn't believe Mr. Blonde would hesitate to kill more innocent bystanders. Not after the way he gunned down poor Charlie. The lodge and a fast car was a much better idea.

His footsteps thudded on the dock. One heavy, the other light. He hit the end, glanced left in the direction of the lodge, and then followed Chloe down the trail leading to cabin five.

Behind him the air exploded. Once. Twice. Three times.

Jake flinched. He pushed harder. The pain in his leg faded. He couldn't outrun three bullets, but it didn't hurt to try. He didn't want to, but couldn't help looking over his right shoulder.

Mr. Blonde, gun in hand, pushed his way through the waist-deep water toward the shoreline, not bothering with the dock, narrowing the angle between him and the trail on which Jake was running. He raised the pistol and fired a fourth time.

CHAPTER 37

IN CABIN FIVE, Cliff Nelson leaned into the table with his weight on his forearms. He studied a pair of eights and three garbage cards between his fingers. Four empty cans of Blue sat on the table near his right hand. Two full beers sat near his left. He tossed the worthless cards into the center of the table, grabbed one of the full cans and took a long, deep slug. After a noisy, smelly belch, he slammed the can on the table. "I'll take three."

He heard three sharp pops.

He straightened on his chair. "You guys hear that?" Six different faces looked at him with expressions ranging from confusion to ambivalence.

"I didn't hear a damn thing," one of them said.

"Who cares? We're playing a game here. I raise. Ten bucks."

"Sounded like lightning. Or thunder. Maybe."

"That wasn't thunder," Jerry said. "Those were gunshots. Some idiot out there hunting, I bet. Not enough common sense to come in out of the rain."

Everyone froze and listened intently to the silence.

Cliff twisted the pinkie ring around his finger a couple of times. Four quick beers to kill last night's hangover, he was a little fucked up, or possibly he was fucked up all over again, but he thought Jerry was right. Those pops sounded suspiciously like gunshots.

"My ears must be going," one hunter said. He wobbled his head like he was trying to clear water out of his ear. "I didn't hear a thing."

Another one of the hunters said, "A bear? Maybe it was a bear?"

"A bear with a gun? For Christ's sake."

"Who cares?"

Cliff snapped, "I care, Jerry. Me. I think Ash was right. I think it was a bear. What else could it be?"

"The weather, maybe? The wind? A branch falling off a tree? Your imagination, you drunk fuck? You in or out?"

Cliff slapped his cards face-down on the table. "I came here to hunt. Not play cards." The legs of his chair scraped across the floor as he pushed himself away from the table. He stood. He hoisted his sagging pants up and slung his only concession to safety—bright orange suspenders—over his shoulders then immediately donned a denim jacket, covering them. Scanning the cabin, he said, "Where's my rifle?"

"We're in the middle of a game here."

"We're playing cards 'cause it's windy and miserable and pouring rain, Cliff. That's why we decided to stay inside today. Remember? Now you want to go out there?"

Cliff pushed out his jaw. "I came to shoot a bear. That's what I plan to do."

"Right now?"

He drained the Blue and slammed the can on the table, crushing it. "Good a time as any."

Ash put his hands on the edge of the table and pushed himself away. "Fuckin' A. I'm with you, Cliff."

"Lock and load, Ash."

Another pop rang out. Louder this time. Cliff wasn't sure what a bear sounded like. He wasn't even sure if the earlier noises came from the weather, a broken branch or his imagination. One thing he didn't have a shred of doubt about—that last "pop" was gunfire. After twenty years living in Atlanta he damn sure recognized the sound of a small caliber firearm. And, when some dip-shit was shooting and the bullets were getting closer, there was only one real choice. You pulled out a weapon of your own and shot back. He grabbed the brim of his Remington ball cap and twisted it on backwards. His voice rose. "Someone out there is shooting. Maybe at a bear. Maybe at us. I'm shooting back."

"Fucking A," Ash repeated.

"Might be a Canadian version of a drive-by," someone said nervously.

"Turn the lights out so they can't see us."

"No. Leave them on so they can. They're Canucks. If they see us, they won't shoot. They're too polite."

"Jesus," Jerry said, his voice filled with exasperation. "Beer me."

"Turn half the lights off."

A beer sailed through the air. Jerry caught it one handed. He popped the top. White foam fizzed out and he nosily slurped it away. "No good reason to go outside when some idiot is playing with guns. Bear or no. Especially not in this weather." With raised eyebrows he asked, "Is the game over? Is that it?"

Cliff tossed him a scornful look and didn't bother answering. He turned his attention to the Browning autoloader in his hand. He slammed the magazine home, tugged the bolt back and let it go, feeding a round into the chamber. "Yee- ha!" He opened the door and walked into the rain. Ash followed closely behind. The door slammed shut behind them.

For a moment, Cliff hesitated. The rain fell in a constant heavy mist. A stiff breeze off the lake tugged at the brim of his cap and punched through his clothes. He shivered. Suddenly the idea of chasing a wounded bear or a dip-shit hunter with piss-poor aim didn't seem like the best idea. But, going back inside the cabin wasn't an option. He could already hear Jerry asking, "What was it Cliff? A bear packing heat? You wrecked the game for a grizzly with a nine, right? Or a .38 maybe?" All the guys laughing…

There was only one real choice.

"Ash," Cliff said, waggling his wrist, two fingers extended, "you go left. I'll go right. Scout the perimeter. Meet you around back."

Ash nodded.

Cliff walked slowly, searching the bush surrounding the cabin. Raindrops stung his chest at the wide V where his wool Stanfield opened. The water quickly sucked the warmth from his hands and the wind muffled the sounds of the forest. His pinkie ring clacked when he flexed his fingers around the hardwood grip of the Browning. He paused long enough to tug up the collar of his denim jacket.

Voices, the words muted and indistinguishable, rose from the other side of the cabin.

Then a gunshot. Not a pop, this time. The sound was too close for that.

"Ash! The fuck are you doing?" Cliff yelled. There was no answer. Cliff shook his head, regretting the last couple of beers. Booze fucked up his aim. Not that it mattered. With a gun as powerful as the Browning BAR .308, he didn't have to hit what he was aiming at. Close counted. "Ash? Ash, you dumb bastard. What's going on?"

No answer.

Cliff spit into the bush, shouldered his rifle and hustled around to the backside of the cabin.

CHAPTER 38

J AKE DUCKED INSTINCTIVELY. The Freak's fourth shot disappeared into the bush behind the first three.

The spit ended at the tree line, and the sand and gravel gave way to a wide hard-pack trail. With stable ground underfoot, Jake pumped his arms for speed and hit the trail in a flat-out sprint, the pain in his knee forgotten. The moment he judged Mr. Blonde could no longer see him from the shoreline, he dodged left into the bush. Hopefully, the man wouldn't go bush-whacking in his expensive Rockports. Hopefully, he'd stick to the trail.

Thick undergrowth forced Jake to slow. His breath came in ragged shallow pants. He paused, planted his hands on his waist and concentrated on inhaling deeply through his nose and exhaling out his mouth. The tension rippling through his body eased. Without his own breath rattling in his ears, a sudden relative silence surrounded him. The trees softened the wind and eased its cutting chill. Rain gently peppered the leaves overhead. Birds, insects, and other wildlife hid from the storm. *They were the smart ones*, Jake thought wryly.

"Chloe," he whispered through clenched teeth, scanning the surrounding bush. Never before had he wanted to hear her speak as badly as he did at that moment. He shivered as a wave of fresh, hot fear washed over him. Why didn't she answer? Where was she? He cocked his head straining to hear the slightest whisper. "Chloe?"

Nothing but rain and wind answered him.

From behind him, on the beach, rocks clacked together. The Freak had come ashore. The fancy shoes and expensive suit would slow him down but they wouldn't stop him. The man was coming.

Jake pushed his way through the bush paralleling the trail. Foliage, heavy with water, soaked him. His head bobbed from side to side, searching, listening. Occasionally he'd whisper, "Chloe?" his voice ranging from anger to fear—where had she gone?

Behind him he heard heavy, labored breathing.

Instantly Jake dropped to his knees. A fresh damp cold saturated his pants from ankle to knee. He rotated his head slowly and peered around the edge of a pine tree.

Mr. Blonde limped down the path, dripping lake water and rain. The pistol dangled alongside his leg in loose fingers. Trickles of dye leached out of his hair and left trails of black down his face like veins of coal. He paused long enough to wipe his forehead with his fist, smearing the blood seeping out of the gash into a pink smudge. He looked at the blood on his hand, muttered, "Fuck," before wiping it off on his jacket.

Hunkered motionless behind a twisted, upturned mound of tree roots, Jake exhaled into the crook of his arm, masking the sound of his breathing. He gave Mr. Blonde a fifteen-foot head start then followed, stepping carefully to avoid cracking branches underfoot. Moss and fallen autumn leaves carpeted the ground and soaked up water like a sponge. Each footstep sent the bitterly aromatic scent of pine needles rising into the air.

Where was Chloe?

The flat trail underfoot began angling uphill. Mr. Blonde's panting intensified. He slipped in the mud and dropped to one knee. Muttering a curse, he regained his footing. He mopped the inside of his arm across his forehead, and swallowed huge, noisy gulps of air. "I hate the bush." Glancing up the rise, he shook his head and doggedly started walking.

Jake's gaze alternated between Mr. Blonde's back and the ground. He pressed his lips into a hard line. Cabin five sat at the top of the slope, surrounded on two sides by water. The closer they got, the less space there was to hide, to run, to maneuver. Time was running out. He fought a rising tide of dread. He needed a plan.

Soon.

Where the hell was she?

Until he knew where Chloe was, he couldn't come up with an idea. His mind was full of static. There wasn't a single clear thought in his head. The more he tried forcing some kind of idea to the surface, the more worried he became. The only thing he could hope for was stumbling across her before Mr. Blonde did. If luck ran their way, they could backtrack and call the police from the lodge.

Or, if Mr. Blonde found her first, hopefully he wouldn't kill her right away, give Jake some time to figure out how to save her.

Had she gone into the cabin? He hoped not. That was an inescapable trap. If Mr. Blonde couldn't find her outside the cabin, eventually he'd look inside. He might not shoot seven hunters to get to her, but there'd be some kind of showdown. If she stayed outside, remained hidden, there was a chance of escaping back to the lodge ahead of him.

A door slammed.

Mr. Blonde dropped to a crouch.

Jake glanced at the cabin. A momentary whisper of blue smoke twisted away from the chimney before disappearing into the rain and wind. Two hunters stood on the porch under the overhang, heads close together. Their voices were inaudible. Jake recognized one of them as the blowhard from the previous night. Cliff Nelson. He wore a gray Stanfield shirt and jeans. Bright orange suspenders peeked out from beneath a denim jacket. And, Jake couldn't believe it, he wore his baseball cap on backward. Cliff had no way of knowing he'd just stepped into a real-life problem. Trying to appear bad-ass wasn't going to do anything for him if he stumbled across Mr. Blonde. Jake couldn't remember the second guy's name. Both men held rifles.

He scanned the tree line on the opposite side of the trail, searching for a scrap of color that didn't belong. Some hint of where she was.

Cliff pointed. The second hunter nodded. He stepped off the porch and took a few tentative steps down the trail, scanning the bush while Cliff walked in the opposite direction and disappeared around the far side of the cabin.

Mr. Blonde rose from his crouch. He slowly swung his arm behind him, hiding the pistol in the hollow at the small of his back. "Hey, friend," he called. "You seen Chloe? I'm trying to check in but nobody's home at the lodge."

"I ain't seen her." There was a moment of silence. "How come you're so wet? You fall in the lake?" The hunter chuckled. There was a long pause. "What happened to your face? It's all black. You're bleeding." He forced a second, unnatural laugh. The tone of his voice became suspicious. "Don't look to me like you're an outdoorsman, wearing a suit like that." He slowly brought his rifle around so the barrel pointed in Mr. Blonde's general direction.

"Is that right?" Mr. Blonde said. "Well, here's the thing, friend. I hate the bush. My definition of roughing it is a hotel without room service. And, I'm not excited about the direction you're pointing that rifle." He shook his head. "All and all, my patience is running thin. You understand? So, I'm gonna ask one question. I suggest you answer it. You seen Chloe?"

Jake held his breath. He'd heard the one question shtick before. It hadn't turned out well for him.

"Screw you," the hunter said. Sudden nervousness laced his voice. He raised the rifle.

Mr. Blonde swung the nine around, levelled it and squeezed the trigger twice. The gunshots were loud, strung together so closely they sounded like one.

The hunter staggered, lost his footing and landed on the ground on his ass. He flopped over sideways, mouth and eyes wide with astonishment. Blood frothed from his mouth. He moaned. His heels drummed the ground. His back arched. Then he lay still.

Jake dropped his chin to his chest and closed his eyes briefly. He groaned. He couldn't let the Freak kill all the hunters. But what could he do to prevent it? Running into the clearing was a kamikaze mission. Mr. Blonde would either shoot him immediately or hold him hostage, forcing Chloe out of her hiding spot.

Perhaps he could work his way around the perimeter of the clearing into the cabin and warn the rest of the hunters?

Macho idiots probably wouldn't take him seriously. Or worse, they would. Every one of them would pick up a weapon and storm out of the cabin and Mr. Blonde would plink them off one by one, like steel ducks at a midway shooting gallery. Jake shook his head. Hunters wearing camo. They all thought they were in Vietnam.

Mr. Blonde twisted his head in a quick quarter turn. He adjusted his tie. "Fuck-wit," he muttered.

Cliff hustled around the cabin. His eyes widened when he saw Mr. Blonde. They immediately narrowed when he spotted his dead companion. "The hell is this?" he said. The barrel of the Browning rose.

"Cliff. No," Chloe screamed.

Jake's eyes cut from Cliff to Chloe.

She rose out of the ground on the opposite side of the trail, waving both hands over her head. "He'll kill you!"

Jake leapt to his feet. He lunged in Chloe's direction. Faster than he believed possible, Mr. Blonde jumped into the underbrush.

Chloe ducked sideways. Mr. Blonde pounced, caught the tail of her fleece and yanked her to him.

Jake dropped to the ground before the Freak looked his way.

What now? He needed something. A plan. An advantage. A weapon. Something. Walking out there empty-handed was a death sentence. The dead hunter proved it. And, it wouldn't help Chloe a bit. Jake stared at the Freak with hatred. He slammed a hard fist into the ground, his mind frustratingly empty.

Mr. Blonde wrapped an arm around Chloe's waist. Holding her like a shield, he walked her out of the bush, back to the trail. He straight-armed the nine, aiming at Cliff.

Cliff wasn't going to make the same mistake as his dead companion. The rifle was at his shoulder, the scope near his right eye. He tracked Chloe and Mr. Blonde as they moved.

"Turn around, friend," Mr. Blonde said. "Take your little toy rifle and go back inside. This don't concern you."

Jake knew Cliff wouldn't. Chloe made an impression on people. Especially macho male hunters. There wasn't a chance in hell the hunter would turn his back on her and return to the warmth and security of cabin five.

Cliff didn't disappoint. "Can't let you take her."

Mr. Blonde arched an eyebrow. "Is that right?"

"That's right."

Jake tensed. Here comes stupid dead hunter number two. Before he finished the thought, Mr. Blonde fired. Cliff dropped to the ground with a soggy thump, dead before the look of comprehension fully formed on his face.

Jake closed his eyes briefly and shook his head. Tourists. All they wanted was a different experience from the concrete rat race they lived every day. A chance to take their guns out of the display cases. Actually use them for the purpose they were…

Jake opened his eyes. His head rose. Instead of looking away from the corpses on the ground in front of him, his gaze sought them out. Two dead hunters. Two high-powered rifles. He let a tight smile touch his lips. He pushed it away. Leveling the odds was one thing. Following through was entirely another.

He rose to a crouch. Staying low, hidden in the brush, he duck-walked toward the edge of the trail where the bush thinned. Cliff's rifle was closer than the first hunter's. It looked powerful. Dangerous. It had a great big scope on it. Made missing impossible.

"Start walking Chloe," Mr. Blonde said. "Before the rest of the fuck-wits come out. And, unless you think you can outrun Mr. Glock," he waggled his gun in her face, "don't bother trying to run." He shoved her down the trail in the direction of the lodge.

Chloe staggered. She flung out an arm. When she regained her balance, Mr. Blonde grabbed her where her neck and shoulder met, holding her captive and controlling her like he had on the dock. They started down the trail toward the dock. "Where's your boyfriend?" he said loudly. "Seems to me two hunters did more than your pussy boyfriend."

Jake knew Mr. Blonde was trying to draw him out. He gritted his teeth in anger, refusing to take the bait. He ran in a low crouch toward Cliff's body. The absurd orange suspenders were beacons in the flat featureless light of the rainy day. Every footstep made quiet sloshing sounds. The soles of his shoes squelched in the mud, slowing him. His breath came in shallow pants.

Don't let him turn around. Not yet.

"If it makes you feel better," Mr. Blonde said conversationally, "those good ol' boys never stood a chance. You see Chloe, a guy picks up a gun, he's got to have the stones to use it. Most guys can't. To be fair, the first time is tough. Was for me, believe it or not. But, just like any job, practice makes it easier. It helps if you love what you do." He paused. "You wouldn't know about that, would you? Seeing as interior design didn't work out, and banging the Boss and spending his money isn't a real job."

Jake wrapped his hands around Cliff's Browning, surprised at its lethal weight, its foreignness in his hands. He took a moment to study it, found the safety button on the trigger guard and pushed it. A red ring appeared, brilliant against the blue steel barrel and the dark walnut stock. Would there be a bullet in the chamber, ready to go? Probably, considering it was Cliff-the-blowhard's rifle, but Jake had no way of being sure. He didn't want to squeeze the trigger and hear nothing but a dull click.

Knowing the sound would alert the Freak, Jake yanked the Browning's bolt backward. It slid easily. A bright brass cartridge spit out the side. When he let the bolt go it slammed forward with a metallic crash.

The Freak froze.

Jake raised the rifle to his shoulder, aiming at the hollow spot between Mr. Blonde's shoulder blades. The slicker became a huge yellow blob, completely dominating the view out the scope. Jake's breath caught in the back of his throat. Not daring to blink, he lowered the rifle enough to look over the top of the scope, down the length of the barrel.

Mr. Blonde swiveled. A genuine smile, perhaps the first Jake had ever seen, played across his face. He pointed his Glock at Jake and dragged Chloe closer, until her body shielded his.

"Jake," Chloe said. She sounded terrified. She twisted under Mr. Blonde's grip. Her face was white and wet. Tears as well as rain Jake guessed, judging from her red, puffy eyes.

"Jake, Jake, Jake," Mr. Blonde mimicked in a high falsetto. "As I was saying, Chloe, you pick up a gun, you gotta be prepared to use it. This pussy missed his chance. Now shut up. You whine worse than his brother."

In a slice of time so brief it couldn't be measured, Jake thought about Marie-Claude lying in the hospital. He saw Chloe tied up in the trunk of a car, her pretty face covered in blood, the fear in her copper eyes. He remembered the beating he took in the wrecking yard. And, he thought about Mark, how his tough-as-nails brother never whined a day in his life.

Killing the Freak would be no problem.

But he had no shot. There was no way of shooting Mr. Blonde without hitting Chloe.

Scare him then, he thought instantly. His heart raced, but strangely the fear was gone, replaced by rational thought that came faster than he ever experienced before. The Freak didn't think he could pull the trigger…

Show him you can. Surprise him.

Jake twitched the Browning's barrel sideways. Squeezed the trigger.

At the same instant the Glock in the Freak's hand jerked. Once.

Jake didn't hear the pistol's tiny bang over the Browning's thunderous boom. He was unprepared for the rifle's recoil. The butt hammered him viciously in the shoulder. He staggered, involuntarily planted his rear foot to compensate and his damaged knee folded in half. He fell hard. Grunted loudly when he landed. The air, where his head was a moment before, buzzed as though a supersonic wasp had just flown by.

Jake looked up. Mr. Blonde stood in front of him with his head thrown back, laughing. Crimson blood and black dye dribbled down both cheeks. His suit looked like wet charcoal and the yellow slicker stood out in bright contrast. He looked like a macabre caricature out of a horror comic. He held the pistol against his thigh in loose fingers. His other arm dangled over Chloe's shoulder, preventing her from escaping.

Confused, Jake narrowed his eyes. Why wasn't he dead? Other than a sore tailbone he wasn't even hurt. The Freak shot at him and missed, likely because the rifle's recoil knocked him on his ass.

But he wasn't dead!

"I haven't laughed like that in," Mr. Blonde paused, cocked his head and eventually said, "years I guess." He wiped tears of mirth away from both eyes with his wrist, the pistol in his hand a contra-diction to the hilarity he found in the situation. "Anyway, back to business." He raised the Glock.

A hard look crossed Chloe's face. Two spots of red anger high-lighted her cheekbones. She opened her mouth and screaming shrilly, raised her foot and scraped the thick, heavy sole of her hik-ing boot down Mr. Blonde's shin from knee to ankle.

Mr. Blonde's eyes widened in pain and surprise. He shoved her away with a howl of rage. In an offhand, distant kind of way, Jake heard the cabin door open and then slam shut behind him, and someone said, "What the fuck?" but from the ground where he sat, the Freak's bright yellow slicker was the only thing of which he was truly aware. Forgoing the scope, he pointed the Browning like he would his index finger and tugged the trigger.

Another ear-assaulting boom.

Another massive blow to the shoulder.

A spurt of red squirted out of the yellow slicker. Mr. Blonde flew backwards, folded in half with an airy grunt and hit the ground, twisting in agony. Frothy red foam spilled from his lips, turned pink in the drizzle and washed away. With a final spasm, his body went limp.

Chloe's hands flew to her mouth, silencing her shriek. A moment later she dropped them, exposing a weak smile.

Someone said, "Holy shit! Jerry, get out here!"

Jake dropped the rifle on the ground. He pushed himself to his feet. Rubbing his shoulder, with the sound of the Browning still echoing in his ears, he walked toward her. She met him half-way. He grabbed her hand. Fingers linked, they stood side-by-side, staring down at Mr. Blonde.

Chloe said, "Is he dead?"

Jake nudged him with his toe. The Freak didn't move. "I think so. That's a pretty big hole in his chest."

"Wow." She sounded surprised, like she couldn't quite believe that months of running, fear and uncertainty could die that easily.

"I know."

For three or four seconds they stood in silence then Chloe said, "What now?"

Jake said, "We have to call the cops. The place is a war zone. Four bodies." His voice trailed away. He and Chloe weren't done yet. In a few seconds, the first of the hunters would come at him with a barrage of questions. After the police arrived, there'd be hours, perhaps days of explanations. He said, "The cops will separate us right away. They'll start asking questions. Lots and lots of questions. They might even toss me in jail—"

"It was self-defense."

"They're not going to take our word on it."

"Maybe you should put the gun in Cliff's hands. Make it look like he shot Dalrymple?"

Jake scratched the back of his head, considering the idea. He could save them both hours of police interviews, explanations, and clarifications. The thing was, other than what he saw on television, he had no idea how a cop investigated a shooting. To what extent would they go? If he started out with a lie, sooner or later it would most likely catch up with him.

"I think it's too late for that," he said. "I think one of the You-Alls saw it all. It's probably better I tell the cops exactly what happened. They'll get the big picture from us. Then they'll interview the hunters and fill in all the blanks with little details, just to make sure the stories jive. You know: 'How'd you get away? I kicked him in the shin. Which shin? The right one.' So they'll look. See if it's scraped. Good move, by the way." He gave her hand a squeeze.

Chloe's worried smile was brief.

"I'm sure they'll cordon off this entire area," he said and swept an arm across the point. "Go over it with a fine-tooth comb–"

"How do you know this stuff?"

"I'm guessing." He became aware of voices behind him, a mixture of shock and anger and questions. He cut a glance over his shoulder. The cabin door opened and a couple more men came out and clustered on the porch. One of them took a tentative step in Jake's direction, followed by a second. Someone said, "I'm getting my gun."

Chloe barely looked at the gathering crowd on the porch. Sounding worried, she said, "Once the police do all that stuff, they'll let you go?"

Jake shrugged. He said nothing. Cliff Nelson stared up at him with vacant, unblinking eyes. His gold and diamond pinkie ring was tarnished with mud. He was no longer the blowhard Jake remembered. Now he was just Cliff, a guy who got drunk and talked too much when he was around an attractive girl like Chloe. Who could blame him? His gaze drifted to the other dead hunter. They'd played cards together the night before. Jake couldn't remember the man's name. He remembered his last passenger, Charlie Cariboo, the Native who just wanted to buy his son some hockey equipment. Now the man lay dead in the bottom of a Lund fishing boat.

A shudder rippled his body.

"Jake? They'll let you go, right?

"All the evidence will prove I had no choice. He was the bad guy. He was going to kill us." His tone was stilted and flat. He sucked in a deep breath and rolled his free hand into a tight fist, controlling tremors that threatened to shake his entire body. "Just like Charlie, and these two idiots and—"

"—Mark," Chloe said softly.

"Yeah. Mark."

The guilt and grief he worked so hard to control exploded like dandelion fluff on the wind. It filled him. Chloe's hand tightened around his. He wanted to squeeze back, smile, reassure her in some way. Nothing came. Her touch that always warmed him was cold and damp. His brother was dead and Jake was too filled with remorse and despair and guilt to feel anything else. There was no room.

"Jake?" Chloe said, her worried expression deepening.

EPILOGUE

THE BIG, SILENT screen flickered in front of Jake, casting its ghostly blue flicker around Tundra Air's lodge. He stared at it but his thoughts were still in the interview room at the police station and he was listening to the cop's explanations, and no matter how much sense they made, he wasn't happy about them.

Mark was dead. Mr. Blonde hadn't lied about that. It had taken a couple of days before one of Mark's colleagues drove by the house, wondering why he wasn't returning calls or showing up for work. That's when the Tampa police finally started their investigation. Some more time went by before they understood Mark's parents were deceased and there was a surviving brother.

About that point Jake had stood up and started pacing the interview room. He tossed his arms in the air. "How hard is it for cops to find someone who isn't hiding?"

"They needed a starting place, Mr. Harris. Mrs. Weatherly thought you were in Montreal." *Oh, and by the way, were you aware she's in the hospital?* "When Tampa authorities found your brother's cell phone with your number in it, they contacted us."

"Four days," Jake yelled. He snatched up his chair and threw it across the room.

One of the cops stiffened, dropping his crossed arms to his sides. The other officer's eyes widened. He didn't move. The side-to-side motion of the toothpick between his lips ceased.

"Four days my brother's lying dead on the hallway floor and I don't know it." He righted the chair and sat down hard. He swiped the back of his hand across his face, surprised to find it wet with tears. The shouts became a mumble. "Four days."

The cop removed the toothpick from his mouth. "We're sorry for your loss, Mr. Harris." He studied the soggy, frayed end. "We're not done yet. We need to talk further about Eric Dalrymple and the events at cabin five."

"How many more times do I have to say it?"

"As many as it takes."

The phone near the entrance to the lodge rang, jerking Jake back to the present. Chloe poked her head around the corner with raised eyebrows. He waved a dismissive hand but otherwise didn't move. She disappeared and the ringing stopped. From the other room, he heard her murmuring voice, the words inaudible.

Minutes after the shooting, the Sioux River authorities were swarming all over the lodge and cabin five. As Jake expected, they had taken him into custody but neither arrested nor charged him. They questioned him for hours, taking him back through the day, through those blurred-together moments when Mr. Blonde walked out of the hut with Chloe. An endless loop. Gradually their questions became less linear, giving Jake the impression he was confirming little details and plugging tiny holes in the narrative. Eventually they released him, telling him to stay available. There might be follow-up questions.

Now, all that remained was the return trip to Tampa. He needed to take care of Mark's affairs and visit Mrs. Weatherly. Hopefully, the old duck was doing okay; a broken hip could be a serious problem for old folk. It was just one more thing for which Jake felt guilty.

"Can I sit down?"

Jake looked up. His breath hitched as it usually did when Chloe walked into the room wearing those faded Gap jeans low on her hips. She slid the fish pendant back and forth on the chain around her neck. The red curls he'd come to love spilled out from beneath her Yankees hat.

He tried forcing a smile to the surface, to somehow prove she was a vision he hoped he'd never get used to. Smiles were still too hard to come by. He settled for patting the sofa beside him.

She flopped down with a noisy exhalation. "What are you watching?"

"I'm not sure."

"Do you know someone named Becky?"

He hiked his shoulders. "Maybe. The name rings a bell." His voice came out in a flat uninterested monotone.

"That was her on the phone. She was calling on behalf of Gary Lewis. Executive Flight Charters? He wants you to call him back. I left the number by the phone."

Deep inside Jake felt a spark of…

What?

Curiosity maybe. It was a tiny flicker, not even strong enough to create a shadow, but significant because it meant there was room for more than grief in the labyrinth of empty black caverns in which he was lost. "Okay."

For several long minutes, they stared in silence at the television.

Chloe nibbled her lower lip. Eventually she hesitantly said, "What happens now?"

He didn't answer right away. "I'm not sure. I can't stay here. It's wrong. Feels strange."

"I know." She flapped a hand at the far end of the bay where cabin five sat, surrounded in yellow crime scene tape that drooped and flapped listlessly in the rain and wind. "Strange is right. I've already packed most of my stuff."

"Sounds like you're ready to leave right now."

"That depends."

"On?"

After a long silence, Chloe said softly, "You."

He cocked his head and looked at her out of narrowed eyes. "Why?"

She reached out and grabbed his hand. Holding it tightly between both of hers she said, "I'm sorry about all this, Jake."

"Not your fault."

She made a face, clearly not convinced. "I can't help thinking if you'd never met me, Mark would be alive. And, if you—"

"If, if, if."

"—and, if you thought the same way, you wouldn't care what I did. As long as I wasn't with you."

Something inside Jake twisted. A second spark flared to life, an unpleasant wave of loneliness this time. It reminded him, as the earlier spark did, that life was more than sadness.

"That's just not accurate," he said, forcing a calm he didn't feel into his voice. "I thought we discussed the next few months in terms of us. You and me." He remembered every detail of the night Chloe invited him upstairs. Perhaps "discuss" was an amplification of their conversation, but they definitely spoke a word or two about the future.

"We did."

"Has something changed?"

"Mark's dead. He wouldn't be if—"

"I know he's dead. Mr. Blonde killed him. I'm talking about us." His voice rose and all traces of calm were replaced by alarm. "Has something changed with us?"

"Maybe. I don't know"

"You haven't gone and convinced yourself this was all your fault, have you?"

"Maybe."

"That I blame you?"

"Maybe."

Jake's voice rose another level, this time in anger. "Well stop it. Listen to fact and stop thinking crazy."

"You haven't said anything in two days, Jake. There were no facts for me to listen to. All I could do was think."

He thrust his legs out, straightening on the couch and dipped his hand into the front pocket of his Levis. His keys jangled when he pulled them out. "Get my car," he said gruffly, still angry but uncomfortable with his outburst. "Back it up to the door. I've got a call to make. After I'm done with that, I'll carry your bags down."

"I get to drive the Mustang? You do love me!"

He knew it was a joke, a way of breaking the tension, and although laughing was still several days away, he came close when he saw the expression on her face, the way her jaw suddenly dropped, and the perfect, startled O her mouth made.

Face pulsing several shades of scarlet, Chloe forced an embarrassed chuckle and stammered, "Jake I was, just…"

He leaned in and kissed her on the tip of her nose, cutting off her babble. "I've got to make a call."

After wrapping up a ten-minute conversation with Gary Lewis at Executive Flight Charters, Jake glanced up the stairs to Chloe's room and hollered, "Chloe? I'm coming up."

"Fine."

At the top of the stairs he leaned on the door jam, crossed his arms over his chest and looked into her room. Her photos were gone. The dresser was bare. The bedside table no longer held a lipgloss. Her aroma was gone too, as though she'd packed her citrus scent in a box and sealed it with packing tape. The room was devoid of her personality, an empty vessel until next spring when Stevenson hired a new hostess. Somehow the idea saddened him. "I liked it better when all your stuff was in here."

The moment the words crossed his lips, Jake winced. His gaze dropped to his feet. He scratched a spot behind his ear. Grief was fine. It couldn't be avoided. Soon it would turn to anger. He'd bump a paint can with his elbow, some shit like that. Enamel would splash all over the floor. He'd melt down and throw tools and punch a hole or two in the drywall. Perhaps smash a window. Holler and yell and swear. And, in the rage there'd be deep, gulping sobs. When he was done, the worst of the pain would be gone and there'd be space for the happy memories.

In the meantime, he needed to quit moping. An empty room was just that and nothing more. Grief was fine. Maudlin was not.

He breathed in and he exhaled and when he looked up, his voice was firm and confident. "I called Executive. Gary Lewis offered me a flying position in Tampa. It's a job I've been chasing since before you and I met."

"That's good news. Congratulations."

He absently nodded his thanks. Hopefully, they'd have plenty of time to talk about the new flying job. For now, he wanted to discuss the two of them, make sure he didn't lose her as well as his brother. "Have you considered what you'll do now that this hostess thing is over?"

"You mean in the forty-eight hours since we spoke about it last? Not really. I've been busy. Psychopaths on my mind."

The sarcasm was mild and inoffensive. He ignored it. "If you're interested in driving to Tampa with me, we could toss some ideas around. When we get there, now Mark's gone..."

Chloe reached out and touched his arm sympathetically.

After swallowing several times, Jake said, "Now that Mark won't be around cluttering up my space... The basement apartment I rent in Tampa is too big for one person."

"Really?" she said cautiously. A small smile played across her face.

"Listen, Chloe. I like you. I like having you around, annoying me with your chatter. I want you to come and live with me in Tampa. I know I'm kind of stubborn. I like things just so—"

"No?"

"And I might be a little moody in the next few weeks—"

"No!"

"This new job will take me out of town several days a month." The words came in a rush, Jake anxious to sell the idea. "You wouldn't have to put up with me too much. You could go to school. Whatever. When I was home, if we happened to have sex–"

She interrupted him a third time with a musical laugh. She tightened the grip she had on his arm. Her pretty, copper-colored eyes brimmed with tears. "Yeah, I think we can make that work."

The End

The genesis of this novel occurred long before the tragedy of September 11th. Before that day, travelling was far easier and much more enjoyable. In the early nineties I travelled from Thunder Bay to Puerto Vallarta via New York and Guadalajara. The friend I travelled with used his Canadian driver's license as identification the entire trip. After all those connections and international borders, the only objection he encountered regarding his identification came from a Canadian customs officer upon our return to Canada. The rules tightened up after 9/11 but it wasn't until 2009 that a passport was required at road crossings for travel between Canada and the USA.

For those people who are familiar with the cities of Tampa, Montreal, and Chicago, I apologize. I've taken huge liberties with geography. That's why it's called "fiction." Sioux River, on the other hand, is an entirely fictional town, a composite of several locations. You won't find it on a map.

Author Bio

Kevin Lamport is an airline pilot by day and by night he (slowly) writes action-adventure novels. Before joining the airline, he flew small float and ski equipped aircraft in northern Canada, including the arctic territory, Nunavut. He is married. Most days happily. His wife continues to be a source of support and inspiration, after more years than either of them care to count. They live with their pets, (Harley and Malibu), in the always sunny Pacific Northwest. On his days off he enjoys hiking, riding his motorcycle, running for fitness, and travelling, which is tricky because he dislikes airports.

Death and a Few Days Off is Kevin's first novel.

Feel free to visit him at www.kevinlamport.com

Follow him on Facebook and Instagram.

www.ingramcontent.com/pod-product-compliance
Lightning Source LLC
Chambersburg PA
CBHW021334250626
47155CB00002B/687